T0031273

PRAISE FOR *THE COLLAPSING WAVE*

'A barnstorming thriller with great action sequences, sympathetic characters, and a wonderful and radical sense of a greater, wider way of seeing life on our planet (and perhaps on others)'
Martin MacInnes

'Terrifyingly plausible ... an excellent allegory for our times, and yet manages never to be preachy ... Doug's writing is addictive and should come with a health warning ... *The Collapsing Wave* has been an absolute joy to read, and I'll be recommending it to everyone' James Oswald

'A powerful and epic multi-layered story. Doug Johnstone is a true literary master' Michael Wood

'Doug Johnstone has the ability to make you believe in the almost unbelievable. He introduces feelings that cut at your heartstrings. He makes you fall in love with the most unlikely of creatures and people. It's a fast-paced story, which picks up to a real crescendo at the end' Sally Boocock, Waterstone's Bookseller

'A beautifully written, engaging story that lasts in the mind long after the final page is turned. I shall wait with no small amount of trepidation for the final part of this trilogy as it will be a very sad day when we have to say goodbye. Definitely recommended'
Jen Med's Book Reviews

'A thought-provoking, gut-wrenching, nerve-wracking and heart-rending story that makes you forget that it's fiction, and sci-fi to boot. The injustice and machismo were hard to swallow at times ... To counter all that, there is such love permeating this story, and a feeling of hope, like maybe mankind isn't entirely lost after all ... A fantastic book in every way, and nothing I can say can do it justice. Just read it' From Belgium with Booklove

PRAISE FOR *THE SPACE BETWEEN US*

SELECTED FOR BBC 2 *BETWEEN THE COVERS* 2023

'A gateway book to sci-fi … I loved it'
Sara Cox on *Between the Covers*

'So readable and accessible … I was really rooting for the characters'
Alan Davies on *Between the Covers*

'The main characters, their lives and their struggles, are portrayed very vividly. I was straight into this, just like a thriller'
Ivo Graham on *Between the Covers*

'All the makings of a film … such relatable characters'
Sunetra Sarker on *Between the Covers*

If you read one life-affirming book this year, make sure it's this one'
Nina Pottell, *Prima* BOOK OF THE YEAR

'This unique read is heart-warming and thought-provoking'
Fabulous Mag

'Prioritising pace, tension and high stakes … a plea for empathy, compassion and perspective … shot through with vivid characters and a sense of wonder' *Herald Scotland*

'An entertaining, fast-paced story of first contact … an emotionally engaging read' *Guardian*

'All the drive, curiosity and wonder of his crime and mystery novels … science fiction gains a new author' Derek B. Miller

'A delicious, demanding departure from Doug Johnstone'
Val McDermid

'An adrenaline-filled ride … laced with empathy and understanding' Rachelle Atalla

'Pay attention, Steven Spielberg! This could be your next film'
Marnie Riches

'Clever and unusual … I was on a journey with these characters, and completely transfixed' Susi Holliday

'A sci-fi novel that is as moving as it is magical and mysterious. Doug Johnstone has hit it out of the park again' Mark Billingham

'An unexpected delight! … Fast-paced yet thoughtful …
a first-contact tale full of heart and high-octane action.
Highly recommended!' D.V. Bishop

'Doug Johnstone held me spellbound in this mesmerising tale of wonder and hope … menace and magic' Marion Todd

PRAISE FOR DOUG JOHNSTONE

SHORTLISTED for the McIlvanney Prize for Best Scottish Crime Book of the Year
LONGLISTED for Theakston's Old Peculier Crime Novel of the Year
SHORTLISTED for Amazon Publishing Capital Crime Thriller of the Year

'This may be Doug Johnstone's best book yet ... Tense, pacey, filmic' Ian Rankin

'Gripping and blackly humorous' *Observer*

'A tense ride with strong, believable characters' *Big Issue*

'The power of this book ... lies in the warm personalities and dark humour of the Skelfs' *Scotsman*

'Wonderful characters: flawed, funny and brave' *Sunday Times*

'A lovely, sad tale, beautifully told and full of understanding' *The Times*

'Exceptional ... a must for those seeking strong, authentic, intelligent female protagonists' *Publishers Weekly*

'Keeps you hungry from page to page. A crime reader can't ask anything more' *Sun*

'As psychologically rich as it is harrowing ... one of the genre's premiere writers' Megan Abbott

'A brooding, intensely dark thriller with a defiant beating heart. Evocative, heartbreaking and hopeful ... STUNNING' Miranda Dickinson

'A noir heavyweight and a master of gritty realism' Willy Vlautin

'The perfect free-range writer, respectful of conventions but never bound by them, never hemmed in' James Sallis

‘Bloody brilliant’ Martyn Waites

‘Pacy, harrowing and occasionally brutal … it had me in tears’ Paddy Magrane

‘If you loved Iain Banks, you’ll devour the Skelfs series’ Erin Kelly

‘A poignant reflection on grief and the potential for healing that lies within us all. A proper treat’ Mary Paulson-Ellis

‘A thrilling, atmospheric book … Move over Ian Rankin, Doug Johnstone is coming through!’ Kate Rhodes

‘An unstoppable, thrilling, bullet train of a book that cleverly weaves in family and intrigue, and has real emotional impact. I totally loved it’ Helen Fields

‘A new outing for the Skelfs deserves dancing in the streets of Edinburgh’ Val McDermid

‘A total delight … Johnstone never fails to entertain whilst packing a serious emotional punch. Brilliant!’ Gytha Lodge

‘Compelling and compassionate characters, with a dash of physics and philosophy thrown in’ Ambrose Parry

‘Dynamic and poignant … Johnstone balances the cosmos, music, death and life, and wraps it all in a compelling mystery’ Marni Graff

THE COLLAPSING WAVE

ABOUT THE AUTHOR

Doug Johnstone is the author of seventeen novels, many of which have been bestsellers. *The Space Between Us* was chosen for BBC Two's *Between the Covers*, while *Black Hearts* was shortlisted for the Theakston Crime Novel of the Year, and *The Big Chill* was longlisted for the same prize. Three of his books – *A Dark Matter*, *Breakers* and *The Jump* – have been shortlisted for the McIlvanney Prize for Scottish Crime Novel of the Year. Doug has taught creative writing or been writer in residence at universities, schools, writing retreats, festivals, prisons and a funeral directors. He's also been an arts journalist for twenty-five years. He is a songwriter and musician with six albums and three EPs released, and he plays drums for the Fun Lovin' Crime Writers, a band of crime writers. He's also co-founder of the Scotland Writers Football Club. Follow Doug on X/Twitter @doug_johnstone and Instagram @writerdougj, and visit his website: dougjohnstone.com.

Other titles by Doug Johnstone,
available from Orenda Books

THE SKELFS SERIES
A Dark Matter
The Big Chill
The Great Silence
Black Hearts
The Opposite of Lonely

Fault Lines
Breakers
The Space Between Us

THE COLLAPSING WAVE

DOUG JOHNSTONE

Orenda Books
16 Carson Road
West Dulwich
London SE21 8HU
www.orendabooks.co.uk

First published in the United Kingdom by Orenda Books, 2024

A catalogue record for this book is available from the British Library.

ISBN 978-1-916788-05-3
eISBN 978-1-916788-06-0

Typeset in Garamond by typesetter.org.uk

Printed and bound by CPI Group (UK) Ltd, Croydon CR0 4YY

For sales and distribution, please contact info@orendabooks.co.uk or visit www.orendabooks.co.uk.

For Tricia, Aidan and Amber

1
LENNOX

Lennox was sitting with the beaten-up acoustic guitar, trying to learn an old Tame Impala song, when the guard appeared at the doorway.

'Time for your eleven o'clock,' Turner said.

He wore his usual combat camos, tactical vest, chunky boots. M27 automatic rifle pointing at the floor. Blond buzzcut, all-American chin and cheekbones.

'Where's Mendoza?' Lennox said.

'Never mind, come on.'

Lennox put the guitar down and stood. 'Mendoza would've knocked.'

He left the living room of the detention block, walked down the hall and out the door, Turner clumping behind him.

He started across the courtyard, taking in the extraordinary view of Loch Broom. Sweeping brown hills across the water, distant islands like knuckles in the loch mouth, steep mountains to the northwest watching over them. And in between, the vast expanse of water glittering like hammered tin in the autumn sun. He thought about Sandy and the other Enceladons in that expanse somewhere, his chest tight with longing.

This was New Broom, the makeshift military base and research centre built a few miles up the coast from Ullapool. The name was someone's idea of a joke, new broom sweeping clean. It was designated American soil, according to Mendoza, not subject to British or international law. The UK government waved the US military in after the revelation of Enceladons coming to Earth and descending into the deep water off Ullapool. The British were technically involved in a support role, but there were precious few of them on the base. All the guards were American marines and most of the research staff were Ivy League careerists.

Lennox reached the door of the research centre. It was a similar building to the detention block, concrete walls, green corrugated roof, small windows. Lennox looked at the high fence surrounding the base, topped with razor wire, double thickness. As well as the detention block and research centre there was a command building, offices, barracks, stockade and a canteen for the guards. Lennox and Heather cooked for themselves in their own kitchen, and were free to walk around the base, but not to enter any other buildings. The two of them had been held here since it was built, kept imprisoned in the nuclear base at Faslane before that. No contact with the outside world.

Lennox wished for the millionth time that there was someone who would miss him, who would ask questions about him. But at least he and Heather had each other.

Turner opened the research-centre door with his keycard, and Lennox shuffled down the hall. Turner never spoke more than he had to. Lennox much preferred Mendoza, who talked about his wife and baby daughter in New Mexico, downloaded tunes onto an old iPod for Lennox, brought them chocolate. He'd even found that old guitar for Lennox, which he was thankful for.

In the large room at the end of the hall Dr Gibson was at his workstation, laptop and monitors, boxes of flashing lights, signal-processing units. A skull cap full of sensors and connectors. Gibson was clean-shaven, blond side parting, wearing slacks and a tight shirt showing his muscles. Stanford and MIT, dripping with privilege but no sense of wonder. To him, the Enceladons were just another move up the career ladder.

'Prisoner Hunt,' Turner said.

Gibson didn't look up, typed on the keyboard, checked a monitor. He waved at the chair facing the huge water tank that filled half the room. The seat had wires running from it to the workstation, like a modern electric chair. Inside the water tank was a creature like a large octopus, but with only five tentacles. It was constrained within the tank in a copper mesh cage, the tips of its tentacles poking out. This was one of the handful of smaller Enceladons the military had captured in the last few months. Normal fishing didn't work as the Enceladons emitted powerful electromagnetic waves to mess with the ship's equipment and electrocute people when they were caught. Instead the soldiers had used some sort of Faraday cage which disabled the creatures' EM powers.

Lennox knew all this from Oscar Fellowes, one of the Brits on the base. He was MI7, the first of the authorities to show an interest in the creatures from Saturn's moon. He'd been there at the big descent, when they came down en masse and sank into the sea. But he'd been sidelined by the Americans, only allowed to do minimal comms trials.

Lennox watched the creature in the tank. No light display, just a dull, throbbing greyness. This wasn't Sandy, the one he'd connected with before. Lennox, Heather and Ava had driven across Scotland at the start of all this, in order to protect Sandy from harm. Sandy disappeared into the water along with the rest of the Enceladons after the big descent, then Lennox, Heather and Ava were arrested. He wondered about Ava – she'd been kept separate from him and Heather, they hadn't heard anything about her.

The Enceladons weren't all alike – these octopus creatures were part of a much larger ecosystem, along with colossal jellyfish beings the size of small boats, all able to absorb each other's bodies and communicate telepathically.

Occasionally, soldiers would get lucky and capture one of the smaller creatures. Some were killed and dissected, others handed over to Dr Gibson, to work out how they communicated. That was key, apparently, to finding out how and why they came here. Lennox knew the answer already – they were refugees fleeing some kind of climate crisis or invading violence in the under-ice oceans of Enceladus. But the military considered the aliens a threat, an excuse to torture and kill. They didn't understand.

'In the chair,' Gibson said.

Turner nudged Lennox in the back and he sat. Gibson placed the skull cap on him. They'd shaved Lennox's afro so that this worked better, and he hated them for it. He squirmed with the cap on, and Turner coughed and tapped his rifle to make a point.

Lennox stared at the Enceladon in the tank. They looked miserable. They couldn't connect or communicate while in the cage, and for an Enceladon that was the same as dying.

Gibson strode to the workstation, worked on the laptop, then flicked a switch. Lennox felt the skull cap power up, a low hum. Another switch and a ripple ran through the cage in the tank. The creature was still stuck inside its mesh, but started a pitiful light display, sepia and grey ebbing and trickling. It was nothing compared to the things Lennox had seen Sandy do in the wild, when they were free.

'Talk to it,' Gibson said.

Lennox didn't want to give Gibson any data, but at the same time he felt the urge to reach out to this poor soul.

<Are you OK?> he sent with his mind, gritting his teeth.

The creature flickered turquoise down their tentacles, then back to grey.

Silence for a long moment, and Lennox wondered if they'd heard.

<We are dying, converting to original energy state.> Their voice in his head was so sorrowful it made him blink away tears. < Pain. Make it stop.>

2
HEATHER

She stood outside the doctor's office, raised her hand to knock, then hesitated. She looked at Mendoza, who threw her a smile. He was a good kid stuck in the wrong military-industrial complex.

She breathed deep then knocked.

'Come in.'

She opened the door and saw Dr Sharp at his desk, pointing at the spare seat. He was early fifties, slim but exhausted, thin black hair slicked back, shoulders hunched, red eyes.

She closed the door and sat down. He opened his drawer and took out a bottle of Lagavulin and two tumblers.

'Wee dram?' His attempt at a Scottish accent was terrible, given he was raised in New Orleans.

'Do I need one?' Heather said.

He poured the whisky into the glasses and slid one over.

'Shit,' Heather said.

The doctor clinked his glass with hers. She noticed that his was more full. 'Sláinte.' Americans loved Scottish culture in small doses.

'Cheers.' Heather drank and felt the fire in her throat move to her belly. She closed her eyes, pictured her billions of cells working to keep her alive. Or maybe not.

'It's back,' she said, smacking her lips.

Dr Sharp nodded. 'It's back.'

He put his drink down and lifted some scan pictures from his mess of a desk. He held one up to the window, shaky hand making it quiver.

'The headaches, nausea and vomiting are because your tumour has returned. As you suspected. Back in the cerebellum and same size.'

Dr Sharp sipped his drink and handed the scans over. She glanced at them, saw the darkness, didn't need to look any closer. She knew her own body.

The doctor ran his tongue around his teeth, made a sucking sound.

'We need to talk about treatment,' he said. 'Obviously, things are tricky here on the base, but that doesn't mean we can't get you the best available. In fact, this might work in your favour. I can request a surgeon be flown from the US—'

'No surgery.' Heather took a drink to buy herself a moment.

Dr Sharp angled his head. 'This is not terminal, Heather, if that's what you're thinking.'

She shook her head. 'No surgery.'

Dr Sharp stared at her for a long beat then raised his eyebrows in acquiescence. 'Then we can arrange chemo and radiotherapy treatments. I can either have you sent to Raigmore under guard, or we can get the appropriate people to come to New Broom.'

'No chemo.'

Dr Sharp sat forward in his chair. The bags under his eyes were big and black and he smelled of alcohol – not just the dram, but stale booze from his pores. We all have our ways of coping, she supposed. He was a widower, had taken a job as a military doctor to lose himself. Dealing with young men was a relief, he didn't have to face his wife's death from cancer. But now this reminder.

Heather had no television or internet, no way of knowing how the arrival of the Enceladons had been received by the wider world. For all she knew, the UK and US governments had concocted a crazy cover story to account for all the phone footage of giant sea creatures descending from the sky into the water around Ullapool. What the hell that might be was beyond her, but anything was fakable, deniable. Or maybe they had gone the other way – open and honest about the first encounter with alien life in human history. *Here are thousands of interconnected, telepathic, aquatic creatures from the seas of Enceladus*. But that wasn't likely. If that had happened, why were she and Lennox still being held here and experimented on?

Dr Sharp shook his head. 'I'm not an oncologist but I asked around, and both surgery and treatment have a decent chance of success. It won't be easy, of course, but you could still have a long life.'

Heather blew a laugh out of her nose. 'A long life doing what? Locked in a military base, experimented on with those poor creatures they dredge from the sea?'

The doctor finished his whisky and poured himself another. He waved the bottle at Heather, who shook her head.

'I'm sorry for the way you've been treated,' he said. 'You know I would let you go in a heartbeat if I could. But I'm nothing in this place, just like you.'

'Am I supposed to feel sorry for you?'

'We all have our prisons, Heather.'

'Spare me.'

But he was right. She would always be stuck in the prison of her dead daughter – Rosie, cancer, teenager. Subsequent divorce from Paul, then her own diagnosis of cancer. She'd refused treatment first time round, her mind still full of watching Rosie go through pain and misery. She'd decided to end it all, stepping into the sea at Yellowcraigs, pockets full of stones, only to be saved by Sandy, the Enceladon who'd rewired her brain and cured her cancer first time round.

Now the cancer was back and Sandy was gone.

'Maybe there's something else we can do,' Dr Sharp said. 'One of the creatures cured you before, right?'

'Sandy.'

'Maybe she'll turn up in the cages.'

'They.'

'Sorry, *they*.' He didn't mean it badly, had just forgotten. The Enceladons referred to themselves in the plural because each creature was a collection of consciousnesses, as well as being part of a bigger entity, a giant organism. In comparison Heather felt alone, disconnected. Lonely. But she was of interest to those higher up the chain here – because of her telepathy and especially because Sandy cured her cancer.

'I'll have to tell them over at the Jedi Council.' Dr Sharp's joke name for the military brass here.

'Of course.'

Heather went to the window, looked at the expanse of water, land and sky. The loch hiding unknowable fathoms of mystery.

Across the square, the door of the research centre opened and Lennox came out, head low, followed by Turner. Heather's heart ached for Lennox, lost without his connection to Sandy. No one even knew they were here. All they had was each other.

'Maybe one of the other poor creatures in the research centre can do the same thing for you?' Dr Sharp said.

Heather watched Lennox scuff across the square, back to their prison home. She turned to the doctor. 'As soon as the Enceladons are captured they close down, you know that. They start to wither away when separated from their community.'

'Understandable, given everything you've told me.'

Heather had occasionally used the doctor as a release valve. Take what you can get in these circumstances. And she wasn't telling him anything they didn't already know higher up. They'd made it clear they would torture her and Lennox if they withheld any information. People resist torture in spy movies, not in real life.

'Maybe this is my body telling me it's done,' Heather said.

'I didn't think you believed in fate.'

Heather drank the last of her Lagavulin, imagined it was poison turning her cells black. 'Maybe I've just had enough.'

3
AVA

The windowless room made her feel ill. If she was going to spend her next years in prison she wanted a last view over the Royal Mile or down to the Firth of Forth.

She tried to calm her breathing. She was in a back room at Edinburgh High Court, waiting for the jury to come back. Her solicitor – a nervous young guy with good intentions but little experience – had plumped for a defence of voluntary manslaughter on the grounds of loss of control. God knows that was true. On the quayside at Ullapool, her husband Michael had grabbed their newborn daughter and told Ava he would have her committed to a mental hospital. It was the final act in a decade of physical and mental abuse, gaslighting and coercion.

When defending Ava, the kid Mathers made a decent stab of laying all of this out, and it had been painful to hear in court. She was ashamed of what she let Michael do. And ashamed of what she'd done to him in the end, a wrench to the back of his head and he dropped like a stone. She felt that shame acutely when she saw Michael's mother in the courtroom gallery. But she was relieved to be free. Even if she spent the next few years in Saughton Prison, it was worth it.

The door opened and Mathers stood aside to let Ava's sister and mum in, then left. Freya looked angry and tired, face drawn. Ava's mum, Christine, seemed smaller these days and her roots were showing. She held Chloe, who was fussing. The baby saw Ava and reached out, and Ava took her and squeezed her tight. She felt something inside her, a message of comfort and happiness from

Chloe. Plenty of mothers talk about having a sixth sense with their babies, but Ava really had something thanks to Sandy in a bathtub somewhere in the Highlands. The creature had connected to both Ava and an unborn Chloe, able to sense both of their thoughts and link them. After Chloe was born, that link persisted without Sandy.

Ava had told her sister about it, and Freya was doubtful. But then she'd never met Sandy, never experienced that incredible being. If only Ava could talk to Lennox or Heather, *they* would understand, the Enceladon had changed all three of them in a profound way. They were something more than human now, and that scared her.

Ava hadn't told her mum about her telepathic link to Chloe, Christine wouldn't understand. She had led Michael to Ava, and was clearly still confused and conflicted about it all. Ava felt sick that her mum doubted her, but wasn't surprised. Christine had experienced decades of a coercive and abusive marriage to Ava's dad, these things were almost impossible to shake off.

Chloe sucked on Ava's finger and Ava knew she was hungry. She sat and began breastfeeding.

Freya and Christine sat too, Freya with her head down, Christine tapping her feet.

'What do you think they'll decide?' she said.

Freya groaned and put her head in her hands. 'Mum, that's not helping.'

'I thought it went well in the courtroom.'

Ava closed her eyes and concentrated on Chloe. The baby had fussed latching onto her nipple, but now that milk was flowing she transmitted a warm glow of satisfaction and love. Ava was overwhelmed by the feeling that her daughter loved her. Imagine if all mothers felt their babies' emotions this strongly? Imagine if everyone knew what everyone else was feeling? Surely the world would be better, we would have more empathy. She knew nothing about Enceladon society but, given that they all communicated like this, it must feel stronger, more connected.

Freya lifted her head. Her curly red hair was an untidy bundle but she still looked more together than Ava felt. Ava had lost weight in prison. No bail, considered a flight risk, despite a new baby. She'd cut her own red hair short, easier to manage.

'It was fucking awful,' Freya said to their mum. 'Making Ava relive all that shit with Michael.'

'Language, Freya,' Christine said.

It sometimes seemed like their mum was from a different planet. Didn't like swearing, didn't approve of Freya's lesbian lifestyle, thought husbands knew best.

Freya shook her head. 'Swearing is the last thing to worry about. Ava could go to jail.'

'It won't come to that.'

'I wish I had your confidence.' Freya looked at Ava. 'Sorry.'

Ave felt detached from the conversation. She was sharing with her daughter, something they might not be able to do for years, depending on the verdict. She pushed her anxiety to the back of her mind. She'd lived in constant fear of Michael for years, she was determined not to let anyone control her anymore.

There was huge public interest in the case, in part because it was tied to the extraordinary events in Ullapool. She was bemused at the British and American governments' attempts to cover things up. After a whole bunch of footage of the creatures descending into Loch Broom appeared online, there was a frenzy. But the fact that the creatures disappeared under the surface meant it wasn't an immediate problem. The UK government hadn't even admitted they were aliens. Only Ava, Lennox and Heather knew they were from Enceladus. Ava thought about Lennox and Heather. She presumed they were being held somewhere, probably the new military base outside Ullapool.

New Broom attracted widespread interest, of course, but the Americans created exclusion zones. Armed troops, no-fly areas, locals moved out of their homes. None of it explained, just vague statements about environmental hazards. It turns out you could get away with anything if you had enough power. According to the authorities, the events were a weird natural anomaly, some previously unknown animals carried by clouds and falling into the sea. Maybe it was meteorological, storm winds from Africa picking up unusually large jellyfish and octopuses into giant clouds and depositing them off Scotland. New Broom was a research station to examine them.

Conspiracy theories were rife, of course, and Ava had scoured them when first allowed internet access in prison. Searching for some sign of Lennox or Heather, looking for the truth. But the lunatic fringe soon took over, creating so much crazy noise that any legitimate concerns were lost.

Ava was distracted by Chloe's discomfort. It was hard to put into words the sensations she received. Maybe it wasn't too different from other mothers and daughters. She remembered Chloe still being attached through the umbilical cord after she was born. Michael cutting that link, separating them. But she still had Chloe and Michael was gone. She smiled.

'Are you OK?' Freya said.

'I'm fine.'

The door opened and Mathers stood there running a hand through his mop of curly hair. 'The jury have gone for the day. We need to come back tomorrow.'

Ava breathed deeply and tried to stay calm.

4
OSCAR

General Ryan Carson was dominating the room as usual. Oscar wondered about the medals on his uniform, if he'd done something heroic in Afghanistan or Iraq. Carson filled that uniform impeccably, fit and muscular despite being in his fifties. He had a gym and steam room built in his accommodation, which no one else was allowed to use. The privilege of power.

He was roasting a junior officer about another fruitless fishing trip, out in their patrol ship trying to catch Enceladons. As Carson tore strips off the poor kid, Jeong, Oscar's hackles rose. He was still angry that the Americans had turned first contact with an alien species into some pest-control exercise. This was the most profound moment in human history, one Oscar had waited for his entire life, and these thick-necked idiots were destroying any chance they had of learning from the experience. They were like Columbus fucking with the indigenous peoples of the Americas.

Oscar looked out of the window. He never tired of this view. The rolling hills on the other side of the loch like hunched giants, sunlight dappling the ripples on the water's surface. He thought about what was underneath. He would never forget what he'd seen in Ullapool. Standing there as countless creatures descended like gods, their light displays and the rushing noise of their movement, the smell in his nostrils like a bakery. He imagined Sandy leaping from the waves outside now, splaying their tentacles and shimmering in the sun before descending. Or one of the bigger jellyfish like Xander, fifty metres long and half as wide, a colossal ecosystem in their own right, powers and intelligence beyond human comprehension.

That's why Oscar was still here – trying to comprehend. But he'd been sidelined by the Americans and was only invited to these meetings as a courtesy, despite the fact he'd been the first one to realise the importance of all this.

He was riddled with guilt. He'd chased Lennox, Heather and Ava across the country trying to track down Sandy and the other Enceladons. And that had led to this, the humans imprisoned and the Enceladons treated like invasive animals – to be captured, controlled and destroyed.

Carson was now ranting at Dr Gibson about another failed experiment. Oscar hated Gibson, he was the opposite of what a scientist should be. He was hurting the few Enceladons they'd captured, subjecting them to endless experiments, control and isolation they found shocking and painful. Gibson was supposed to be investigating how they communicated telepathically, but it was going nowhere. All he did was work on the poor souls until they gave up and died. Then he dissected them in a pathetic attempt to work out their biology, like something from the Dark Ages.

Oscar would've done things differently but he got very limited time with the Enceladons, or with Lennox and Heather. When he'd spoken to Lennox or Heather they'd been understandably hostile, given his role in this whole shit-show. He didn't blame them.

'We need more specimens,' Gibson was saying now.

Carson leaned his fists on the table. 'You've done nothing with the specimens we've captured.'

'I just need more time.'

Carson shook his head. 'Our top priority is why they're here. We've been asking the same damn question since they arrived, and we're no further forward.'

'You know they're refugees.' Oscar was surprised that this was his own voice.

Carson glowered at him. 'Dr Fellowes. Enough with the bleeding-heart liberal stuff. That's what they want us to think.'

'They're incapable of lying,' Oscar said, clearing his throat. 'That's what Lennox said.'

'And you believe Hunt and Banks? They're collaborators.'

'It's not us versus them, I wish—'

Carson thumped the table. 'Enough. Unless you want your time with the specimens removed.' He leaned closer. 'Let me remind you that you are here out of the generosity of my government. If I had my way you'd be off this base today. So it would serve you well not to irritate me further.'

Oscar's cheeks reddened. He was impotent here and everyone knew it. He'd spoken to his bosses at MI7 but they said their hands were tied. The UK government had been steamrollered by their American counterparts, who refused the international community access to these waters, citing security issues. Having the biggest guns in the world made a difference.

Carson turned to Gibson. 'As for more specimens, we might have good news soon.'

Gibson perked up. 'What do you mean?'

Carson threw a thumb down the table.

'Flores in R&D has almost finished a much-improved fishing rod for these things. Flores?'

Flores was tall, dark and handsome, like a lead in a romance movie. The fact he was a research scientist was ridiculous.

'Final testing happening right now, sir. We should be good for a trial run in the next couple of days.'

'What is this?' Oscar said.

Flores checked with Carson first, who nodded. 'A much bigger version of the Faraday cages, with some mods. Tweaking the EM bursts, adding targeted sonic emissions. The aim is to trap one of the scyphozoa.'

Oscar shook his head. 'The giant ones? General, these are the first creatures from another—'

'Enough.' Carson didn't even have to raise his voice.

Oscar swallowed his anger.

Carson spoke to Flores. 'Let me know when it's ready. I want to catch me a big alien fish.'

5
LENNOX

Lennox cleared the plates as Heather got the cards out. They had a routine – one cooked, the other cleaned up. Tonight Heather had made chicken balti with a kick, the smell of coriander in the air.

When he'd finished washing up in the kitchen, he walked back to the living area. Not much in here – a bookshelf of memoirs and fiction that Mendoza had picked up from a charity shop in Ullapool. A cheap sofa and armchair, the square dining table and two chairs. The view out of the window was the best thing, sun setting over the sea, shadowed fingers reaching behind the mountains.

Heather had dealt his gin rummy hand. He didn't particularly like card games, but there was nothing else to do except play guitar. They played a few hands, Heather won and looked sheepish about it.

A fifty-year-old woman and a teenage boy thrown together was weird, but he liked Heather's easy way of talking, that she cared. He wasn't used to that. This could've felt like a home if they weren't surrounded by armed guards and razor wire.

'How did it go today?' Heather said, dealing.

Those poor fucking creatures, what these bastards were doing to them. Heather and Lennox could sense their pain, as if they themselves were being tortured. If we could all feel each other's pain, none of this shit would happen.

'Bad.'

<Who was it?>

<Leia.>

It was natural for them to switch between speaking out loud and in each other's minds. Lennox couldn't have explained it to someone who didn't have it. It wasn't an open transmission, like you were flooded with someone's every thought. It was directed, though he couldn't say how. It was still possible to keep secrets, stay individual. He was happy about that, but also happy to have this bond.

Heather shook her head. <They're not doing well.>

<No.>

The Enceladons didn't have names, or at least not ones that made sense to Lennox and Heather. It was tied to the idea that they were all part of the same ecosystem and didn't think of themselves as individuals. That was why they faded away and died when captured. Being separated from the group was intolerable.

Heather and Lennox had devised a naming system using characters from *Star Wars* – Luke, Han, Chewie and Leia to begin with. Sadly, only Leia was still alive. More recent arrivals were Rey, Kylo, Finn and Poe.

Heather fanned her cards. 'Do you think they'll live much longer?'

Lennox put his cards on the table. 'We have to do something.'

<Like what? We've been over this a million times.>

<It feels like we're complicit.>

Heather took his hand. <You can't ever think that.> 'We tried to save Sandy and the rest. We did the right thing. These bastards...'

She looked so tired. He remembered something.

<How did it go with the doc today?>

Heather squeezed his fingers and smiled. <Fine.>

<Do they know what it is?>

She shook her head. 'Need to do more tests.'

Lennox put out feelers with his mind, to see if she wanted to send something she didn't want to say out loud. Their telepathy meant they were closer than normal people, but Heather was still a mystery. He sensed nothing.

'That's bullshit.'

She got up from the table. <I'm feeling a bit tired, might turn in.>

<Of course.> He got up too, gave her a hug, watched her walk to her bedroom and shut the door. She moved slowly, touched the doorway for support on the way past.

He walked down the hall to the front door and opened it.

'Hey.'

Mendoza turned and smiled. 'Hey, compadre.'

He was shorter than Lennox but weighed twice as much – all muscle. His combat vest made him look even bulkier. Shaved head, dark-brown eyes, tattoos of birds on his neck and hands. His rifle was across his body, pointing away.

'How's it going?'

'Good.' Mendoza pointed his chin at the sunset. 'Nice evening.'

'OK if I go for a walk?'

'Sure.'

Turner never let him do anything, but Mendoza let him roam. He was grateful for the exercise and fresh air.

He patted Mendoza on the back and walked across the large square. Two soldiers made their way to the canteen, but it was otherwise empty. Lennox walked towards the fence nearest the sea, stood there for a while, then sauntered to the right until he was hidden behind the meeting room. It would be empty this time of day. He walked to the corner of the fence in the gloaming, the sun now behind the western hills. The small Rhue lighthouse on the headland wasn't lit and looked lonely.

He closed his eyes and concentrated. <Hello?>

Nothing.

<Sandy?>

He sighed but kept trying. Thought of poor Leia earlier, asking for the pain to stop. He hoped Sandy was swimming far away through the cold Atlantic so they would never be caught. But he also wanted them right here. His life had been transformed by that creature. Only Heather and Ava understood.

<Sandy, please, if you can hear me.>

'Hey.'

He jumped and opened his eyes. A girl stepped from behind a rocky outcrop on the other side of the fence. She was around his age, tall and lanky. She had long black hair cut into a fringe, green eyes that seemed to glow in the darkness. She wore gym shorts showing off long, tanned legs, thick socks and walking boots, a black waterproof with green trim and a small backpack.

Lennox looked around to check they weren't being watched.

'It's OK,' she said. 'I'm careful.'

Lennox couldn't speak. This was the first person he'd seen apart from the authorities and Heather in months.

'I'm Vonnie,' she said.

'Lennox.'

'What were you doing?'

'What?'

She mimicked him by scrunching her eyes shut, furrowing her brow. 'All that.'

'Nothing.'

'Meditating?'

'Kind of.'

'I meditate. Helps with all the bullshit.' She stepped closer to the fence. 'I guess you've got a lot of bullshit in there.'

Lennox wondered if he was hallucinating.

'Yeah,' he said, feeling stupid. 'Who are you? I mean, where did you come from?'

She nodded behind her. 'My dad owns the Ardmair Holiday Park up the coast. I get out of there when I can, long walks along the shore. Escape all those weirdos.'

'Weirdos?'

'You don't get to see the news in there?'

Lennox shook his head.

'How long since you heard anything?'

'Six months.'

'You and the blonde woman?' Vonnie had been watching them. 'Is she your mum?'

'No.' But she *was* the nearest thing he had to a parent.

'Why are you in there?'

Lennox didn't know where to start.

'Is it to do with the visitors?'

'What do you mean?'

Vonnie sucked her teeth. 'The weirdos have made a camp up the coast. Some of them are paying Dad for berths, but loads just camp on the beach and the side of the road. They call it Camp Outwith. Reckon they've all had a message from the visitors to go there. They stare out to sea for hours at a time.'

'Camp Outwith?'

'If you've met the visitors, they'll be jealous.'

'What do you know about the visitors?'

Vonnie stuck out her lip. 'Just rumours, what the Outwithers talk about. They're from another planet, a sea world, octopuses and jellyfish, weird powers. They can make folk have strokes, electrocute them, give them hallucinations.'

Lennox smiled. 'It's all true.'

Vonnie considered that. 'Maybe the Outwithers aren't so crazy after all.'

'Can you help us?' Lennox said. 'Can you tell people we're being held here?'

'Like some Guantanamo shit?'

'Do people know about this place?'

'I mean, they know it exists,' Vonnie said. 'But no one knows what's going on. They don't allow drones, no shipping, the roads closed for miles.'

Lennox frowned. 'So how did you get here?'

She smiled. 'I know what I'm doing.'

Lennox heard a noise behind him, footsteps across the square, getting louder. Vonnie heard them too.

'You'd better go,' he said.

Vonnie took a step back, fished something out of her pocket. It was a folded piece of paper. She flicked it nonchalantly over the fence. It landed at Lennox's feet and he picked it up.

'I'll see you again. Take care, Lennox.' She stepped behind the rocks and was gone.

The footsteps got louder as he picked up the paper and unfolded it. It was a pencil drawing of him, lifelike and generous, mouth smiling, eyes shining, like he had hope. Underneath she'd written: *Vonnie xxx.*

6
OSCAR

He pulled into the layby between campervans. Switched his engine off and stared at the bonfires on the beach. He got out, felt the sharp air on his face, smelled seaweed. There were a dozen fires, each surrounded by people, shimmering shapes in the firelight. Beyond them, the mouth of the loch was darkness.

Camp Outwith had grown up in the wake of the Enceladons' arrival. Months ago, Carson took the first few arrivals in for questioning. But none of the Outwithers had met any of the aliens, so they were useless. They'd simply been drawn here by some dream, a sense it was vital. Two months ago, soldiers cleared out the camp, sending vans, motorhomes and campers away down the road. But they all came back the next day. Carson didn't waste any more resources on a bunch of deluded hippies, as he saw them.

Oscar was more interested. He'd come incognito a few times, sat at a campfire and listened. They weren't what he expected, not hippies at all. They were ordinary folk from all walks of life, some had left jobs and families to be here. He was reminded of religious visions, they all spoke about a higher meaning, a sense they had to be here. He was envious. The chatter from the campfires gave him a pang in his heart. The sense of community here was the opposite of New Broom.

'Welcome.'

He jumped at the voice and turned. Jodie Becker – she wouldn't call herself the leader here, but that's what she was. Oscar had read her file back at base. Prior to this she made jewellery on Skye, after arriving from London in the nineties. She was black, sixty but looked younger, short and lean in a red boilersuit and Docs, grey quiff, warm smile.

'Hi.'

'You're welcome to join us.'

Oscar shook his head. 'I'm OK.'

She narrowed her eyes. 'You've been here before, right?'

He looked away.

She rubbed her chin. 'It can take a while. I didn't believe when I first felt it.'

'I haven't felt anything,' Oscar said.

She looked at him. He was self-conscious about his suit and plummy accent. He opened his car door and hesitated.

'If you change your mind, you know where we are,' Jodie said.

'Of course.' He climbed into the driver's seat and cleared his throat. Started the engine and watched Jodie in the rear-view mirror as he spun away and drove towards Ullapool.

He finished his Ardbeg and ordered another double. The barman at the FBI was a big lad, red beard and ponytail, lion rampant tattoo on his forearm. Oscar tried to hide his English accent when ordering.

He sipped his dram and looked around the pub. The FBI was busy, a handful of locals and tourists, an old timer playing mournful accordion by the fireplace. The Ferry Boat Inn also did rooms upstairs, but it was mostly just a pub with a stunning view down Loch Broom.

Oscar looked outside at the ferry sitting in dock and remembered the first time he came here. When the journalist Ewan forced his SUV into the water to prevent them chasing Sandy and his human friends. How Ewan died, shot by one of Oscar's special-forces goons, who'd died himself, knocked out and drowned in the submerged car.

Oscar cringed with guilt, anxiety crawling up his throat as he sucked down whisky to fight it. He'd been blinded by his selfish enthusiasm for the Enceladons, had allowed shameful things to happen. People were dead because of him, and for what? The great revelation of first contact had dissipated thanks to the meatheads intent on shooting first and asking later.

A sliver of moonlight painted a shimmering line down the loch outside, and he remembered the giant jellyfish and octopuses descending from the sky into that peaty water. How he'd felt then that anything was possible.

'Can I get you one?'

A young woman with an open face, dark-brown eyes and strawberry-blonde hair in a bun, tight vest top and jeans.

'Excuse me?'

She nodded at the barman. 'Same again, Robbie, and for me.'

Robbie raised his eyebrows but got the drinks. He put them down and didn't ask for payment, which meant they knew each other.

'Sláinte.' She held eye contact as they clinked glasses. 'You're Oscar Fellowes, right?'

Of course, it was too good to be true that a pretty young woman was into him.

'No.'

She sat next to him. 'Yes you are. I'm Vicky McLean, freelance journalist.'

He stared at her for a long time. 'How do you know my name?'

'It's my job to find things out.'

'I've got nothing to say,' he said, nodding at their glasses. 'Except thanks for the drink.'

'Can you confirm that people are held against their will at New Broom?'

He delayed answering by drinking, loving the heat in his belly. 'No comment.'

'Or that you've captured some of these creatures and are experimenting on them?'

He cleared his throat. 'No comment.'

'Or that some people can communicate with them. That they're not from Earth.'

'I just work in research. The animals are an unknown species, but they're definitely oceanic in origin.'

The standard line. It worked fine in press conferences in London and Washington, but here, in the place where weird shit was going down, it was harder to keep a straight face.

'But you have an astrobiology background, a double first from Oxford. Work for the secret service.'

'I'm just a civil servant.'

Vicky smiled and drank. She could certainly handle her malts. Oscar liked her.

'Why would an astrobiologist who worked for the secret service be involved in a top-secret American military base next to the location where thousands of creatures literally fell out of the sky?'

'No comment.'

Vicky finished her drink. Oscar was lagging behind.

'Rumour has it you've been sidelined by the Yanks.'

He lowered his glass. Who the hell had she been talking to? 'No comment.'

She shifted her weight and her bra strap showed on her shoulder.

'OK,' she said. 'Then what do you make of the guys at Camp Outwith? A bunch of kooks?'

'I don't know anything about them.'

'But you've been there a few times.'

He finished his whisky and put his glass down on the bar harder than he intended. 'Have you been following me?'

Vicky smiled again. 'Just keeping my ear to the ground. Local knowledge and all that. Do you deny it?'

All he'd wanted was to get quietly shit-faced and feel sorry for himself, and now he was being manipulated by a cute journalist.

'Well?'

He noticed something over her shoulder, outside. Dancing lights shifting and swirling in the sky, stretching down the length of the loch. Green and blue, red slashes coming and going, oranges ebbing and flowing. It reminded him of the Enceladons' light displays in the wild.

'Northern lights,' Robbie said.

Oscar left the pub along with a few others, Vicky behind him somewhere. He crossed to the shore, stepped over the wall and onto the beach, the crunch of stones. The display overhead was sumptuous, sinewy, iridescent. As if the cosmos was trying to communicate some deep meaning, something transcendent.

He stepped into the water and felt the sharp cold on his feet. His trousers stuck to his legs as he went deeper. He knew there were people behind him, probably laughing, but he kept going, up to his crotch, his stomach. He wanted to dive in, go deep underwater and meet the Enceladons, mirroring the aurora with their otherworldly light show. He wanted to speak to them, connect with them.

But he just stood there up to his waist in freezing loch water, feeling empty, the northern lights dancing across the sky above him.

7
HEATHER

Oscar looked terrible, bloodshot eyes, saggy skin, a cloud of existential dread hanging over him and last night's whisky breath. He was sweaty but shivering.

'Big night?' Heather said.

She looked around his office. Giant maps on one wall – a maritime one of Loch Broom feeding into The Minch then the Hebrides, another one of the icy surface of Enceladus. Heather had done plenty of reading about both while she'd been here, Dr Sharp had rustled up some relevant books for her on the sly. The Minch was the site of the largest meteorite impact on Britain, a billion years ago. She recalled the meteor flashing over her head a few months ago as she stood in the water off Yellowcraigs Beach, ready to go. How she'd been embraced by Sandy.

'Not really,' Oscar said.

She'd originally thought of him as Fellowes, that's how Ewan referred to him when he was chasing them across the country. But he'd insisted at New Broom that she and Lennox call him Oscar, and she was annoyed that it had worked. Using his first name made him seem more human, and she resented that. Oscar was at least partly responsible for Ewan's death, and Heather could never forgive him. Ewan gave his life to save the rest of them. He died, while this hungover shit got to sit in his office feeling sorry for himself.

'Did you see the aurora last night?' Oscar said, taking a large drink of water from a metal bottle. He pressed the bottle against his cheek and sighed.

'Of course.'

She'd grown up in East Lothian, had only seen faint glimmers over the Firth of Forth on rare nights. The display last night was amazing – stunning folds of aquamarine and countless other shades, a sea of colour in the sky. She'd gone outside and stared upward with Lennox until her neck ached.

Oscar drank some black coffee. 'Amazing, wasn't it?'

'Why am I here?'

'Can't we just catch up?'

Heather snorted with derision. 'We're not friends, if that's what you think. You're keeping us here against our will.'

'I told you before, I can't do anything about that.'

'I doubt you've tried very hard.'

'I don't…' He looked out of the window. Almost every building on the base had an astonishing view except the research lab and the R&D centre. Presumably because they had stuff to hide.

He shook his head. 'I don't have a voice here.'

'You've got more of a voice than we have.'

Turner was outside the office with his machine gun. She was fifty years old but still pretty fit, reckoned she could get round the desk and throw a few good punches at Oscar before she'd get hauled off or shot.

She looked at the map of Enceladus's surface. The Enceladons had all lived in the oceans underneath, warmed by volcanoes on the ocean floor. She presumed thousands of scientists were suddenly interested in Saturn's moon, pointing telescopes, analysing spectra, sending new probes. This was the biggest thing to happen to humanity, and it had exposed us as pitiful. She quite liked that. Human exceptionalism had fucked Earth, it was the reason for climate change, imperialism, wars, slavery, capitalism. Once you think of another being as less than you, you can do whatever you want to them. Like those poor Enceladons they captured, experimented on and killed. Oscar had told her he was against all that but he was still here, one of the oppressors, sitting in meetings and taking a salary. Fuck him.

Heather sat forward. 'Why am I here?'

Oscar ran a hand through his tousle of hair and sniffed. He reached into the bottom drawer of his cheap desk and brought out a small cardboard box, slid it over.

'This is for you.'

She didn't move to take it.

Oscar pointed with his chin. 'It's Ewan's ashes. He was cremated in Inverness three days ago.'

Heather blinked heavily. Remembered the first time she met him, the morning after all this started, when he came to her front door in Dirleton, chasing the story. She'd taken him to the pub along the road to lead him away from Lennox and Ava hiding in her house. She felt responsible. He was on their side and she'd let him put himself in danger so they could escape. Now he was in a cardboard box.

'Why have you got him?'

'No next of kin.'

'What about his wife and kids?'

'Ex-wife, now in New Zealand. She wasn't about to drop everything for this.'

'I don't think I should have them.'

'You're the closest he had to family, you and the others.'

'He's dead because of you.'

Oscar shifted in his seat. 'I didn't kill him.'

'You didn't put a gun to his head, but you're responsible.'

'That's not how it was.' Oscar swigged water from his bottle, put it down with a clank that made him jump.

Heather stared at him. 'Typical of you privileged Oxbridge types, swanning through life with no repercussions.'

'I've said before how sorry I am for what happened, how things went. If I could go back and do it differently, I would.'

'Talk is cheap.'

Oscar was pale, like he might be sick. 'Look, do you want his ashes or not?'

She could keep arguing, make him feel more guilt, but she was suddenly tired, throbbing pain at the back of her neck. The tumour letting her know it was getting ready to kill her.

She leaned forward and opened the box. A pile of grey dust, small fragments of charred bone nestling amongst it. It could be anything, anyone.

'I want to perform a scattering ceremony with Lennox,' she said.

'Of course.'

'Into the loch.'

'I can't let you leave the base, you know—'

'I don't give a shit about the rules,' Heather said. 'You were responsible for his death, the least you can do is let us say goodbye to him properly.'

He looked worse than Heather felt, and she was glad. He *should* feel bad.

His shoulders slumped. 'You'll have an armed guard, you know that.'

'Fine. This morning.'

Oscar nodded as if he couldn't wait for this conversation to be over. He pointed at the box. 'Take him and go.'

8
AVA

She watched the jury members file into rows and wondered about their lives. Did they have wives and husbands, families to go home to? Had any of them ever been abused, fought cancer, lost a loved one? Did they have compassion in their hearts or had they been hardened by their lives?

The courtroom was bright, blonde wood everywhere. Ava smiled at the judge on her raised bench, but the judge avoided her gaze. Mathers had said Judge Newbold could be lenient, but she'd been unreadable during the trial. Maybe that made her a good judge.

Ava looked at the public gallery, rising rows of fold-up seats like a cinema. She imagined the folk there munching popcorn, moaning at the lack of action. She saw Freya holding Chloe and her heart sank. Freya smiled and waved Chloe's hand, but she looked terrified. Their mum was next to her, holding a tissue at her nose already.

At the other side of the gallery were Michael's family. His mum, Margaret, stony-faced, and his two older brothers, who looked just like him. She remembered the times Michael had beaten her, and saw the same hatred in his brothers' eyes right now. She wondered about those three Cross boys, beaten by their own father, the abuse passed down through the generations. But that was no excuse, at some point you had to drag yourself into the modern age, had to break the cycle of bullying and violence, had to become a better person. Or die.

The clerk of court conferred with the judge like gossiping teens at a party, then the little man started talking in a loud voice, overstuffed legal language that Ava didn't understand. So much needless ceremony to endure in order to find out if she was screwed.

Eventually the foreperson of the jury stood. She was a middle-aged woman, round in the hips, straggly brown hair in a ponytail. She looked nervous.

'We, the jury, find the defendant guilty of manslaughter due to loss of control...'

The rest was lost to Ava, her head spinning. She sensed uproar in the gallery but didn't turn, didn't want to see their faces. The juror was still talking, the clerk and the judge too, as if they were discussing going out for drinks.

Ava swallowed hard and kept her head down, focused on her breath, closed her eyes and tried to shut out the noise.

She thought hard. <Help me. Please help.>

She hadn't heard Lennox, Heather or Sandy in months, no reason why she would now.

The judge was talking, looking at her, but she couldn't hear. Just a rushing noise in her ears like she was drowning. The judge smiled and Ava thought that was weird, then there was more noise from the gallery. Mathers approached Ava and smiled, touched her elbow.

'...the best we could've hoped for.'

'What?'

Mathers frowned. 'Four-year suspended sentence, Ava. You can go home.'

She wasn't going to prison. She felt sick. Her throat closed and she struggled to breathe. Eventually she sucked in air and saw Freya grinning, jiggling Chloe in her arms, who was fussing because of the noise. Next to Freya, Christine was sobbing into her tissue, holding Freya's arm, her chest rising and falling in stutters.

Across the divide, Michael's brothers were standing and pointing at her as a security guard stepped towards them. Margaret glowered with her lips puckered and her forehead creased. She gripped her handbag tightly as if that was the only thing keeping her upright.

Ava stared at the handbag, remembered hitting Michael across the head with a wrench, wondered how she would feel if someone cracked Chloe's skull like that.

Ava clutched Chloe to her chest, felt Freya's arms around her. She and her sister had been estranged for years before all this. Freya saw Michael for what he was much earlier than Ava did. When Ava left him and ran from the authorities with Lennox, Heather and Sandy, she asked Freya for help and they put their differences behind them. After her arrest, Freya had moved to Edinburgh to care for Chloe as their mum fell apart. Ava would always owe her.

They were in the foyer of the high court, gowned solicitors blustering by, security guards frisking people at the entrance. Christine was here too, subdued and quiet. She'd been controlled by her husband for their whole marriage and this was all hitting hard.

After the court verdict, Ava had been escorted to a room where she and Mathers signed a bunch of paperwork, she had no idea what. But she was free, as long as she didn't break the law in the next four years. She hugged Chloe, felt deep relief.

There was noise down the corridor, and Ava saw the Cross brothers being escorted out by security. They shouted at her, red-faced, and she blushed. She'd killed their brother, and she would always feel that. Margaret walked over to Ava, but Freya stepped between them.

Margaret took in Freya. 'Fucking dyke.'

Freya smiled. 'A fucking dyke who will flatten you if you take another step towards my sister.'

Margaret stared at Ava. 'I hope you can live with yourself.'

She didn't wait for a reply, followed her sons out of the building.

Beyond her, Ava saw a scrum of reporters and photographers, TV cameras too. Blue skies behind them on the Royal Mile. Tourists would be walking up and down, wondering what all the fuss was about, maybe someone famous.

She felt a hand on her back and turned. Mathers looked so happy, like this was the last day of school. He saw the crowd outside and nodded the other way. 'You can go out the side entrance.'

Ava couldn't believe this posh lad had saved her life. She put an arm around him and kissed his cheek. He looked flustered and ran a hand through his hair.

'Thank you,' she said, 'for everything.'

'Just doing my job.'

He led them down a long corridor and through two sets of doors. They walked past a storeroom and a toilet, some admin offices. Ava recognised the way from when she arrived each morning from prison. Chloe squirmed in her arms and she sensed discomfort.

They turned and walked through more doors, then Ava saw the exit. Mathers pressed the release and they were outside in the fresh air, yellow paintwork of St Giles Café across the road, tourists at the small tables outside. A delivery truck was double-parked outside a seafood place down the road. Two large men in suits were getting out of a large SUV with tinted windows parked a few steps away. Ava watched them walk towards her, then one pulled a taser from his pocket and stunned Mathers, who crumpled to the pavement, while the other pushed Freya and Christine against the wall. Taser guy grabbed Ava's arm and pulled her towards the SUV. She screamed and he punched her in the face, blinding pain engulfing her. It took all Ava's energy to keep hold of Chloe, who was crying. She felt blood in her nose and tears in her eyes as the guy dragged her, tried to push her head down into the SUV.

She glanced back, saw Freya break from the other guy and run over. She grabbed Ava's arm and try to prise the thug's fingers away. He tasered her and she fell into Ava, who protected Chloe as she was knocked against the car. For a moment, Freya's mouth was at her ear.

'Take this,' she said, slipping a phone into Ava's pocket. 'I can track you.'

The guy tasered Freya again. Her legs wobbled and she fell, body trembling on the concrete. Ava slid the phone into her underwear while the guy was looking at Freya on the ground. The guy turned and ripped Chloe from her arms, and Ava screamed and scratched as she was shoved into the car. The guy handed Chloe to another man Ava hadn't seen before, then pushed in behind her and punched her again, so hard that she felt faint then passed out.

9
LENNOX

His Converse high tops weren't made for this terrain. He and Heather scrambled over rough rocks towards the shore, Turner and Mendoza behind them. Heather had on walking shoes, the guards in their army boots and him in his slippy trainers, gliding over mossy rock.

They reached the Rhue lighthouse and Lennox looked back at the camp. A vomit of manmade shit in the middle of this natural beauty, everything wrong with the human race. The landscape was so beautiful it hurt his brain, and dumped in it were tons of concrete, prefab buildings and fencing, military boats in the dock. It was a large base, but compared to the surroundings it was a tiny speck. Being outside like this must make the guards feel vulnerable. They couldn't even understand what was out there, Turner and Mendoza hadn't seen the Enceladons when they landed. Lennox had been up in space with them before they descended. He still struggled to get his head around it.

He squeezed his eyes shut.

<Sandy? Hey.>

'What are you doing?' Turner said, nudging him with his gun.

Lennox followed Heather to the tiny bay near the lighthouse. Slipped down a grassy slope to a grey, stony beach. Heather was at the water's edge and he squelched over seaweed to her. She removed her small backpack and unzipped it, lifted out a cardboard box and placed it on the shingle.

Turner and Mendoza stepped onto the beach but stayed above the high tide line.

Heather looked at Lennox. His feet were damp inside his shoes.

'Do you want to say anything?'

Lennox thought about it. He'd never seen a dead body until Ullapool, then Ewan and Michael died in front of him. He'd seen a few Enceladons close to death in the research tanks. He looked at Turner and his automatic weapon, imagined how many people he could kill with it. He got a smile from Mendoza.

He turned back to Heather, shook his head. 'No.'

She looked up and down the loch, then at the box. She picked it up, opened it. Stared for a long time.

'Ewan, I remember sitting in the pub, lying to you. You knew I was lying, and I knew you knew, that's why we got on. You were smart and selfless. You gave your freedom so we could escape.' She paused and looked back at New Broom. 'And you gave your life to save ours. That was so brave. It's hard to do the right thing, but you did the right thing.'

She faltered and Lennox wondered if there had been something more between them. They were the same age, both with marriages that had fallen apart.

Heather wiped at her cheeks and Lennox realised she was crying.

<Are you OK?> he sent.

She didn't register that she'd heard him, but he knew. She'd left herself open and he could feel her grief, waves of sadness, not just for Ewan but for her teenage daughter, Rosie. It was so strange to be so connected with someone like this, to understand what another person was thinking. He didn't feel human anymore, he felt like part of something bigger.

<I'm fine.> She sniffed and glanced at him.

Turner and Mendoza stood watching, not knowing they were communicating. Lennox felt sorry for them, isolated in their own minds, stuck in their individual bags of meat.

Heather took a handful of Ewan's ashes from the box, stepped to the water's edge and scattered them. The grey powder peppered the surface then sank, some grains drifting in the ebb and flow. Lennox stepped forward and did the same. Then he took a larger handful and walked into the water up to his knees. He remembered before when he'd gone swimming with Sandy then Xander in this loch, met the others in their community.

'Hey.' This was Turner, chin up, watching. Mendoza touched his arm.

Lennox took the box from Heather and walked further in, upending what was left into the water, the grains circling his knees.

<Sandy-Lennox partial!>

He yelped at the voice in his head, a voice he'd dreamed of hearing for six months, a voice he never thought he'd hear again.

<Sandy!> He looked around the water. Calm.

Turned to see Heather wide-eyed. She'd heard them too.

<Sandy-Lennox-Heather partial. Sandy-Ava partial not apparent.>

<Sandy, where are you?>

<Here.>

He saw a familiar ripple of lights under the surface, slipping through the wash at incredible speed, then two tentacles were wrapped round his ankles. Lennox tried to keep his face calm as he glanced at Turner and Mendoza. Turner narrowed his eyes and took a few steps down the beach.

<So happy to be connected again,> Sandy said in his mind.

<Sandy, where have you been?>

<With Enceladon tribe, hiding from other humans. Looking for Lennox-Sandy partial.>

<I've been locked up by the other humans.>

<Both of us.> This was Heather in his head, like fingers in his mind.

<Sandy-Ava-Chloe partial?>

<We don't know where they are.>

Sandy squeezed his ankles. <Come with us.>

Lennox looked at Heather, who'd taken a step into the water.

<We can't,> she sent.

Lennox frowned. <Why not?>

<They'll shoot us.>

'Hey.' This was Turner again, closer.

Lennox saw Sandy's other tentacles rippling through the water as if tasting it. <Former Ewan energy?>

Heather shook her head. <You can sense that?>

<Ewan-universe eternal.>

'Hey!' Turner was running, stones crunching underfoot.

<Get out of here,> Lennox sent.

<Sandy-Lennox-Heather partial connected.>

<Go.>

Turner was splashing through the water, Mendoza close behind him. They could surely see Sandy's tentacles, their head throbbing in blue-green flashes.

'What the fuck?' Turner said, turning to Mendoza. 'It's one of them.'

He grabbed Lennox's arm and hauled him away. Sandy's tentacles let go as he fell backward into the shallows. Turner stumbled but righted himself as Heather ran to Lennox, Mendoza splashing into the water behind.

Turner unslung his gun and flicked the safety.

Sandy darted to the left in a haphazard movement, then switched direction.

<Lennox-Heather partial, we will return.>

Turner let rip, spraying bullets into the loch in a sweeping arc, wider and wider.

<We will connect again soon.> And Sandy was gone, deep underwater.

Lennox burst out laughing.

10
OSCAR

A rap on the office door broke Oscar out of his stupor. 'Come.'

It was that blowhard Turner. 'There's been an incident, sir.'

He was surprised the American troops still called him 'sir', but they imbued it with a huge amount of disrespect.

'What sort of incident?'

'Hunt and Banks are in the stockade.'

He should've known the ceremony for Ewan was a ruse. 'Did they try to escape?'

'No, sir, they encountered an illegal.'

It angered Oscar that the soldiers referred to the Enceladons as 'illegals', like they were refugees crossing the border. Just another way of dehumanising them.

'What?'

'At the lighthouse. One came right up and contacted the boy. I attempted to shoot it—'

'You what?'

'I fired on the—'

'Oh, for fuck's sake.'

Oscar grabbed his jacket and made for the door.

A thick-necked guard was at the desk in the small room to the front of the stockade. He checked Oscar's ID.

'I'm part of the research team,' Oscar said.

'Your name isn't on the list.'

'It's last-minute.'

'It's against regulation, sir.'

Oscar stuck his chest out. 'Do you want me to call Carson, get him down here? I don't think he'd appreciate being disturbed for something this trivial.'

The guard took a picture of Oscar's ID then handed it back. 'Number two.'

He pressed the release on the heavy, barred door and Oscar heaved it open, went through. It was a short, bright corridor, strip lights overhead, barred doors either side. He waited at number two until it clicked open then went in.

Heather was sitting on a bench, Lennox lying on the thin bed. They both opened their eyes at the sound of the door.

'Why are we here?' Heather said. 'We've done nothing wrong.'

Oscar looked for somewhere to sit, but there was nowhere. 'Tell me what happened.'

Heather shot a glance at Lennox and smiled. They were sharing something. Oscar knew they were telepathic with each other even without Enceladon help, but had kept that from the Americans. Gibson was only interested in how the Enceladons communicated with humans, it had never occurred to him the humans could communicate with each other. If Carson knew, they would start experimenting on them.

'Jesus, I know you're talking to each other.'

Heather shook her head, looked sorry for him. He hated that condescension, but it was well deserved. He was just an ordinary man, they were something else.

'Why should we tell you anything.'

'Look, I'm just trying to do the same thing as you,' Oscar said, hands out. 'I want to make contact.'

Lennox ran a hand over his buzzcut. 'You're part of all this.' He waved at the small, barred window. 'You're one of them.'

'That's my point,' Oscar said. 'It shouldn't be us and them. I want to feel what you feel.'

Heather and Lennox shared another look, something more conciliatory.

Oscar leaned against the wall, trying to look nonchalant. 'I'll get you out of here, I just need to clear it with Carson.'

'Do that first,' Heather said, 'then maybe we can talk.'

Oscar drummed his fingers against the wall then looked at Lennox. 'OK, just tell me – was it Sandy?'

Lennox rubbed the back of his neck, glanced at Heather.

'Turner said he shot at them,' Oscar said. 'Maybe I can help them if they're in trouble.'

'They're not in trouble,' Lennox said.

Oscar pushed away from the wall. 'How do you know, did they tell you they were OK? What else did they say?'

The plural thing made perfect sense to Oscar. If you were part of an ecosystem that communicated seamlessly between parts, you would be plural too.

Lennox shook his head.

Oscar turned to Heather.

'Get us out of here,' she said. 'Then we'll see.'

He stumbled over peaty banks in his brown brogues. The air was cold but the sun high, a constant breeze from The Minch in his face.

The Rhue lighthouse looked bigger from far away, paradoxically, it seemed to shrink in the landscape as he reached it.

He climbed down to where Heather and Lennox had been with Ewan's ashes, according to Mendoza. He stood on the shingle and looked out to sea. The wind ruffled the water and he thought about energy transferring from wind to wave. Energy all around him that he couldn't see with his pathetic human senses. Birds navigated by sensing magnetic fields, some fish sent electrical messages, dogs lived in a world of scents. In one way, it wasn't surprising the Enceladons had telepathy, just another extension of the animal kingdom's sensory experience. And here he was, stuck with his limited human brain, trying to understand it.

He closed his eyes and listened to the wind and waves. The philosopher Thomas Nagel wrote a famous essay in the seventies called *What Is It Like To Be a Bat?* Even if we could communicate with other animals, our different experiences of the universe would make it impossible for us to understand each other. The limits of the human imagination. We can no more comprehend what it's like to be a bat or a dog or a fish than they can know what it is to be human. So where did that leave the Enceladons, creatures from another world who communicated through thought? He had to *try* to understand. To connect. Otherwise why was he here?

He saw something in the loch, wondered if it was Sandy or Xander, one of the others. As it got closer, he recognised it. The cardboard box that Ewan's remains were in, soggy and falling apart. Ewan committed to the sea, already a part of the universe again. Where was his consciousness now?

Oscar watched the water for a long time, hoping for something to happen.

11
AVA

She was underwater, swimming around and looking for Chloe. She dived deeper towards lights in the distance, saw Sandy, Xander and thousands of other aliens having a party, giant paper hats, streamers, thumping beats pulsing through the water. She tried to talk to them, ask where Chloe was, but they ignored her. The dance music made her head pound and her mouth was dry. A force dragged her away from the party towards the surface. Alongside her were different whales – blue, humpback, sperm – and dolphins, seals, basking sharks. They all swam upward and she was their leader, then they breached and spun in the air.

Her head bumped against the window and she opened her eyes. She was in the back of the SUV with the two muscle-bound guys in suits. They both had handguns in holsters under their jackets and wore shades like they were in a Hollywood movie.

She closed her eyes, head throbbing with pain, and tried to swallow. Stretched her fingers and toes, shifted her weight, sensing for injuries. Her wrists were tied together. The pain was in her face and head, her nose crusted with blood, a lump on the back of her head. She raised her hands to check her nose.

'You OK?'

She opened her eyes again. This was the guy opposite her. He was shorter than the other one but wider, spent more time in the gym to compensate. He had a neatly trimmed moustache and buzzcut brown hair.

'Where's my baby?'

Moustache removed his sunglasses. 'She's being taken care of.'

East Coast American accent, calm voice.

'She's my daughter, I need her here.'

'She's travelling separately.'

Ava glanced outside at the countryside. They were on a high moor, brown scrubland either side, tiny burns lacing the rolling hills. The road was like a black scar through the landscape.

She looked down at the plastic restraint on her wrists. Not so tight it was cutting her, but tight enough.

'Travelling where?'

Moustache held out a water bottle. 'Drink this.'

Ava shook her head but her mouth was so dry, her tongue swollen. 'Where are we going? Who are you?'

Moustache waggled the bottle. The other guy hadn't moved. He had a pink scar along his square jawline. Moustache leaned forward. She pictured leaping up and punching his face, how far she would get before being tasered or shot.

She grabbed the bottle and drank, cold water like sunshine in her throat.

'Small amounts,' Moustache said.

She ignored him, kept glugging. Eventually she stopped and wiped her lips, held on to the bottle.

'What did you give me?'

Moustache shook his head. 'Just a little sedative.'

'You roofied me?'

'It was best that you rest for the journey.'

'Best for who?'

Scarface nodded. 'I told you we should've given her a bigger dose.' A different American accent, Texan maybe.

Moustache gave him a look.

Ava remembered being in court, the guilty verdict, confusion afterwards, the dream state she fell into, signing papers, holding Chloe, escorted out. Then these guys taking the law into their own hands.

'I was released,' Ava said. 'I was free.'

Moustache looked apologetic. 'We're nothing to do with that.'

'You mean you're above the law.'

'I prefer to think we're outside Scottish jurisdiction.'

Ava waved her bound hands at the window. 'And yet we're in Scotland.'

She realised that she recognised the landscape. They'd passed the head of a loch, the land spreading out and up either side in a familiar U-shape, like a funnel towards the ocean. This was the head of Loch Broom and they were driving towards Ullapool.

'Where's Chloe?'

'I told you—'

'When can I see her?'

'Soon.'

She'd been separated from Chloe since her birth except for when Freya brought her to prison visits. Mathers had pleaded with the authorities that Ava be allowed to go to her mum's place under house arrest, but no dice. And now, just as she thought the nightmare was over, they were apart again.

'We're going to New Broom,' she said, staring at Moustache.

He nodded. 'Yes.'

She'd read as much as she could about what was happening there. Lennox and Heather had been arrested along with her in Ullapool, but then they were separated. They hadn't been charged with anything but she knew they couldn't have been released or they would've come to see her. She'd tried communicating with them but came up blank, which meant they were somewhere far away. She'd seen the stories about New Broom being built and realised they must be there. Where else? The media furore about the base died down, the news cycle moving on to other stuff.

But the base was the key. They were doing something there, with Heather and Lennox, maybe with Sandy and the others. And now her and Chloe.

The vehicle sped down the slope into Ullapool and she remembered the last time she was here, heavily pregnant, full of stress about the baby, Michael, Sandy. But at least then she had her daughter with her.

The SUV slowed as a supermarket truck signalled to turn into a filling station. Cars coming round the corner in the other direction were making it wait.

They were right next to the water, a huge shimmering expanse flanked by hills. She imagined opening her door and leaping the small wall, running into the water and … what? Swimming off with her hands tied together to a happily ever after?

She realised her fingers were touching the door handle, glanced at Moustache.

'Don't be stupid,' he said. 'Chloe is waiting at New Broom.'

But her fingers lingered on the handle all the same.

Scarface cleared his throat. 'Plus, we'd kill you before you got out of the car.'

She sat back in her seat and waited for what was to come.

12
HEATHER

She walked from the kitchen to the living room with two plates of scrambled eggs on toast. Lennox ate like a horse and she liked that. Rosie had been the same – long-legged after a growth spurt, suddenly rangy in an impossible way. She walked with a self-conscious swagger, simultaneously full of newfound confidence and cripplingly uneasy with her new body. It had been glorious and painful to watch. After her cancer diagnosis that swagger disappeared, and within months she could barely shuffle from one room to the next. Heather couldn't bear it, yet she and Paul had had to – hospital visits, chemo and radiotherapy, the state of her afterwards, how it sapped her life. The injustice filled Heather with rage, which had never left her.

Lennox had almost finished his lunch and she'd barely touched her own. She pushed egg around and thought about earlier, Ewan's ashes, Sandy in the loch, Oscar at the stockade.

Lennox raised his eyebrows at her, his mouth full. <We have to get back to that beach.>

She was briefly startled at his voice in her head. Maybe at sixteen years old you could easily get used to new powers, but at fifty she wasn't sure if she was made for this. It was the future and she wasn't convinced she wanted to be part of it.

She looked at him as he mopped up egg on the plate. <We can't.>

'What?' He pushed his plate away. <We have to, you heard what Sandy said.>

She shook her head.

Lennox stared at her. <They said they'll come back for us.>

She chewed on a piece of toast and tried to think.

<It's like you don't want to get out of here,> Lennox sent.

<It's not that.> She looked outside.

'Then what?'

Lennox leaned forward on his elbows. Freckles across his nose, big brown eyes. She thought about his life, bullied and harassed as a mixed-race kid. He'd told her stories about the shit he got at school, in the children's home. And she thought about how the Enceladons were being treated here. Humanity was a shitshow.

'Sorry, I just...' She didn't know what to say.

Lennox took the plates to the kitchen. <I think Oscar will help us.>

He returned and picked up the guitar from the sofa. Strummed a few chords as he waited for her to reply.

Heather shook her head. <I don't trust him.>

<He got us out of the stockade.>

<He has no *real* power.>

<But he believes in the Enceladons, right? He knows they're the future, he understands they're not the enemy.>

Heather walked across to him. 'He killed Ewan, have you forgotten?'

'He didn't actually kill him.'

'Oh come on, you're not that naïve. Ewan was shot because of Oscar. You're very quick to forgive and forget.'

Lennox put the guitar down and stood. <I'm not forgiving or forgetting anything. We just need to look at what's happening now.>

'We're here because of Oscar.'

Lennox looked at her with sorrow in his eyes, maybe pity. She couldn't take that. After everything they'd been through together.

Lennox shook his head and walked to the window, tapped on it, pointing outside. <We've found Sandy again, that changes everything. While we were separated, I couldn't stand it, like having part of myself removed. But now we know Sandy is OK, they're all OK.>

'We don't know what they've been doing,' Heather said. 'Maybe they're ill, maybe the seas here don't suit them. There are a million reasons why they might not be thriving. You've seen the ones that have been captured, they die.'

<That's *because* they're captured.> Lennox ran his hand over his head. 'Why are you so down on this? Why are you against thinking of the future?'

Heather pressed her lips together. She didn't want secrets between them. <My brain tumour is back.>

Lennox stared at her then reached out and held her hand. She felt his smooth skin against her own, imagined the cancer spreading between them. She tried to take her hand away but he held tight.

'Sandy can cure it again, right?' he said. 'That's even more reason to get together. To save your life.'

Heather pulled her hand away. She closed her eyes, easier not to see his face.

<Maybe I don't want my life saved.>

13
LENNOX

Lennox knocked on the front door from inside. Mendoza opened it and smiled, and Lennox went outside and closed the door behind him. Heather had gone to her room, and Lennox wondered about what she'd said. How can anyone not care if they die?

'Hey,' he said, scuffing his trainers in the dirt.

'Hey, Little Man.'

This was a joke about Lennox's greater height.

Lennox lifted his head. 'That was something earlier, huh?'

'Sorry about Turner, man. He's a trigger-happy jerk, could've shot you.'

Lennox shrugged. 'It's OK.'

Mendoza gave him a sideways look. 'What are those things like? I've only seen them locked in cages, looking half dead. That was different this morning.'

'Honestly? They're incredible. Like nothing else.'

'What do they want?'

'I think they just want to be left alone.'

'Then why did they come all this way?'

'No choice. Their homeland was taken over by something else. They're refugees.'

Mendoza pressed his lips together. 'I get that.'

He stared across the compound and Lennox followed his gaze. The sun was high in a clear sky, the sharpness of the light making the loch seem almost hyper-real, like the setting of an epic fantasy.

'So it's not like *Independence Day* or shit?'

Lennox snorted a laugh. 'That's a terrible movie.'

'I liked Will Smith in it.'

Lennox didn't know how to explain. That was last century's thinking, an archaic idea of aliens. Now that it had really happened, all those movies were redundant.

'Do you think Turner killed that one today?' Mendoza said.

'No.'

'You sound pretty sure.'

'I know he didn't.'

Mendoza narrowed his eyes. 'So they *do* speak to you, huh?'

Lennox lowered his head, but nodded all the same.

'What's that like?'

Lennox thought for a long time. It had redefined him, made him into something different. But he couldn't communicate that. 'It's fucking crazy.'

Mendoza laughed. 'I bet.'

Lennox let silence fall over them for a minute. 'Can I go for a walk?'

Mendoza sucked his teeth. 'I don't know, man. Fellowes said to keep an eye on you two.'

'Fuck Fellowes,' Lennox said automatically.

'That guy has your back, bro. I heard he argued with Carson to get you out the stockade, said it wasn't anything *you* did. Turner bullshitted some but I told Carson the truth.'

Lennox pulled at his earlobe. 'Maybe.' He looked up. 'So can I go for a walk?'

Mendoza pointed at the fence along the south side of the compound. 'Stay out of the courtyard. If one of the officers sees you, I'll probably get shit.'

'Thanks.'

'Go on.'

Lennox skipped down the step and away from the main square. When he reached the fence, he turned and waved at Mendoza, then walked parallel to the fence. The sun was warm on his skin in the shelter from the wind.

He walked behind the supplies store, out of view of Mendoza. Closed his eyes and tried hard.

<Sandy. Please, Sandy, can you hear me? Sandy-Lennox partial is stretched, need to reconnect.>

Nothing. He opened his eyes, watched seagulls drift in the sky, circling on thermals. He wondered what they were thinking, if he would be able to understand.

He stared at the sea. <Sandy, you said you'd come back. I need to speak to you, hear your voice.>

Silence.

He walked to the end of the building and round the corner. He remembered last night, reached into his pocket and took out the picture Vonnie drew of him. He touched her name at the bottom of the picture with his thumb, imagined her popping up again from behind the rocks.

He stared at the land outside the fence for a long time thinking on what she'd talked about – Camp Outwith. There was a bunch of folk up the coast who'd had some kind of experience. Maybe the Enceladons were somehow choosing people who understood. Who were open to the idea of taking humanity somewhere new.

He thought of Vonnie's black hair, green eyes, long legs. Stared for a long time through the fence trying to conjure her into existence.

14
OSCAR

He scoped the binoculars in a low, wide sweep across the water. The light was fading, the loch in shade now. He lowered the glasses and scanned the horizon from Ben Mor Coigach to Annat Bay on the peninsula. Stared at Isle Martin for a moment, raised the glasses, just waves on the shore.

He'd been out in the army RIB for two hours, taken it into open water as far as he dared. He'd powered around the Summer Isles, along the coast to Achiltibuie, past Horse Island, Bottle Island and Priest Island. Saw a colony of grey seals on the low rocks at Càrn Deas, soaking up the last rays. Spotted a basking shark in the narrow inlet between Horse Island and the rocky outcrop to the southeast. Three black knives through the water – snout, dorsal and tail fins – flicking languorously in the shallows.

But no Enceladons.

He'd taken the boat without asking, flashed his ID and put on his best Oxford-graduate pomp when questioned.

Now he was back at the loch mouth, skimming the shoreline at Ardmair. A few fires were lit along the beach at Camp Outwith. Oscar killed the engine and looked through the binoculars as he bobbed in the water. Saw faces smiling, talking, someone cooking over a fire, another with a barbecue, chugging a can of beer. Like they were on holiday. They didn't understand how the world worked – you can't just abandon everything, turn up here and expect aliens to jump out of the water into your lap. You had to work for these things.

He lowered the glasses from his face and looked around. Saw a small object in the water and swung the binoculars round. Just a seal staring at him inquisitively. He wondered what it was thinking. Who is this idiot out on a boat at twilight, expecting to find something that big military vessels couldn't?

'Fuck off.'

He laughed at the sound of his own voice and gunned the engine. He rounded Rhue Point and saw the lights of New Broom, spotlights in the gathering gloom, as if they could keep darkness at bay. As he reached the dock, he saw two soldiers with their weapons raised.

He briefly thought about turning round, making for The Minch, out into the Atlantic with the whales and dolphins, sharks and seals and Enceladons.

Instead he slowed and docked, tied the boat up and stepped onto the boardwalk.

'Carson wants to see you,' the taller soldier said.

They walked him across the courtyard to the general's office, waited outside as he knocked and entered.

Carson had a large tumbler of whisky in his big paw, sat behind his desk with a table lamp on. Outside his big window, the land across the loch was a sinuous black curve against the mauve sky, like the outline of a fantastical beast.

He nodded at Oscar to take a seat. 'What am I going to do with you, Fellowes?'

Oscar didn't speak.

'Taking RIBs without permission now. After I let your little friends out of jail.'

'Sorry, sir, I was just having a last look for them before dark. I know you had people out earlier after the incident, but I thought—'

'You don't think.' Carson took a slug of whisky. The bottle of Bruichladdich on his desk was half full. He smacked his lips. 'One of the saving graces of this place, they make a fucking great Scotch.'

'Yes, sir.'

Carson pulled a glass from his desk drawer, poured a few fingers from the bottle and slid it over.

'I like it with ice,' Oscar said.

'Just drink.'

It slid down easy, then set his guts on fire.

Carson chuckled. 'I'm thinking of having you sent home, Fellowes.'

'Sir, no. I'm valuable here.'

'We both know that's not true.' Carson stared at him. 'You're not in step with what we're doing. You're on their side rather than ours.'

'It's not about sides.'

Carson sipped his dram. 'It is *absolutely* about sides. I'm a military man, you understand? It's always us and them, otherwise it makes no sense.'

Oscar cleared his throat. 'Maybe if our governments discussed it a bit more, if they consulted with the scientific—'

'You're living in a goddamn dream world, Fellowes. That's way above our pay grades. They talk, consult, whatever. Then we get our orders and carry them out.'

'But don't you see our approach isn't getting any returns? We're no further forward than when we started.'

'We're working on that.'

'The bigger cage, you said. That won't make a difference.'

'You haven't seen it.'

Oscar felt the need for more whisky. 'Does it work?'

'Of course.' Carson downed the remainder of his drink. 'But that's not what I'm talking about.'

'Then what?'

Carson shook his head. 'None of your concern. You're transferred as soon as I get the paperwork sorted out.'

'Please don't do that, sir. I'll toe the line, I just want to be part of this. I need it.'

Carson regarded him and Oscar felt like he was at boarding school again, being hassled by the prefects. 'I've made up my mind. You're gone in a few days.'

Oscar felt like crying. He couldn't believe this was the end. 'If I'm going, tell me what you're working on.'

Carson poured himself another whisky. 'We have a new subject, the third person involved in initial contact.'

'Ava? What do you mean you have her?'

Carson waved a hand in the air. 'Special rendition, of a sort.'

'You snatched her.'

'Needs must.'

'But how is she any use? You've seen the other two, they hide their communication with the Enceladons. I'm sure Ava will be the same.'

'Not her,' Carson said with a grin. 'The baby.'

15
HEATHER

She pulled the plug from the sink and watched the water drain. Dried her hands on a towel and stared out at the Rhue lighthouse. She thought about their encounter with Sandy, Turner shooting. The joy she felt at Sandy's voice in her head.

She stared at the lighthouse in the gloom. It wasn't lit, ships had no need of its warning anymore. Beautiful constructions from a different time, now redundant. Eventually, the rest of our culture would go the same way. She remembered sitting on Yellowcraigs Beach all those times she needed to be alone, when Rosie was going through chemo. She loved the lighthouses of the Firth of Forth – Fidra, Bass Rock, Isle of May – their complex sequences, a language only sailors could decipher.

She heard the front door open and waited for Lennox. She felt sorry for arguing with him, but he was so relentlessly positive about Sandy and the Enceladons, and she was so weary. She wanted to share his enthusiasm for what might come, but she'd learned with Rosie never to get her hopes up. The same for her own brain tumour. She wondered if Sandy could really cure her again. The fact that the tumour was back so soon suggested Sandy's intervention was temporary.

'Hello?'

Not Lennox but another voice she recognised straight away.

She turned and saw Ava in the kitchen doorway, tears on her cheeks.

Heather strode over and wrapped her in a hug. Ava sobbed and buried her head in Heather's chest. Heather just held her and breathed calmly. It was a trick she'd used when Rosie was a toddler, just hold them and wait, don't say anything.

Ava's breath caught in her throat but Heather felt her begin to calm.

She remembered hugging Rosie in a hospital bed, both of them knowing she would die.

Eventually Ava pulled her head up, but kept her arms around Heather's waist.

<It's so good to see you.> Ava's voice in her head, clear as a bell.

<And you.>

Ava touched a finger to her temple. <I haven't done this in months. Since I got arrested.>

<What about with Chloe?>

<It's not the same, it's feelings, moods.>

'Where is she?'

Ava burst out crying again. 'They took her from me. They won't let me see her.'

Heather looked at her. Ava's hair was short and shaggy, dark bags under her eyes. She'd lost weight, her collarbone jutting out at the edge of her blouse.

'What's happened?' Heather said. 'We don't get any information here. Last I knew you were arrested for Michael's murder.'

Ava looked around. <Where's Lennox?>

Heather tilted her head. <Outside somewhere.> She ushered Ava to the table, put the kettle on. <Tell me everything.>

Ava waved at her smart clothes. <I was just in court. My trial.>

Heather threw two teabags into the pot. 'Have you been in prison all this time?'

'No bail. They thought I was a flight risk.'

Heather shook her head as the kettle boiled. She poured water into the pot and brought it to the table with two mugs.

'I was found guilty of manslaughter, but got a suspended sentence,' Ava said, wiping her face. 'I was free, had Chloe in my arms, I was outside.' She swallowed. 'Then these guys attacked me and shoved me into their car, took Chloe. They drugged me. When I woke up I was almost here, and they said I would never see Chloe again if I didn't cooperate.'

'Jesus.'

Ava shook her head. <What about you and Lennox? You're prisoners, right?>

Heather poured the tea and shrugged. <They do whatever they want here. What does the rest of the world know about New Broom? Do they even know it exists? What about Sandy and the Enceladons? Surely the world's gone apeshit?>

Ava took her mug and stared at the curls of steam.

Heather had a sinking feeling. She'd hoped that people cared, that they would find a way out. That folk were campaigning for their release.

'The news was crazy for a while,' Ava said, hands wrapped around her mug. 'The footage of the Enceladons coming down over Ullapool. But the backlash kicked in pretty quick – that the footage was fake or a hoax, or distracting from something else. Folk know about New Broom, but the government said it's just a research station looking into new aquatic species. There were early rumours about aliens, but that got drowned out by online bots and trolls claiming it was hallucinations caused by vaccines or pollutants, something the military were testing. I guess locals might think differently, but the rest of the world has moved on.'

It was a post-truth world now, full of lies and misinformation. The idea that aliens came to Earth and no one knew or cared made Heather furious.

A headache throbbed at the base of her skull. She would be sick soon, felt her stomach roil.

The front door opened without a knock and Heather recognised the scuff of a soldier's heavy boots. Turner appeared at the doorway and pointed his gun at Ava.

'You're wanted in the research centre.'

Ava looked at Heather, then shook her head.

Turner flicked his thumb over his shoulder. 'Your kid's there.'

16
AVA

The guard marched her across a dusty courtyard, lit by bright spotlights, casting shadows into the nooks of buildings. She could sense the mountains all around, felt them looking down on her. To the west, the sky was still light on the horizon, the sea shimmering below.

They reached a low green hut, and Turner opened it with his security card and waved her inside. She hesitated then stepped in, past an empty reception desk to a large room dominated by a huge water tank.

She spotted a man about her own age, smart shirt and trousers, neat hair.

'Dr Gibson,' Turner said.

He looked up, then across the room, and Ava followed his gaze.

Chloe was strapped into a recliner, wiggling her feet in the air and playing with her toes. She wore a small skull cap with wires coming from it.

<Baby! Mummy's here.>

Chloe smiled at her and Ava's heart dissolved. She felt the warmth of recognition from her daughter, mixed with an undercurrent of anxiety.

Chloe pushed her hands out towards Ava, who ran to her, only to feel Turner's grip yanking her back.

'Please sit,' Gibson said, pointing at an empty seat a few feet from Chloe.

'Let me go to my daughter,' Ava said through her teeth.

'All in good time, we don't want to taint the experiment.'

'Experiment?'

Gibson smiled and it was utterly hollow. 'Little Chloe has already given us some interesting readings.' He was standing at a desk with an open laptop, a stack of electronic boxes with lights flashing.

Ava looked at Chloe, who smiled and giggled.

When Chloe was first born, this ability to directly experience her emotions had overloaded Ava. But she got used to it quickly, learned to tune in and out, arrange a mental filter to allow her a little distance from her daughter. Then, gradually, she lowered her defences, let more of her daughter's signals into her mind, made them part of herself.

At times in prison, it felt like part of her own body had been ripped out when they were separated. As soon as they were in the room together, it was like she was whole again. The size of all this scared her, but it was also thrilling.

She yanked her arm away from Turner's grip and ran to Chloe, who stretched her fingers out and rocked in the recliner.

Ava was almost at Chloe when Turner hauled her backward so hard she fell over. Chloe cried, Ava feeling the baby's swell of emotions as she rubbed at her scuffed knees and stood.

Turner was pointing his gun at her.

'Now, now,' Gibson said behind them.

Ava sent a feeling of reassurance to Chloe, who shoved her fist in her mouth.

'Let her go,' she said to Gibson. 'Whatever this is, I'm happy to cooperate, just don't do anything to Chloe.'

'No harm will come to her,' Gibson said. He pointed at the chair. 'Sit.'

She glared at him, then Turner, then smiled at Chloe and walked to the chair. Gibson strapped her wrists to the armrests, placed a skull cap on her head. She felt a fizz in her scalp and thought of executions. She knew that some in the olden days hadn't worked right, needed umpteen goes to kill someone.

Gibson went back to his desk and typed on the laptop, and a small cage emerged from the gloom in the water tank, an Enceladon trapped inside.

<Sandy?> she sent towards the tank.

Gibson smiled. 'It can't hear you, the cage prevents comms.'

Ava looked at Chloe, who was back playing with her feet, content for now.

'What are you trying to prove here?' Ava said. 'That creatures in captivity are sad? I could've told you that.'

She knew that too well from her childhood, her marriage.

Gibson shook his head. 'Your friends have been hiding their talents, and I expect you to do the same.' He nodded at Chloe. 'But my instinct is that the baby won't have the same reticence.'

'Leave her alone,' Ava said, steel in her voice.

Turner stepped up, just to remind her he was there.

Gibson pressed a button on one of his rigs and a spark rippled round the cage in the water tank. The creature jolted along with it, then wriggled its tentacles around. The suckers reached for the glass wall of the tank.

<Sandy?>

<Help.> It wasn't Sandy's voice, someone else.

There was a buzz to her right and Ava saw Chloe jolt in her seat and start crying. She turned to Gibson.

'What the hell?'

She felt Chloe's distress. The Enceladon reached out to Chloe sending reassuring messages, and Ava's heart filled up. Even imprisoned and tortured, this creature's first instinct was empathy. Ava was overwhelmed by emotions flowing between the Enceladon and Chloe, a shifting pattern of feelings so deep and rich she couldn't keep up. She realised this was how Sandy communicated with other Enceladons, it wasn't just telepathy but on another level. Having to communicate in words with Ava and the others must feel so primitive to them.

'Interesting,' Gibson said, staring at his laptop screen.

The door to the room opened and Fellowes walked in.

Gibson raised his eyebrows.

Fellowes took in Ava in her skull cap, Chloe across the room.

'What's going on here?' he said.

17
LENNOX

By the time Lennox returned to the detention block he was cold and tired. He'd spent hours walking around the fence, trying to get something from Sandy. Nothing. The guards had changed over, Mendoza replaced by Turner, which was never good. Lennox nodded at him and Turner scowled.

Lennox heard a baby crying as he came inside. He got to the living room and saw Heather with the baby in her arms, singing a lullaby under her breath.

<Hi, Lennox.>

He turned. Ava was in the kitchen doorway, wiping her hands on a dishtowel.

Lennox grabbed her and hugged. She was bony, thinner than the last time he saw her. He held on longer than he meant to, but something about her made him feel hopeful that things were changing. Eventually Ava eased away from him and took Chloe from Heather. The baby instantly calmed.

Ava turned. 'She's a bit bigger than last time you saw her.'

Chloe spotted Lennox and waved her chubby arms. He put a finger out and she grabbed it, and he laughed.

'She's amazing.'

'She is.'

He got a sense of something from the baby and turned to Ava. <Can she talk to you?>

<We sense moods and feelings from each other.>

Heather cleared her throat. 'It's why they're here. They want to experiment on Chloe, because she isn't as guarded as us.'

'Shit,' Lennox looked at Chloe, then at Ava. 'What about the court case?'

Ava sighed as Chloe released Lennox's finger. 'I'll tell you later. Turns out the verdict didn't matter, they were always going to bring us here.'

'Bastards.'

All three of them watched Chloe for a moment. Lennox thought about what it must be like at that age, without the words to understand your own experience. It was mind boggling that humans eventually linked feelings to words, expressed themselves. Understood each other. He wondered about Sandy and the Enceladons – if they were born telepathic, how did that impact their ability to communicate when younger? How would Chloe's abilities impact her life?

He heard the front door open. Probably Turner come to hassle them some more.

He stepped into the hall and there was Sandy, upright on three of their tentacles, the other two waving in the air, their head inflated. They pulsed colours up and down their body in patterns and shades that felt like home to Lennox, aquamarine, blending into reds and oranges, a spectacular aurora within their skin.

<Lennox-Sandy partial.> Sandy's voice in his mind was like a hug, warmth and adrenaline. Sandy scuttled forward and launched into an embrace, wrapping their tentacles around his waist, shoulders and head, pulling Lennox towards him and squeezing.

<Sandy.> He closed his eyes and laughed as Sandy squeezed him joyfully.

Sandy pulled away, trailing their tentacles across Lennox's cheek in a show of affection. Dots and stripes spun and flickered across their body, and Lennox was drawn into their large black eyes, the golden rims growing and contracting hypnotically.

Sandy saw the others through the doorway and threw out tentacles in their direction. <Heather-Ava-Chloe-Sandy partial.>

They pulled Lennox into the room. <Lennox-Heather-Ava-Chloe-Sandy complete.>

Chloe stared at Sandy and giggled. They wrapped their tentacles around all of them, then ballooned their body, stretching their skin thin to make a membrane encircling them. Lennox felt like he was inside a tent, snug and safe with the danger outside.

<How did you get in here?> he sent eventually.

Sandy reduced in size and stood with a tentacle on each of their shoulders. Lennox remembered what he'd read about earth octopuses having semi-autonomous 'brains' in their limbs. Thought about that collective consciousness. Wondered how humans would cope if we let our arms and legs make decisions for us. The idea of a central control system was embedded in our physicality, our DNA, and affected how we saw everything. But Sandy and the Enceladons saw the universe differently.

<Simple displacement of materials.>

Heather frowned. <You made a hole in the fence?>

<What about the guards?> Lennox sent.

<EM signal created dream state.>

Lennox had seen Sandy put someone to sleep before. He'd also seen them accidentally kill someone.

<Sandy-humans complete leave enclosed area?>

Heather and Ava looked at Lennox wide-eyed.

'Do they mean break out?' Ava said. She threw a worried look at Chloe.

'It sounds like we can just walk out,' Lennox said.

Sandy removed their tentacles and scuffed to the door. <Simple leaving?>

Lennox had to think.

'Where would we go?' Heather said, touching Lennox's arm.

He thought about Vonnie, Camp Outwith up the coast, full of outsiders who would do anything to meet Sandy, definitely on the Enceladons' side. 'I know a place.'

'I'm not sure,' Ava said, cradling Chloe.

Heather angled her head. 'If you stay, it'll mean more experiments on Chloe. Maybe more invasive.'

They all shared a look and Chloe picked up on the vibe, let out a whine.

<Sandy-guard partial not dream-state for long.>

Lennox looked for approval, got it. <Let's go.>

They followed Sandy down the corridor to the front door, where Turner was slumped against the wall, eyes closed.

'Should we take his gun?' Lennox said.

Heather looked at him. 'Would you ever shoot it?'

Lennox thought and shook his head.

'There's your answer.'

The four of them followed Sandy, creeping along the outside wall of the detention block. They reached the corner then had to make a break for it across open ground to the bottom edge of the perimeter fence.

Sandy was a few yards ahead, then Lennox, Ava with Chloe gurgling next, and Heather bringing up the rear. The overhead lights made Lennox wince as they crouched and ran.

They were about three-quarters across when Lennox heard a noise behind, turned and saw Heather sprawled in the dirt. Ava was trying to help her up with one hand, Chloe under the other arm. The baby was crying, Heather getting her breath back, wiping at her face as she got up.

'Hey.' This was a guard fifty metres away, lifting his gun to his line of sight. 'Stop right there.'

'Come on,' Lennox said.

Sandy rushed back and ushered Heather along, Ava and Chloe as well.

'I'll fire,' the guard said. There were other voices now, and an alarm.

They ran towards the fence and Lennox saw a large hole through both layers, burn marks around the edge.

A burst of gunfire made him duck. He turned to check on the others, panic in their eyes. A spotlight was trained on them from one of the guard towers, following their clumsy moves to the fence. More voices over the siren, the sound of boots on the dirt, the click and chunk of guns loading.

'Fuck,' Lennox said.

More gunfire made him wince and duck.

Then they were at the hole in the fence. The others crouched and went through then Lennox followed. It was darker, the spotlight beam diffused by the fence. The voices got closer. Then there were other bright lights, soldiers' torches, and more bursts of gunfire, so close Lennox thought he would have a heart attack.

He felt disorientated and staggered towards the shore, stumbled and fell down a hole, sliding into a peat bog. He struggled out and couldn't see anyone in front, just the torch beams behind.

<Ava,> he sent. <Heather? Sandy?>

More voices telling him to give himself up. He couldn't go back that way. There were voices left and right along the shore too. He backed away to the edge of the loch, water lapping at his heels.

He saw a light from the far left, barrelling through the soldiers, Sandy, flashing blue and green.

<Sandy!>

<Sandy-Lennox partial must leave.>

<Where are the others?>

<Unclear, but we must leave now.>

Gunshots split the air. Sandy launched themself at Lennox, enveloping him in their expanded body. Lennox felt a warm glow, then the two of them fell into the dark water and swam away faster than a speedboat, diving deep into blackness.

18
OSCAR

Oscar was pouring his third glass of Barolo when the alarm made him flinch. He went to his window and saw searchlights sweeping the perimeter fence and the rocks beyond. Soldiers throwing on jackets as they emerged from their quarters and running towards the fence.

He took a gulp of wine and headed out the door, stopped a passing guard. 'What's happened?'

'Breakout.'

'What?'

'The three prisoners,' the guard said, impatient to go. 'An illegal made a hole in the fence.'

Oscar hurried to the perimeter, bathed in garish light. He saw the hole in the fence, like it had been burned with an acetylene torch.

He looked at the detention block, in comparative darkness, ran over there and found Mendoza helping Turner to his feet. He shook his head and ran a hand over his face. His gun was on the ground.

'What happened?' Oscar said.

Mendoza gave Oscar a stare as if this wasn't the time.

Turner looked confused, then saw Oscar and scowled.

'An illegal came out of nowhere and attacked, tentacles on my face...' He rubbed at his neck then looked at his hands. 'Next thing I knew, Mendoza was waking me up.'

Oscar looked through the open door to the corridor inside.

'All three of them are gone,' Mendoza said. 'And the baby.'

Oscar wondered if this was down to him. He'd insisted that Gibson stop experiments on the baby and return them to the detention block. But help had come from outside – an Enceladon, maybe Sandy. Most likely arranged when they met Lennox at the beach.

He walked back to the hole in the fence, a soldier guarding it now. He heard shouts outside the perimeter, saw torches spreading out. If he went outside the fence, he'd probably get shot.

A soldier appeared at his side and cleared his throat.

'What is it?'

'General Carson would like to see you, sir.'

'Thank you.'

The soldier didn't move. 'Immediately.'

Oscar sucked his teeth and stared at the soldier. Then he walked across the yard to Carson's office. Halfway there he glanced back, saw that the soldier he'd spoken to had gone through the fence to help with the hunt.

He changed direction towards the front gate, kept walking. He reached the gatehouse and waved his security pass at the guard inside.

'We're in lockdown, sir.'

'You think I don't know that? Carson asked me to get the files on the escaped prisoners, they're in my car.' He pointed at his BMW outside.

The guard hesitated.

Oscar stared until he released the gate lock.

He pushed through and went to his car, got in and started the engine. He didn't look in the rear-view mirror as he drove away from the base, along the single track that ran the length of the peninsula. He got to the T-junction, thought about where he would go if he was them. South was Ullapool but it was a distance away, and the trek around the coast wasn't easy. North was Ardmair Beach and Camp Outwith. Closer, and probably easier terrain. Plus some like-minded souls to take you in.

He turned north. The road was twisty and hilly with blind corners. He drove too fast, thought about the wine he'd drunk.

The road straightened at the top of the headland peak and he saw the camp's lights down on the shore a couple of miles ahead. There were two turn-offs at either side, a few empty holiday rentals. He pulled over in a layby and got out, looked at the lights of Camp Outwith. It was a beacon in the night, brooding hills behind it visible against the starry sky. He stared into the darkness in the other direction. New Broom was over the brow of the headland. He wondered how long it would take to walk from one place to the other in the dark, in difficult terrain, being chased by armed guards.

He got back in the car and pulled into the road. He presumed Carson would have the same idea soon, would send a truck full of soldiers to Outwith. Oscar wanted to get there first, speak to Lennox and the others. Maybe he wanted to get one over on Carson, maybe he actually wanted to help them. He hadn't untangled that in his mind.

The road levelled off as he reached Ardmair.

He glimpsed something emerging from a tumbledown cottage on the right, a white flash in the darkness. The sheep scrambled in front of him in a panic, caught in his headlights as he yanked the steering wheel, sending the car onto the verge then over it, bumping over grass then gravel, stones and seaweed, as the car thumped onto the beach, its nose burying into the shore at the water's edge.

19
AVA

She stumbled over rocks and worried she would drop Chloe. She couldn't see much in the darkness, only a splinter of moonlight overhead. Torch beams played over the ground behind her.

'Lennox?' She spoke in a loud whisper. The guards were still a distance away, fanning out along the shore. 'Heather?'

She felt a swell of excitement from Chloe, and wondered about that. How crazy that babies don't understand what's happening. She was suppressing her own anxiety and fear, trying hard not to transmit them to the baby. That's what motherhood was, pretending everything was OK when it wasn't. Acting like no harm will come to your child, the world is a safe place. But Ava knew the truth and there were armed men chasing her to prove it.

<Lennox? Heather?>

The guards spread in each direction along the coast. She was inland, crouching in moss and heather, Chloe tight to her chest. There was a hill behind her. High ground is an advantage, right? Plus it was the only place the guards weren't searching yet.

<Sandy? Anyone?>

Where the hell were they? She'd been ahead of them coming through the fence, glanced back a couple of times but kept running. Then when she looked back a third time she couldn't see them. She wondered if they'd been captured. This was such a mess. Less than twenty-four hours ago she was released from court and given her daughter back. Now she was running for her life.

Chloe made a burbling noise, and she sensed the baby was starting to absorb some of her terror, felt her get anxious. She crouch-ran up the hill, stumbling as she went, the ground uneven and wet, her shoes squelching in the mud. She splashed into a burn, her knee jarring, and stopped at the other side, panting. Chloe grumbled and she recognised the start of something bigger. She tried to send calming vibes, but she couldn't convince herself, let alone her daughter.

She staggered forward through deep bracken whipping at her shins, and sank into thick moss. She heard a noise to her left and tensed, saw the dirty white flash of a sheep's arse bobbing as it ran away. The sheep bleated and she cringed at the noise.

She jogged up the slope, the ground underfoot more solid, thin scrub grass and some rocky outcrops. Chloe made more noise in her arms. She shushed the baby and jiggled her, but Chloe kept fussing.

<Please, it's OK, stay calm.> She knew words didn't work, but hoped the sentiment would come across. 'Shhh, Chloe, shhh.'

Some torch beams were coming her way now, spreading inland.

She turned and ran as fast as she could, the ground rockier. She glanced back and saw three torches in a line, all heading towards her. Her ankle turned as she tripped over a rock and fell, pain shooting up her leg as she held tight to Chloe, turned her body to land first and cushion the baby.

Chloe let out a yelp then a sustained wail.

'Shhhh, please.'

'Hey.' American accent, one of the guards. The torch was pointing at her but still some distance away.

She tried to stand and felt burning pain in her ankle. Just a sprain, but she couldn't run. She limped sideways hoping to lose them but knew it was useless. She zigzagged up the hill and across, torch beams getting closer.

'Lady, we don't want to shoot you.'

It had been stupid to run, she couldn't escape, not with Chloe, what the hell was she thinking? She felt resigned, then realised this was how Michael had made her feel.

She staggered up the hill but they were closing. She glanced past the torch beams at the huge black expanse of the loch. She wondered if Sandy and the others were out there, free and clear.

She felt something sharp against her thigh, looked down and saw she'd run into an old barbed-wire fence, which had torn her trousers and cut her. She saw black blood in the thin moonlight and cried out from the pain. Chloe echoed her, wailing and sobbing. Come and get the stupid woman and her baby, the pathetic, useless cow who can't do anything right, the idiot who allowed herself to be abused for years, then went to prison for her husband's murder, then let herself be taken, then couldn't even break out of a camp when there was a big hole in the fence.

She slumped to her knees, pain in her ankle and thigh, Chloe worked up into a frenzy. Tears came to her eyes. She blinked them away and rocked Chloe in her arms, trying to calm her, trying to protect her from the shit of the world.

<Sandy? Lennox, Heather? Please. Help.>

Torches shone in her face now and she turned away, shielding Chloe. She looked at the sky, cloudless, slice of moon, a spray of stars. She thought about the unimaginable distance to Enceladus, the journey they'd made to come here, to be dehumanised and persecuted, just like her.

'Come on,' the nearest guard said, not unkindly. 'Let's get you back.'

He reached out a hand and she stared at it for a long time. Eventually she took it and stood then walked, bleeding and limping, back to the base.

20
HEATHER

She crouched behind a boulder on the slope of Meall Mòr and watched the action below. Her feet were soaking and her heart hammered in her chest like a panic attack. She saw torches further down the hill congregating on a single point, heard Chloe wailing.

<Ava, it's OK.> She wasn't sure she was getting through. Heather had practised her telepathy with Lennox for months, nothing like that with Ava.

She saw Ava in the torch beams, Chloe in her arms as she was led back to base.

<Ava, I don't know if you can hear me, but I'll come back for you. I promise. Just hold on.>

More torch beams danced up the slope towards Meall Garbh, the peak to her right. She'd studied the map over and over, knew the Gaelic names but didn't know how they were pronounced.

The guards were moving fast. She turned and scurried across the rocks on the side of the hill. At the peak was a radio mast. She wondered about the signals it was sending out.

She stumbled over a loose stone but righted herself and continued. She was in the dip between the two hills now, a small burn burbling somewhere. Eventually she caught a glimpse of Ardmair Beach ahead. She'd cut across the headland and come out the other side. The flicker of lights from caravans rippled on the black water of the bay. She thought about Lennox. She'd seen him back outside the base, swept up by Sandy and taken into the water. She was angry – was Sandy only here for Lennox? Save one of them but let the others flounder? But she was being stupid, if they'd all stayed together, they would be back in New Broom.

She turned away from the loch. The boggy terrain gave way to a footpath, then she approached two empty houses. B&Bs or holiday rentals, no lights on. It was a stupid idea to hide in the first house she came to, but she tried the front door, unlocked. She ran in, looked around in the dark. Went to the kitchen sink and gulped down a glass of water, breathed heavily, rested her hands on the edge of the counter.

She was fit for her age but not invincible. She couldn't run forever, had to be smart. She grabbed the biggest kitchen knife from the block on the counter and left.

She went to the next house, also unlocked, God bless Highland folk. She rummaged through the drawers in the kitchen and bedroom, didn't find anything useful. This was definitely a rental, no personal possessions.

She left and reached a road, checked both ways, nothing in the darkness. She looked behind, caught a glimpse of torches emerging from the pass between hills, still some distance away. Across the road was a narrow lane and she ran up it, saw a few more houses. She tried the first two, more empty rental properties.

She approached the third house, knew straight away that someone was living there. Car parked outside, dirty boots stacked on the front step. She tried the door – open. Jesus, these people were trusting. She went inside, crept down the hall. All the lights were off. She walked to a bedroom door, pushed at it, heard heavy breathing, saw an old couple sleeping. She moved down the hall to the kitchen then the living room. Saw a large handbag on a sofa. Dived in and raked through it. A purse full of bank cards and cash. Wet wipes, tissues, keys, lip balm.

A mobile phone.

She woke it up, felt a thump in her heart as she realised it wasn't locked. Beautiful, trusting old people. There were three bars of signal and half the battery left. She pocketed it and crept out of the house.

She saw the torches dancing behind her, spreading out. Two went into the first house she'd visited. She realised she was still holding the knife from there.

She stepped into the roadside ditch to hide and saw something up ahead. A tumbledown cottage covered in vines and moss. She went round the back and part of the wall was missing. There was sheep shit all over the floor. She found a dark corner and hunkered down. Pulled out the phone, punched in a number.

Waited. Thought about the time. He would be in bed with her.

Eventually she heard her ex-husband's voice.

'Hello? Who is this?'

'Paul, I need help.'

21
LENNOX

He was strangely warm in the Scottish water, surrounded by or inside Sandy's body, somehow. This wasn't the first time, he'd done the same in Loch Ness and off the coast of Ullapool with them. And one far more crazy experience inside Xander, up through the Earth's atmosphere and into space.

They darted through the dark water. He saw through the sheen of Sandy's stretched skin, their light display of green and blues, speckles and arrows and spirals. They swam to the bottom of the loch, spiralling and pirouetting, stretching and billowing, Lennox sharing Sandy's sensations through their body. Conflicting yet coalescing experiences from their limbs and torso that somehow made a coherent whole.

He saw some gloomy fish floating near the sea floor, and sensed something from them when they saw Sandy. Could he understand fish now? They were surprised but not frightened, knew Sandy wasn't a threat. They rose to shallower waters and Lennox saw a pair of seals darting after a larger fish. He sensed the exhilaration of the mammals, the anxiety of the fish, all part of a community that he was part of too.

<Sandy, we need to go back.>

<Sandy-humans tried to change Sandy-Lennox partial energy.>

Sandy even felt affinity with the guards trying to kill them. They would never understand that humans were isolated in their stupid skulls, that some of them meant harm to the Enceladons and anyone who sided with them. Anyone who challenged the status quo, who threatened their power.

<I have to help the others. We need to find Ava and Heather.>

Lennox had lost his bearings and had no idea where they were relative to New Broom. Sandy swam upward and broke the surface, and Lennox saw lights along a curved beach, caravans and campers. Must be Camp Outwith, that Vonnie talked about.

<There.>

Sandy shifted through the water to the shore and Lennox weirdly slid out of their body and stepped onto the beach. He stumbled and felt dazed as he stood there, after the lightning-quick movement through the water.

Lennox was at the bottom end of the beach, away from the bonfires. He looked at Sandy, shimmering in the darkness, lights flashing up and down their body. Sensed their excitement at being reunited with Lennox, and shared it. But he had to find Ava and Heather. He had to take a chance with the Outwithers. If anyone was willing to help them, it was these guys.

He didn't know if Ava and Heather had escaped. If they were back at the base, Lennox and Sandy would have to come up with a plan to get them out. If they were still free, maybe they'd find their way here.

<Ava? Heather?>

He looked at Sandy. He didn't know how he was going to do this – just walk over to the campfires and introduce themselves?

'What the fuck?'

He turned and saw Vonnie a few feet away, staring at Sandy. They were rummaging through the stones, suckers sticking to the pebbles, head ridged and throbbing yellow and orange. The most alien thing Lennox had ever seen in his life.

'Hey,' Lennox said.

Vonnie held her hands out. She was wearing three-quarter trousers and big boots, a thick jumper and waterproof, hair in braids. 'Is that one of them?'

Lennox didn't know where to start. 'This is Sandy.'

'Sandy?'

'That's just the name I gave them.'

'Does it talk?'

Lennox took a step towards her. Her eyes were big and bright in the darkness. 'Not vocally.' He tapped his temple. 'We hear each other's thoughts.'

Vonnie laughed then covered her mouth. 'Sorry, this is just so…'

'I know.' He looked around the beach, waiting to hear voices or a boat motor, see searchlights strafing the water, helicopters thudding overhead. But there was just the three of them in the darkness, water lapping on the shore and the ruffle of Sandy exploring their surroundings.

<Unknown human?>

Lennox flinched at Sandy's voice in his head, then laughed. <She's a friend.>

'What's so funny?' Vonnie said.

'They were just asking who you were.'

Vonnie grinned and took a step forward. In the light from Sandy's skin, Lennox could make out a spread of freckles across her nose and cheeks.

'You said "they"?'

'That's the pronoun they use. They're plural. To be honest, I have no idea if they have genders.'

Vonnie pressed her lips together. 'Where are they from?'

'You wouldn't believe me if I told you.'

'Try me.'

'A place called Enceladus, it's—'

'The sixth largest of Saturn's moons.' Vonnie grinned. 'Five hundred kilometres in diameter, covered in ice, but with a moon-wide ocean underneath. Volcanic and tidal-heated, the cryovolcanoes spew stuff into space from the south pole, right?'

Lennox stared at her.

Vonnie shrugged. 'I have a thing about space.'

She'd been getting closer to Sandy, who lifted two tentacles to her. They raised their body up on the other tentacles, expanded their head and widened their eyes.

Vonnie was mesmerised by Sandy's gaze, and Lennox knew that feeling.

'An animal from Enceladus.' She glanced at Lennox. 'Why are they here?'

Lennox wondered how to answer, decided to keep to what he knew for sure. 'They're refugees.'

'From what?'

'I'm not sure.'

Vonnie nodded, like this was normal.

She held out a hand, but when Sandy touched it she snatched it away. 'Are they safe?'

'Unless you try to harm them. Or me.'

Vonnie angled her head at Lennox. 'So you two are buddies?'

'Something like that.'

'Did they break you out of prison?' Vonnie waved a hand around the beach. 'Last time I saw you there was an eight-foot fence between us.'

'Yeah, they cut a hole in the fence and helped us escape.'

'Us?'

'The other woman you saw, Heather. And another, Ava, with her baby daughter.'

Vonnie looked around. 'Where are they?'

'That's what I need to find out. We got separated.'

'Maybe Jodie can help.'

'Who's Jodie?'

'She's the leader of this place, I guess. She's here because of them.' Vonnie pointed at Sandy.

Sandy raised a tentacle and Vonnie reached out. Lennox saw the suckers attach to her skin. He waited to see if Sandy would give her a vision, but Vonnie just smiled at Sandy, then Lennox.

'I can't take Sandy over there, they'd freak out.'

Vonnie stuck her lip out. 'I didn't.'

'You're different.'

Vonnie shifted her weight. 'I've got somewhere you can stash them for a bit, while you speak to Jodie.'

She didn't wait for agreement, just walked up the beach, crunching stones underfoot. Sandy followed her. Lennox watched them go and felt something in his heart.

22
OSCAR

He smelled whisky and skunk, felt the warmth of a fire, and wondered if he'd died and gone to heaven. Opened his eyes. He was sitting on a low deckchair by a large, crackling bonfire. The smell reminded him of his dad burning leaves in the garden in autumn. He was a long way from that little boy.

A handful of people sat around the fire, and he recognised Jodie. She smiled and leaned towards him, offering a hipflask.

'Drink this.'

He took it and had a sip. Felt the burn in his throat down into his stomach, the taste of seaweed and pepper. Good stuff.

He offered it back but Jodie shook her head. 'Keep it. You look like you could use it.'

Oscar took another hit and shook his head. 'What happened?'

'We found you over there,' Jodie said, nodding down the beach. 'In your car.'

'Shit.'

The sheep in the road, his slow reflexes, the feeling of flying for a moment.

He looked at the contented faces around the campfire. They needed to be here, they felt *a part of something*.

'You keep coming back,' Jodie said. Her skin glowed in the firelight as she swept her quiff back from her eyes. She was in the same red boilersuit and Docs, thick, puffy jacket over the top.

'Sorry.'

Jodie stared at him until he felt awkward.

'Don't be sorry,' she said, waving a hand around the fire. 'We're all drawn here for a reason. None of us can explain it.' She looked out to sea, the strip of moonlight tearing a slash in the black surface.

Oscar shook his head. 'I'm not like you.'

Jodie smiled and put on a sarcastic voice. '"We're all individuals!"'

Oscar was surprised that a black woman in her sixties was able to quote from a scene in *Monty Python's Life of Brian*. But that was his own pathetic biases kicking in. Just because the movie was made by posh English white guys like him, didn't mean it was his alone.

'I haven't felt anything,' he said.

These people didn't know anything about Sandy, had no idea they were from Enceladus, a billion kilometres away. That they were telepathic, refugees, an entire community living in the water here. They only knew what they'd seen on the news, read on conspiracy sites, what they'd felt.

That was the sickening thing for him – he had knowledge, but they had a connection. Lennox, Heather and Ava were connected to Sandy. He was so jealous it made his teeth clench.

'Any newcomers recently?' he said to Jodie.

She swigged from a can of Guinness. A twig in the fire crackled and spat, and Oscar jumped.

Jodie narrowed her eyes. 'You're from New Broom.'

Oscar shook his head. 'No.'

'We heard the alarms.' She pointed at the headland. 'We've seen them searching on the loch before. I thought they were all American.'

'I'm not one of them.'

'Yes, you are. But you're different too. You care about them, that's why you're here.'

'You've got me wrong.'

'I don't think so.' Jodie accepted a joint from a young man next to her. The guy was dressed like a nerdy hillwalker.

She took a toke and Oscar smelled it, flashed back to smoking weed in Oxford, down by the river one night, a lifetime ago, it seemed.

She offered him the joint and he hesitated. Made a show of examining it.

Jodie laughed. 'It's not poisoned.'

He had a toke, felt his head expand. He had a million things to do, serious things. Track down Lennox, Heather and Ava. Find Sandy. Face Carson. Sort out his crashed car. But it felt good, for a moment, not to deal with any of it.

'Christ,' he said, passing it back.

'It's fairly heavy duty.' Jodie took a small puff and passed it along. 'So, who escaped?'

Oscar shook his head.

Jodie smiled. 'You're the enemy, I should have you kicked out of here.'

'Why don't you?'

'I've never spoken to anyone from the base. Only heard rumours. Would love to know exactly what you're up to. And why they have a posh English dude hanging out there.'

'What rumours have you heard?'

'That you're experimenting on them. You're keeping the kid and the woman against their will. They haven't been seen since the descent, very suspicious. And now the one who was up for murder. Rumour has it she was taken in the street in broad daylight. I wonder who could be behind that.'

Oscar wanted to tell her it wasn't him, he wasn't the bad guy. But he wasn't sure that was the truth.

'Interesting,' he said, sounding lame.

Jodie nodded. 'So now, I think at least one of those people has escaped, and maybe some of the creatures.'

'No.'

'You don't understand.' She lowered her voice so that he had to lean in to hear. 'You can't *contain* this. It's so much bigger than you can imagine.'

'What makes you say that?'

She waved around the fire. 'We've all felt things.'

Oscar forced a laugh. 'Feelings aren't facts.'

'No, they're much more important. That's what you'll never understand.'

23
HEATHER

'Heather?'

She jolted from a dreamless sleep and swung a fist towards the voice. Her knuckle cracked as she connected with something, and she scrambled into the darkest corner of the building, away from a torch beam.

'It's OK,' the man said in a soft voice.

She shook the fog from her brain and realised who it was. 'Paul. Fuck, sorry I hit you.'

'Sorry I woke you.'

She looked through the window frame at the road outside, beach and sea beyond. 'Switch the torch off.'

He did and she caught a glimpse of him in the pre-dawn light. Still solid and handsome.

He offered a hand and helped her up. She shook the pins and needles from her legs. Her neck was stiff and her hair was a mess. She ran a hand through it and wrapped him in a hug. He smelled of vetiver and sandalwood, the same smell she'd loved for twenty years. But he wasn't hers to smell anymore, that was for his new wife.

She held on for longer than she should and imagined she was somewhere else, decades ago, when they first met, before they got married, had Rosie, watched her die. Before their divorce, her cancer, their reunion months ago when he helped them all.

He knew her like no one else ever would, and she loved and resented it.

'Did you see anyone out there?'

Paul shook his head. 'All quiet.'

'What time is it?'

He checked his watch, the one she gave him for his thirtieth birthday. 'After five. The sun's coming up.'

'We need to find the others.'

'Others?'

'Lennox, Ava and Chloe.'

Paul put a hand on his hip. He was wearing black jeans and black Nikes, thick-knit jumper and brown leather jacket. 'What's going on, Heather? Who are you hiding from? Where have you been?'

She'd explained nothing on the phone, just begged him to come. She was secretly pleased that she still had that power over him – she could call him in the middle of the night, get him out of his warm bed next to his pregnant wife, make him drive across the Highlands. She knew that was stupid and childish, but she needed it right now.

'We need to get somewhere safe, first. Can we go to yours?'

Paul gave her a look that she understood. 'You know we can't. If you're wanted by the authorities, it won't be long before they turn up at our place. I won't do that to Iona, not again.'

'No,' Heather said. 'I'm sorry.'

Paul looked around. 'Where then?'

Heather led him out of the crumbling building and pointed. 'There are houses in the hills. Most are empty. The soldiers will have searched them all by now, so maybe we can hole up in one until we think of something.'

'Soldiers?' Paul shook his head. 'Heather, what the fuck have you got into?'

Heather laughed and Paul did too, and it felt good, like home.

'Come on,' she said.

◈

The view from the living room was beautiful, west over Ardmair, Loch Kanaird, Isle Martin and beyond. A light haze made everything look fuzzy and unreal, or maybe that was just Heather's mind. Sunlight from the east had caught the peak of Ben Mor Coigach, setting it on fire.

This was crazy. Sitting in a B&B with her ex-husband, clutching hot mugs of tea, staring at the calm expanse. She felt tiny, like she didn't matter, and she liked it.

Paul puffed out his cheeks. 'Wow.'

She'd spent ten minutes filling him in on everything she'd been through since they last saw each other. He had met Sandy back then, but she'd told him as little as possible to protect him. He'd seen the footage from Ullapool harbour later, presumed Heather was involved. But he hadn't heard from her since and thought she was OK. Now he knew everything.

'Enceladus,' he said, closing his eyes.

'I know, it's crazy.'

'You're sure?'

She nodded.

'And that thing helped you escape last night?'

'Burned a hole through the fence like it was nothing.'

Paul took a sip of his black tea. No milk, not in an abandoned B&B. 'Makes you wonder what else they can do.'

'I don't think we've even scratched the surface,' Heather said. 'That's why the military are interested.'

'And it speaks to you?'

'They.'

'What?'

'I told you, they're plural.'

'Right, right.'

He was easy-going, had always been her anchor, which was why she'd turned to him for help now.

'Telepathy,' Paul said, shaking his head.

'I know how it sounds.'

He stared at her for a long time, vestigial love in that look. 'I believe you. So what now?'

'I need to find Lennox. I think Ava is back at the base, she didn't make it. But I'm sure Lennox and Sandy got away.'

Paul looked at her and she raised a hand to her hair like a schoolgirl. Jesus.

'You can't go anywhere, obviously, with armed soldiers hunting for you.' He tried on a smile and she remembered his face when she told him she was pregnant with Rosie.

'But I can try to find out stuff.'

'Where?'

'I can start with the camp down the road. Maybe Lennox and Sandy went there. Or I can ask around in Ullapool.'

He finished his tea and walked to the sink, rinsed his mug and put it on the draining board.

'You should get some rest,' he said.

She laughed, too high, awkward. 'Do I look that bad?'

He gave her a look full of compassion. 'Just get some rest.'

24
LENNOX

He bolted awake and his first thought was Sandy. It took him a moment to realise he was in Vonnie's bedroom, fully clothed on top of her bed. The last thing he remembered was Vonnie leaving to talk to the woman from the camp about him and Sandy. He'd put his head down for two minutes and now it was six hours later. And Sandy wasn't here.

The room wasn't large, just a bed with yellow covers, matching drawers and desk. The desk was covered in art stuff – drawing pencils, notebooks, paints. The walls were covered in astronomy posters – one of the solar system, a large picture of the moon's craters, a detailed depiction of the Milky Way, picture of a nebula that looked like fingers reaching to heaven.

Lennox saw the telescope by the window, remembered looking through it last night as Vonnie showed him Saturn. He could see the rings. He knew from Sandy that some of their dead ancestors made up one of those rings. Giant plumes of vapour ejected from Enceladus's south pole into space, and that debris made up Saturn's E-ring. When an Enceladon died, or when their 'energy changed', as Sandy put it, their body was placed in the currents of the jet stream, propelled by volcanic activity upward through the hole in the ice sheet and into the blackness. It was burial in space, effectively. The Enceladons thought of it as returning their essence to their god, Saturn. But that wasn't quite right, Saturn was one of infinite gods. The volcanoes at the bottom of the ocean were gods, so was the giant ice sheet that covered the moon, so were the creatures they shared an ocean with. Their god was in everything.

'Hey.'

He jumped at Vonnie's voice and turned to her in the doorway. She wore loose trousers and a baggy purple UHI sweatshirt.

'I came back earlier to take you to Jodie, but you were zonked.'

'You should've woken me.'

'You needed to sleep.'

'Where's Sandy?'

Vonnie smiled. 'In the bath.'

She left and Lennox followed down the hall. 'Are your parents not around?'

'It's just my dad,' Vonnie said. 'And he's not here much.'

Vonnie opened the bathroom door. Sandy was splashing in the tub in six inches of water, tentacles playing with the taps and shower curtain, running up the tiled wall. Their light display sparked to life when they saw Lennox and Vonnie, blue-green flourishes, shimmering orange between.

<Lennox-Sandy partial happy.>

Lennox had a warm feeling at their voice. <Yes.>

'Your dad didn't see Sandy?' he asked Vonnie.

'Of course not.'

They both looked at Sandy for a long time in the bath, occasionally glancing at each other.

'So,' Vonnie said. 'Enceladus, eh?'

'Yeah.'

'And they talk to you?'

Lennox tapped his ear. 'When we first met, they showed me things. Then they put something in my ear and I can hear their thoughts.'

Vonnie scratched her cheek. 'Can I talk to them?'

Lennox grinned. 'Try touching their tentacle.'

Vonnie hesitated then pulled the sleeves of her sweatshirt up a little. She crouched by the bath. Sandy's skin showed spots then stripes, red and blue. Vonnie reached out and Sandy wrapped a tentacle around her fingers and up the wrist, then reached out another limb to wrap around Vonnie's neck and shoulders.

Vonnie jolted and closed her eyes, slumped to the floor, her eyes glazed over. Lennox thought of his first encounter with Sandy, when they showed him where they'd come from and asked for help.

He heard the front door of the house open.

'Vonnie?' Woman's voice, soft London accent.

He stared at Vonnie in a trance. He tried to close the bathroom door without drawing attention, but the woman pushed it from the other side.

She was short, late-middle age, and her eyebrows almost hit the roof. She stared at Sandy and Vonnie, connected between hand and tentacle. Eventually she dragged her gaze away.

'Lennox?'

This was presumably the woman Vonnie talked about, the Camp Outwith leader.

She pointed at the bathtub. 'And this must be Sandy.'

Sandy released Vonnie's hand and she fell back and opened her eyes. Took a moment to focus.

'Jodie.'

Jodie nodded at the window. 'You have to go, soldiers have arrived at the camp. They're turning everything upside down to find your friend. They'll come to the house.'

Vonnie struggled to her feet. Lennox remembered his own dislocation after his first encounters with Sandy.

'But where can we go?' Lennox said.

Vonnie blinked and smiled. 'I have an idea.'

25
AVA

The guard unlocked the door to her cell in the stockade. 'Shift.'

She stared at his keycard dangling on a lanyard from his pocket. This was the same guy Sandy knocked out last night, Turner. He seemed to have recovered fine. She looked around the bare room, out the barred window.

'Where's Chloe?' she said.

'Just move.'

He took his gun in both hands, reminding her he was in charge.

She stood. 'I want to see my baby.'

'Maybe you will if you fucking move.'

Ava stepped close to him. 'Does this make you feel like a real man? Threatening innocent women?'

Turner's face didn't change. 'Innocent? I heard you murdered your husband.'

She swallowed and remembered the moment, bringing the wrench down on Michael's head, blood spurting as he dropped, Ava casually lifting Chloe from his arms.

Turner stepped aside and Ava walked ahead. He opened the outer door and marched her across the courtyard.

'Where are we going?' she said.

He shook his head.

She looked at the fence where they'd escaped, already fixed. She gazed beyond to the lighthouse and the loch.

They arrived at an office building, nameplate on the door said General Carson. Turner knocked then stood back.

'Come.'

Turner ushered Ava in then was waved away by Carson behind his desk. Fifties, fit, strong jaw, handsome in a buttoned-down, silver-fox kind of way. The kind of dominating authority figure she might've wrongly fancied in the past. But that was all gone now.

He stood and pointed at a chair. 'Ava Gallacher, please sit.'

She was slightly impressed he'd used her maiden name – folk in prison kept referring to her as Ava Cross, as if she was still the property of her dead husband.

She sat and he smiled.

'How are you?'

'Where's my baby?'

He angled his head. 'Chloe's safe and well.'

'I want to see her.'

'You will.' He pulled at his cuffs and cleared his throat. 'If you behave yourself and cooperate.'

'What do you mean?'

Carson stared out of the window. She watched him for a moment, the sharp line of his chin, then followed his gaze. The mouth of the loch opened into the sea, and she wondered where Sandy and Lennox were. Where Heather was. If they were thinking of her.

Carson walked to the window and peered out, as if he might see the others out there.

He turned back to Ava. 'It's a strange coincidence.'

'What is?'

'We've been here for months, fishing for our little alien friends. Going about our business without any interference.' He touched the knot of his tie. 'Then on the day we bring you here—'

'Abduct me off the street, you mean?'

He took her in.

Ava straightened her back. She wasn't going to play nice anymore. She'd sucked it up for months, been the good little girl in Saughton Prison, awaiting trial. Not saying anything controversial. Be sweet, act contrite and sorry, and you'll get your old life back. The last twenty-four hours had revealed what a lie that was.

She imagined grabbing the glass paperweight from his desk and smashing his skull open like she did to Michael.

Carson cleared his throat. 'On the same day we bring you here, one of the creatures breaks into our facility and helps you all escape. It makes me wonder if you have some special connection with these things.'

Ava stood up, balled her fists, didn't know what to do with the anger fizzing in her fingers. 'I just want to be with my daughter.'

Carson sucked his teeth. 'That's not possible.'

'Why not?'

Carson waved a hand at the window. 'We need your help with the illegals.'

'Illegals? These creatures are from another planet.'

Carson looked at her like she was stupid. 'And they're here illegally.'

Ava laughed. 'Human laws don't mean anything to them.'

'They will, I'll make sure of that.'

So Lennox, Heather and Sandy were still out there. Good. She hoped they *did* forget about her. She hoped they ran and swam until none of these bastards could ever find them.

'Anyway, like I said, strange coincidence that this all happened as soon as you arrived,' Carson said.

'I had nothing to do with it.'

Carson walked back to his desk. He placed his knuckles on the wood and leaned forward like a silverback asserting dominance.

'Maybe it's not you,' he said softly. 'Maybe it's little Chloe.'

Ava's cheeks flushed. 'Keep my daughter out of this.'

Carson straightened up, a smile on his face. 'I'm afraid that's not possible.'

26
LENNOX

The breeze on the water was biting. Vonnie sat at the stern, guiding the small boat, gunning the throttle on the outboard motor. They were round the other side of the Ardmair headland, out of sight of the camp, and had taken the boat belonging to the Isle Martin Trust, locals who looked after the island in the loch. Once they cleared the headland, they would be exposed for a while, if anyone with binoculars happened to look their way. But there were often boats out on the water, folk checking crab pots and lobster creels, working at the salmon farm to their right.

Sandy was in an old holdall of Vonnie's. It was amazing how easily they squeezed into small spaces, then at other times ballooned to three times their normal size. Now, two of Sandy's tentacles were poking out of the zipped bag, tasting the air.

Vonnie pointed the boat north as they cleared the headland, pulled her hood up. Lennox did the same and didn't look back. After a few minutes they turned west to a small hook of land on the east of the island. Lennox saw a low pontoon and a large, whitewashed house in the sheltered bay.

'The Mill House,' Vonnie said as they arrived.

They reached the pontoon and she tied the boat up.

Lennox grabbed the holdall and they walked to the house. Inside were dorm rooms with bunkbeds and a basic kitchen.

'The trust rent it out sometimes in the summer, for uni field work,' Vonnie said. 'No one's been here for ages, though.'

Lennox looked east to the mainland. You couldn't see Camp Outwith from here. 'And the army doesn't know about this place?'

'I don't know how they would. No one lives here.'

He flicked a light switch and nothing happened.

'No electricity or hot water,' Vonnie said. 'Just a fireplace and wood. It's basically a big bothy.'

Lennox felt a wriggle in the holdall and put it down. Sandy unzipped it from inside and sprung out.

<Sandy-Lennox partial seek Sandy-Ava-Heather partial.>

Lennox felt the burn of guilt. Sandy was right, they should be looking for the others. But they had to lay low for now, avoid capture, work out what their next move was. Lennox didn't even know if they'd escaped New Broom, no one at Camp Outwith had heard anything. He felt shame at having left them behind.

<Not right now. We're hiding.>

Sandy waved a tentacle at Vonnie. <Sandy-Vonnie partial is good energy?>

Lennox smiled.

Vonnie narrowed her eyes. 'What are they saying?'

'They're asking if you're good energy.'

'Shit, I hope you said yes.'

<Yes.> 'Yes.'

Sandy rippled ridges across their forehead, down their flanks. Inflated their head a little, spreading rings of brown and green up and down. One day, Lennox would understand what all their light displays meant.

<Would Sandy-Lennox-Vonnie partial like to meet Xander-Enceladus whole?>

Lennox grinned at Vonnie. 'Fancy a swim?'

He stripped to his shorts, the cold wind cutting across the pontoon. Vonnie tied her hair in a bun and started to undress, and he looked away, felt blood rush to his cheeks. Sandy was between them on the pontoon, tentacles trailing in the water below.

'OK,' Vonnie said.

He turned. She was in matching black underwear, hands on her hips, skin goose-pimpled in the cold.

'What now?'

<Sandy? Let's go.>

He reached out his hand and she took it. Her skin was soft and warm, despite the cold. 'Trust me?'

'Do I have a choice?'

'No.'

<OK, Sandy.>

Sandy expanded their body, stretching their skin until it was opaque, blood vessels visible in the multicoloured spaces in between, dark and light patches melding and shifting. They wrapped themself around Lennox and Vonnie, and Lennox sensed Vonnie panicking.

'Relax, it's OK.'

Sandy launched themself into the water with Lennox and Vonnie inside them, slipping fast through the loch, curving round the bay to the north, diving deep into darkness, spiralling as they swam.

Lennox looked across and saw Vonnie wide-eyed. They were cloaked in Sandy's skin, breathing part of their body or breath, Lennox wasn't sure. But it felt like they were a part of Sandy now and Lennox loved it.

They swam past the salmon farm he'd seen earlier and Lennox sensed Sandy's sadness at the fish stuck in a tiny space. Everyone should be free.

They darted up and down in the water, turned northwest towards the Summer Isles, dived deeper. Lennox saw two seals up ahead and squeezed Vonnie's hand. She looked at him, then the seals, and grinned. The seals tumbled over each other in the water, racing alongside Sandy for a while. Lennox sensed their happiness, the simple pleasure of being active and alive.

They travelled faster, the mainland coast somewhere to their right. They passed more islands, swerving and chicaning through them, and

Lennox caught a glimpse of something else in the water alongside. Dolphins, a pod of around twenty, swimming in synch with each other and Sandy. Then Vonnie squeezed his hand and he followed her look, saw a whale of some kind, a giant presence in the water, effortlessly keeping pace, its white underbelly visible in the light from Sandy's body. And then porpoises and more seals, all the animals flanking Sandy as they dived deeper and deeper.

They turned round a rocky outcrop into a giant, hidden undercut. Lights in the distance grew bigger and brighter very quickly. Vonnie squeezed his hand and he squeezed back.

<What the fuck?>

Lennox was shocked at Vonnie's voice clear in his head, and she looked surprised too. Must be possible because they were both connected through Sandy.

<It's the Enceladons.> Lennox grinned. <All of them.>

Sandy sped up as they reached the outskirts of the congregation, thousands of creatures like Sandy swimming between and around giant jellyfish, forests of dangling tendrils, the whales, dolphins and seals playfully swimming around and through them. It seemed to Lennox that they were communicating with Sandy and the others, but he couldn't hear anything in his mind.

Sandy led them through the maze of animals, Vonnie staring goggle-eyed, Lennox laughing. They came to one particular jellyfish creature. and Lennox felt Sandy's love spread through the water. He was sure Vonnie felt it too, as she shook her head and squeezed his hand and didn't stop.

They darted through Xander's tendrils and approached a smooth part of their underbelly. Sandy touched Xander's skin and seemed to sink into them, as if they were one single creature.

<Lennox-Sandy-Xander partial.> This was Xander's voice in his head, deep and reassuring like a hug.

<Hi, Xander.> There was a pause and he wondered if Sandy was talking to Xander, maybe they were examining Vonnie.

<Hello, Vonnie-Lennox-Sandy-Xander partial. Human-Enceladon complete. Good energy.>

Vonnie laughed. <Good energy.>

Lennox felt the truth of that.

27
HEATHER

She took a shower and tried to relax, but all the time she was listening for the front door, the clump of soldiers' boots, expecting to be dragged out naked and wet, thrown in the back of a truck.

She switched the shower off and dried herself, stared at her body in the mirror, thinner than she used to be, not in a good way. She looked like her mother, which made her think about all the people she'd lost, especially Rosie. She touched the back of her neck and thought about the stroke that started all this with Sandy. They said it was some kind of electromagnetic contact signal that was 'wrongly calibrated'. So wrong it killed a dozen people. She thought about what she'd seen Sandy do – accidentally kill a council worker on Yellowcraigs Beach, deliberately knock out Ava's husband. Cure her own tumour, for a while.

Part of her wanted Sandy back in her life so they could cure her cancer again. But another part of her wasn't sure. It was like she was fighting the inevitable, fighting herself. Maybe she needed to embrace the tumour as another part of *her*, a vital part of her self, even if it killed her.

She pulled on her clothes and stepped out of the bathroom, rubbing her hair with the towel. She walked to the window and peeked out. She took in the view of Ardmair Bay, the loch opening to the sea, different shimmering currents out there, infinite light and shade on the water, the Enceladons underneath somewhere. The island just offshore only highlighted how vast the expanse of water was, and she thought about how three quarters of the planet were covered in oceans. Creatures from another world would presume that life on Earth was water-based, with good reason. She wondered why her ancient ancestors ever thought it was a good idea to climb out of the primordial swamp.

The sound of the front door made her freeze. She had nowhere to go, just a wet towel to defend herself.

'Hey.' Paul's voice.

She relaxed her shoulders.

'Look who I found.'

Paul appeared from the hall with Freya, Ava's sister. She looked tired and nervous, Heather could relate to that.

Heather, Lennox and Ava had stayed with Freya in Ratagan at the start of their road trip. Freya never saw Sandy, they'd kept them hidden in the camper, but she'd been supportive and let them hide out, no questions asked.

'Hey,' Freya said. She was shorter and more curvy than Ava, the same shade of red hair, only hers was a mess of curls.

'What are you doing here?'

'I followed them,' she said, glancing at Paul. 'They took Ava off the street in the middle of Edinburgh. I managed to give her my phone, and I tracked it using Mum's.'

She dug an old iPhone out of her pocket and held it up. 'The phone stopped moving when it got to New Broom. Does she still have it?'

'She never mentioned it. They would've searched her when she arrived.'

Freya sat on the sofa and picked at the armrest. 'Did she escape with Chloe?'

Heather sat next to her on the sofa, touched her hand. 'She tried but they caught her and Chloe. She's back at the base.'

Freya shook her head. 'I can't fucking believe it. How can they do this? How can they just do what the hell they like?'

Heather didn't know what to say.

'Ava needs her life back. She should be free, she's done nothing wrong.'

'I know.'

Paul went to the window and looked at Ardmair. 'The soldiers came this morning, turned the camp over.'

Heather felt her heart in her throat. 'They didn't find Lennox or Sandy?'

Paul shook his head. 'I don't think so. I was watching from up the hill.'

Freya looked at him. 'Sandy – that's one of the creatures, right?'

Heather nodded.

'It was with you,' Freya said, 'when you were at my place. Ava said.'

'Yes. They helped us escape from New Broom.'

'Well, it didn't help Ava.'

'It was chaos, Freya. At night, in the dark, it was confusing and scary.'

'Think how my sister felt, alone with her baby. And now back with those dickheads.' She got up from the sofa and rubbed at her wrist. 'We have to do something.'

Heather came over to her. She wanted to wrap her in a hug but she was worried Freya would burst into tears or throw a punch.

'What can we do?' Heather said. 'Maybe if we found Lennox and Sandy...'

She tailed off because she couldn't think of a way to end that sentence.

'We have to let people know what's happening here,' Freya said. 'They're holding prisoners illegally.'

Heather shook her head. 'But how? They'll just deny it, talk about conspiracies. And if we expose ourselves, they'll come for us next. No one cares.'

Freya rubbed her wrist again. 'If people really knew what was happening, they'd care.'

Paul cleared his throat. 'I have an idea.'

Heather had been so focused on Freya she'd almost forgotten he was in the room.

'I asked around at Camp Outwith. I was careful, didn't give anything away.' He looked at Heather. 'But there's a journalist in Ullapool who's interested in New Broom. Maybe if we talk to her anonymously, we can get her help.'

Freya looked at him then Heather. 'What have we got to lose?'

Heather took them both in. 'Everything. But let's do it anyway.'

28
OSCAR

They were in the meeting room. Carson had gathered all the senior personnel after the escape. Oscar was surprised he got an invite, given Carson's antipathy towards him. Carson was currently raging at Sergeant Blackthorn, head of security, for allowing three humans and a goddamn baby to escape right under his nose. Oscar felt sorry for the guy, just a verbal punchbag.

Oscar tuned out and stared outside, thought about last night, his conversation with Jodie Becker in the early hours. What he'd seen out on the water, just as the guards from New Broom came through the place. The size of the loch made him appreciate how insignificant he was. One of the reasons he'd been obsessed with alien contact all his life was that it put the human experience in perspective, opened up the universe. There were other beings out there, other consciousnesses. They probably called themselves the equivalent of humans, because of course they did. They weren't *other* in their own world.

Sitting here now, Carson's shouts filling the room, he felt so depressed to be part of the human race, this pathetic, meaningless stuff we thought was important. Politics, diplomacy, arguments, vendettas, warfare, subterfuge, deceit, lies, hate, conspiracies, and on and on. There was something pure about the Enceladons, they interacted in good faith with the universe around them, unable to lie, didn't understand the concept, at least according to Lennox and Heather.

Maybe that was delusional. Maybe they had intrigue and politics and hate, just hid it better. Maybe he was idealising them because he was so disillusioned with his own place in human society. He used to think he was destined for greatness – Oxford University, a prestigious post-grad, a research job in astrobiology, then headhunted by the government for a secret department looking at unexplained phenomena. It was like living *The X-Files* for real. But the job had become a desk-bound grind, a series of dead ends and scams, years of wasted time.

Until the Enceladons.

Now he was getting kicked off the project, kicked off the base, just when it was getting interesting.

'And you,' Carson said, turning to Oscar.

He cringed and shrank into his seat.

'Would you like to explain to me what the hell you were up to last night?'

So that's why Oscar had been invited, another punchbag.

He thought about what he'd seen, what he knew. He could tell Carson, get himself off the hook. He had a trump card, but he was keeping it to himself for now.

'I was out trying to find them,' he said eventually, turning his hands palms up in acquiescence.

Carson snorted. 'You left New Broom in the middle of a lockdown. You tricked an idiot guard into letting you drive away. Then our troops found you this morning while sweeping that hippy camp, drinking tea with their so-called leader, your car on the beach.'

Oscar shook his head. 'A sheep jumped out. The people at the camp found me after the accident. They were helping me.'

'Bullcrap,' Carson said.

He walked slowly around the table putting on a show. Oscar had expected this, but in Carson's office or the stockade. But Carson needed a public scapegoat. He couldn't stomach that an Enceladon had broken in so easily and helped the humans escape. It highlighted how out of his depth he was here. So he needed to shout at Oscar in front of everyone to remain in charge.

'How do we know you weren't helping the fugitives? They could've been in the trunk of your car.'

Oscar let out a laugh. 'Have you seen my car?'

Carson straightened his shoulders. The two officers nearest him edged away. 'You think this is a goddamn joke?'

Oscar looked down.

'I have to speak to the vice president in a moment, with two of the fugitives still at large. What a shitshow.' He pointed around the room. 'I cannot believe a high-security facility was breached by an illegal so easily, that the might of the US military were running around like headless chickens, and only managed to find a young woman and her baby.'

'They're not illegals,' Oscar said.

Carson narrowed his eyes, simmering with rage. 'I beg your pardon?'

'There's no law against them being here.'

Carson stared for a long time and Oscar thought he might attack him.

'We make the law here. That's something you Brits never understood. We run this place and I say they're illegals.' Carson pointed at him. 'You can consider yourself very lucky you're not in the stockade.'

Oscar's cheeks flushed. He didn't want to be locked up, not now. Because he'd seen them. When he was at Camp Outwith, the soldiers tearing through the site, kicking over bonfires and rummaging through tents and campervans. Oscar had stood on the shore and seen a small boat puttering across the waves to Isle Martin, and he was pretty sure Lennox was one of the two figures on board.

29
AVA

Ava could hear Chloe crying from outside the research block. Her breasts were leaking at the painful noise, her body tapping into millions of years of evolution.

She grabbed Turner's arm at the entrance. 'What's going on in there?'

He shrugged her off and raised his gun.

She stuck her chin out. 'Are you going to shoot me? An unarmed woman?'

He slapped her hard in the face. Tears rushed to her eyes, her cheek stinging, burning shame burrowing into her. Michael had beaten her but always been careful, marks or bruising that could be explained away as an accident. She recognised the same look in Turner's eyes.

Chloe was still crying inside the building, making every nerve in Ava's body sing.

Turner stared at her breasts and she crossed her arms over them.

She tried to send reassurance to Chloe, but wasn't sure if it was getting through. She still wasn't sure how their telepathy worked, what the limits were.

She tried to keep her voice calm. 'Are we going in or not?'

Turner smiled and swiped the door, ushered her inside. Same walk to the room as before, another secure door to open, Chloe's cries getting louder. Ava's heart hammered against her ribcage.

Inside, Gibson was back at his table, looking at his laptop. The room was filled with Chloe's cries. She was lying in a cot this time, ankles and wrists in restraints attached to the edges of the cot. Her head was also in a secure restraint, a kind of built-in helmet. She was opening and closing her fists, toes wriggling, face purple, snot running from her nose. The head of the cot was raised, pointing towards the water tank. Several Enceladons were swimming around, sending a flurry of messages to each other, too much for Ava to untangle. They were darting in and out, tentacles reaching for and tangling with each other.

Chloe must be getting the same overwhelming jumble of noise in her brain. Imagine being a six-month-old baby and having this beamed directly into your head.

Ava tried to run to Chloe but Turner held her back. She tried to wriggle free but he backhanded her again. Tears streamed down her face. She tried to send calming vibes to Chloe, but couldn't even hear herself think above the noise in her mind.

She turned to Gibson. 'What are you doing? Let my daughter go.'

Gibson glanced up and smiled. 'She's doing very well.' He nodded at Turner. 'Let the kid see its mum.'

Turner roughhoused her over to Chloe. Ava tried to shake off his grip but he held firm. He smashed the butt of his rifle into her side and she doubled over, then righted herself and held a hand out to Chloe.

'Baby, please, it's OK.'

Chloe was struggling and screaming and Ava couldn't take it.

She turned to Gibson. 'Please.'

Gibson spoke quietly. 'I think I've found a way of amplifying the signals, as well as blocking. At the moment I'm blocking the kid, but amplifying the illegals.'

'I can hear them, it's too much.' Ava put her hands over her ears as if that made a difference.

Chloe was reaching out, hands grabbing thin air, and Ava felt sick.

'What's the point of this?'

Gibson sucked his teeth. 'We're testing emotional response, what better way than between mother and daughter.'

Ava reached out to Chloe but Turner pulled her back.

'Honey, it's OK,' she said.

She couldn't think because of the chaos in her brain, a hundred migraines at once. Her vision blurred and she saw flashes and sparks of light. She closed her eyes and focused on Chloe, sent as strong a message as she could – Mummy was here, everything was OK. If Chloe was experiencing half of what Ava was, she must be going mad.

Ava felt something from Chloe, an overwhelming scream in her mind that made her stagger backward until she tripped and fell against the tank. The scream had obliterated everything else in her mind, a howl so furious she couldn't comprehend it.

Chloe instantly calmed in her cot and stopped crying. The silence was deafening.

Ava heard a thump behind her, then another and another. She turned and saw all the Enceladons throwing themselves at the wall of the tank, tentacles spread out, suckers gripping the glass. She heard something in her mind, they were singing a song as one, desperate to get to Chloe and comfort her. All of them were stuck to the glass, drawn to the baby.

Ava glanced at Gibson, staring at the water tank.

'I thought you blocked her,' she said.

He looked at Chloe. 'I did. Very interesting.'

30
LENNOX

Lennox stirred the beans in the pot, placed it back on the portable gas stove they'd found. He'd also found a packet of stale crackers to dip in the beans.

They were in the kitchen of the Mill House, which looked out towards the mainland. Lennox couldn't see any signs of life except the salmon farm, if you called that living. He remembered the feeling he got from Sandy as they swam past it, sadness and incomprehension.

Sandy was in the kitchen sink, splashing water on the window and floor. Drops splattered over Lennox and sizzled in the stove flame. Sandy's light display was ambient turquoise, a kind of default contented vibe.

'I like a man who can cook.'

Vonnie walked in, towelling her hair. He remembered her in her underwear at the pontoon earlier and felt flushed.

'I would hardly call this cooking.'

She peered into the pot. 'I've eaten worse.'

'It could do with sausages or something.'

Vonnie wrinkled her nose. 'I'm vegan.'

He felt a shiver of embarrassment but also acknowledgement that she was right. Knowing what he knew now, eating animals was unethical. He'd never thought about it until he met Sandy. Now his eyes had been opened to how other creatures felt, what they thought.

Vonnie pointed at the beans. 'Watch they don't burn.'

He removed them from the stove and switched it off, poured them into a couple of small bowls and chucked a few crackers in each.

'Yum,' Vonnie said.

'Sorry.'

'Don't apologise, it's great. I always used to get hungry after a swim when I was wee.'

'I never really went swimming.'

'Didn't your folks teach you?'

Lennox swallowed some cracker and beans. 'I don't have parents. At least, not any I know.'

'Oh. Sorry.'

He waved that away.

Vonnie ran a hand through her damp hair. 'Must've been tough.'

'Everyone has it tough.'

Vonnie nodded. 'My mum died when I was a baby.'

'Sorry.'

Vonnie laughed. 'Shit, we really need to stop apologising for nothing.'

They ate in silence and watched Sandy, who was gazing out of the window.

<Why are those fish in cages?> Lennox jerked at Sandy's voice in his head. One day he would get used to it.

He sighed. He didn't want to explain. It was like explaining the horrors of famine or war to a kid, that life was just unfair and we had to get used to it.

<It's a salmon farm,> he sent.

'Are you talking to them?' Vonnie said.

'Yeah, about the fish farm.'

Vonnie nodded. 'Sandy gets it.' Then she considered for a moment. 'What do they eat?'

Lennox was embarrassed that he'd never thought to ask.

He remembered Vonnie's thoughts in his head while they were swimming with Sandy. It felt good. Personal, close like family. 'Do you want to ask Sandy directly?'

'Fuck, yeah.'

'Are you sure?'

Her eyes lit up. 'Of course, are you crazy?'

<Sandy, can you connect with Vonnie?>

Sandy turned from the window, reached a tentacle to Vonnie's face, another round her back. Vonnie put out a hand and her eyes glazed over as the suckers of Sandy's tentacle attached to her skin. Lennox knew that Sandy was asking permission, they always needed consent for anything invasive. Vonnie gave a nod and the tip of Sandy's tentacle crept into her right ear. She straightened her shoulders then relaxed them. Lennox wondered that he hadn't heard their conversation, maybe it was private until they both agreed to let him in. There was so much about this he needed to learn.

Sandy removed their tentacle and Vonnie opened her eyes, stared at Sandy then Lennox. Her eyes seemed impossibly green, like a colour that had just been invented.

<Holy shit.>

Sandy flailed a tentacle. <Meaning unclear.>

Vonnie and Lennox burst out laughing.

'It's nothing,' Vonnie said, then realised she'd spoken the words. <It's nothing.>

'You'll get used to it,' Lennox said.

'I hope not.'

Sandy turned back to the window, looked outside. <Accessing human-tribe story.> They puffed their head out a little. <What is farm?>

Lennox sighed. <Humans breed animals to eat.>

<In cages?> Sandy slapped a tentacle against the worktop.

<Yes.>

Vonnie shifted her weight. <Sandy, what do you eat?>

Sandy narrowed their head. <Tiny creatures on Enceladus offer energy to Enceladus whole. Like your zooplankton on Earth.> They looked outside. <Farm is torture.>

Vonnie nodded. <You're right, it's inhumane.>

Sandy looked at her. <Humans torture?>

Lennox rubbed at his eyes, suddenly tired. <Yes, humans torture.>

<Humans torture Enceladons in New Broom?>

<Yes.>

Sandy's light display became animated, purple and red sweeping across their body, their smooth skin ruffling into ridges and furrows. <Humans convert Enceladon energy to original state?>

They meant kill.

<Yes. I'm so sorry.>

Sandy's skin was a cascade of darker hues, black and brown, ending in maroon patches. <We must help Enceladon-partials. Reunite Enceladon-whole.>

'But how?' Vonnie said.

<We can't just go in there,> Lennox sent. <They'll kill us all. Convert energy to original state.>

< Sandy-Ava-Heather partial is in New Broom?>

Lennox felt ill. Here he was, safe and sound, and for all he knew Ava and Heather could be dead.

<I don't know,> he sent.

Sandy shimmered green and purple. <Must reunite Lennox-Ava-Heather-Sandy partial.>

Lennox swallowed, glanced at Vonnie. <It's not that easy.>

Sandy deflated, tentacles shrinking towards their body. <Must consult with Enceladon-whole. Confusion of human behaviour.>

Vonnie gave Lennox a look. 'They've got that right.'

There was silence for a few moments, then Lennox heard Vonnie's voice in his mind, soft and friendly.

<Sandy, how is this possible? Talking with our minds?>

Lennox was again embarrassed he hadn't asked before. Vonnie was so much more forthright and inquisitive than he was. He thought about the astronomy posters on her bedroom wall, the telescope at her window.

Sandy changed to oranges and yellows, pastel shimmers across their skin.

<Accessing human-tribe story.>

'What does that mean?' Vonnie asked Lennox.

'It's the internet.'

'They've got Wi-Fi?'

'Yeah.'

They both laughed at the weirdness of all this.

Sandy shuffled towards them, tentacles waving.

<You call it relational quantum mechanics. The state of a quantum system is observer-dependent, that is, the state *is* the relation between the observer and the system.>

Lennox was no clearer. <What does that mean?>

<Pre-observation, quantum state is all possible wave functions. Upon observation, quantum state collapses wave into single state of observer-observed partial.>

'I don't understand,' Lennox said, looking at Vonnie. 'You're into physics, does this make sense?'

'Maybe.' She reached out and touched the end of a tentacle. <How does that make you telepathic?>

Sandy slunk a tentacle round her wrist. <Enceladons simply collapse the wave to make the connection.>

Vonnie narrowed her eyes then looked at Lennox.

'It's a weird thing about quantum physics – all certainty goes out the window. You can never know exactly where a particle is, instead you have to describe it as a bunch of probabilities of finding it somewhere – that's called a wave function. It turns out that observing something actually collapses that wave. It makes the particle decide where it is. That's the whole idea behind Schrödinger's cat. Observing what happens to it makes that thing happen. It means that there's no such thing as objectivity or separation in the universe. At a basic level, things don't exist on their own. Reality is not *things*, it's the connections *between* things. We've always been connected. The collapsed quantum wave function is the connection. The Enceladons found some way to tap into that.'

Lennox still didn't fully understand, but he felt his heart swell at the idea.

31
HEATHER

This was a mistake. She was too exposed coming to Ullapool, there were soldiers everywhere. She'd been covered in the bed of Paul's truck, Paul and Freya up front, and they got lucky, the soldiers were mostly searching the vehicles leaving town rather than the ones coming in. It was Paul's idea to do it this way rather than have the journalist come out to the B&B, which made sense.

Paul and Freya had booked a room at the Ferry Boat Inn then smuggled Heather in through the delivery entrance to the restaurant, her hoodie pulled tight.

Now she felt claustrophobic in the little room – two single beds squeezed into the space, stripey wallpaper and patterned curtains, the heating on, making her sweat. She walked to the small window looking over Loch Broom and turned the radiator off. Stood to the side and gazed towards the head of the loch. A flat, black expanse flanked by undulating brown hills like waves themselves, contours overlapping.

She appreciated being here, for all her anxiety. She'd been cooped up in New Broom for months, then hiding in the guest house. She wanted to be free, wanted to be out there wandering down the street, hearing the chatter of tourists, the clank of the boat masts as they bobbed in the water, the engine growl of the ferry sitting in the dock.

The rhythmic knock on the door made her jump, but it was what they'd arranged.

She let in Paul, Freya and a shorter woman in her twenties, blonde hair in a pony, brown eyes, compact body.

'Vicky McLean,' she said holding out her hand.

'This is a mistake,' Heather said.

'No, it's OK. Please.'

Heather heard a noise outside, went to the window and saw a squad of four soldiers patrolling down the promenade, stopping passers-by and showing them a picture.

'They could be here in two minutes,' she said.

Paul came over to her, spoke softly. 'No one saw you come in. But we can go whenever you want, just say the word.'

The room felt even more claustrophobic with all four of them here. Paul had got Vicky's name and details from the woman who ran Camp Outwith, but none of them knew if they could trust her.

'I believe you wanted to tell me something,' Vicky said.

Freya stood in the bathroom doorway to make room. Paul stood at the window glancing outside, in case soldiers came into the FBI bar downstairs. Vicky pointed at the dressing table and stool underneath.

'Please,' she said.

Heather sat on the stool and Vicky sat on the bed opposite. Heather could smell her perfume, light and airy. She wondered if Vicky could sense her anxiety.

'I understand you're wary of me,' Vicky said. 'But I'm just trying to expose what's happening at New Broom, and you want that too, right?'

Heather cleared her throat but didn't speak, smoothed out the material of her jeans.

'OK,' Vicky said, looking round the room. 'Why don't I tell you what I have so far.'

She touched her ponytail nervously and Heather wondered what her life had been like. She had a strong Highland accent, local girl done good, but she wanted more, Heather could see that in her eyes.

'This is all officially denied, of course,' Vicky said. 'But we know that the US military are running New Broom. Stupid name, by the way. Anyway, they're investigating these creatures, the ones from the descent six months ago. The official line is that these are sea creatures blown off course and somehow lifted into the clouds in a freak storm, then dropped over the water at Loch Broom. Anyone with common sense knows that's bollocks. I was here that day—'

'You were?' Heather narrowed her eyes.

'I saw you. With Lennox Hunt and Ava Gallacher, all arrested once the creatures disappeared into the water. Ava was charged with murder, you and the boy disappeared from public sight. So I assume you've been held captive at New Broom.'

Heather nodded.

'Ava was abducted upon release from the High Court yesterday, and I assume she was brought to the base.'

Heather nodded again, looked at Freya, who clenched her fists at the mention of her sister.

'Then last night there was an emergency of some kind, alarms blaring, soldiers searching the surrounding countryside. And now here you are.' Vicky smiled. 'I suspect the creatures are extraterrestrial in origin.' She looked at all three of them in turn, but no one spoke. 'Usually when I say that, folk burst out laughing. So this is something new.'

Heather glanced at Paul.

'So.' Vicky waved a hand around the room. 'What do you want to tell me?'

Heather sighed. 'OK.'

Vicky reached for her phone. 'Can I record this?'

'Sure.'

She looked at the glowing red button on Vicky's phone and felt herself fall into a trance as she started talking and couldn't stop. She tried to say everything that had happened to her in the last few months as clearly and cleanly as possible, in chronological order. Her grief, meeting Sandy, going on the run, communicating with them, the alien curing her cancer, saving all their lives, the Enceladons running for *their* lives, refugees coming to Earth to survive. Then what happened to her afterwards, muscled into custody in Faslane, transferred to New Broom once it was built, the experiments, initial shock turning to mundane routine. It was amazing how you got used to having no hope. The cancer returning, then Sandy returning.

Paul knew some of this, Freya very little. Vicky listened as Heather kept talking, not looking at anyone in case she burst out crying. After a while she didn't even know what she was saying, just that she needed to tell someone. But more than that, she wanted someone to understand how different she felt compared to a few months ago. How she felt when she was with Lennox and Ava, when she could hear their voices in her mind. When she was with Sandy everything was as it should be, she was part of something in a way she'd never been before.

Eventually she ran out of energy and stopped. Her eyes were wet and her throat dry. She felt like an empty shell. She wanted to go to sleep in one of these saggy beds and forget everything.

'Wow,' Vicky said, ending the recording 'That's something else.'

Heather rubbed at her face with both hands. 'Yeah.'

She raised her head and looked around in the room. They didn't understand, not really, and she felt the loneliness of that.

32
OSCAR

Low sunlight made the water shimmer and the mountains glow as he guided the RIB towards the island. He glanced behind but no one was following, he'd managed to take the boat without anyone noticing. He pushed his hood down against the biting wind. He spotted three seals lolling on the rocky southern edge of the island, then followed the coast. Camp Outwith was to his right, lights coming on in the gloaming. He turned left and spotted the pontoon and three buildings marked on the OS map. He got binoculars out and checked for movement on the shore – nothing.

He got to the pontoon and tied up, then stepped ashore. Saw a thin ribbon of smoke coming from one of the houses. He walked over to it and looked in a window – empty kitchen, bowls and a pan in the sink. Walked round the house, through long grass and piles of bricks, to the room where the fire was. Saw Lennox and a girl in front of the fireplace, arms entwined, staring at the flames. Sandy was moving around the room, lifting things from a shelf – books, ornaments, a teddy bear – shimmering blues and greens across their body.

Oscar walked round the house and in the front door. He heard the crackle of the fire, smelled the wood, a salty tang in the air too.

He knocked on the open door.

Lennox and the girl jumped off the sofa and backed away as he held his hands out. Sandy stood on all five tentacles, head inflated, blades of red light down their limbs.

'I didn't mean to frighten you,' Oscar said. 'I'm not here to harm you.'

The girl looked at Lennox in confusion.

Oscar turned to her. 'My name is Oscar Fellowes, I work at New Broom. I know Lennox.'

'You're the reason I was locked up,' Lennox spat.

Oscar took a step and Lennox lifted a coal shovel from the fireplace.

'I'm sorry,' Oscar said. 'I was wrong, I see that now.'

'Ewan is dead because of you.'

Oscar sighed. 'Look, I'm here on my own, OK? I could've told Carson and he would've sent troops to get you. I don't mean you any harm.'

The girl narrowed her eyes. 'How did you find us?'

'I was in Camp Outwith when the soldiers came through. I was with Jodie. Crashed my car and she rescued me. I saw your boat heading for the island and recognised Lennox.'

Sandy had come over to Oscar, two tentacles raised. He thought about how easily they could hurt people. How they burned a hole in a fence like it was nothing.

'I just need to understand,' Oscar said, looking at Sandy.

Their iridescent display was hypnotising. He felt like his whole life had led to this point. When he chased them all across the country he hadn't realised what Sandy was like. His time at New Broom had made him realise and he'd turned, he knew that now. He'd ignored the nagging in his belly for too long, the sense that he was on the wrong side. He wanted to be here in a bothy on an island with the most extraordinary creature he'd ever seen, an alien who had experiences he couldn't comprehend but desperately wanted to understand.

'I hope you can forgive me,' he said to Lennox.

The girl stared at Lennox with raised eyebrows.

'I never caught your name,' Oscar said.

Lennox held out an arm as if to protect her. 'Don't.'

'I'm Vonnie,' she said, chin jutting in defiance of them both.

'I want to help you,' Oscar said. 'I want to help Sandy and all the other Enceladons.'

Lennox stared at Vonnie, then they both looked at Sandy. Oscar took a moment to catch on. 'Are you talking to each other through Sandy?'

Vonnie straightened her shoulders and stared at him.

Oscar lowered his voice. 'What's that like?'

Silence in the room. He didn't know if they were discussing him.

Eventually Lennox spoke. 'We need to get everyone out of New Broom. Heather, Ava and Chloe, all the Enceladons there. We need to break them out.'

Oscar shook his head. 'Ava and Chloe are there but Heather isn't, she wasn't recaptured. But I can go back and work on the inside. I can help them escape.'

He didn't know how long he would still be at the base, and wanted to help as much as possible in the time he had left.

Sandy moved towards Oscar, tentacles raised to his face. He thought about that Nagel essay, what *is* it like to be a bat? Even if we could talk to them, how would we understand?

'Sandy, be careful,' Lennox said.

Sandy reached out a tentacle to Oscar's upper arm, wrapped around it. Another touched the side of his face.

<Do I have permission?>

Oscar's legs went weak. He reached for the tentacle and stroked it, felt the smoothness of Sandy's skin, ripples of energy underneath.

'Yes,' he said, then tried something. <Yes, I give permission.>

He left the room and fell through a black hole to an icy-blue ocean, water in every direction, light-blue ice a ceiling above him, glimmers of smouldering red below like a network of veins across the moon's core. Enceladus. He'd read so much about it and now he was here somehow, arms turned to tentacles, his body vibrating, skin stretching and contracting with energy, thrusting through the water, meeting similar creatures, heading to a group of large jellyfish, overwhelming colour displays. He tasted the water through his tentacles. Tiny microorganisms passed through him, some becoming part of his biome, just as he was part of the jellyfishes' ecosystem, all of it in synch and connected. Emotion welled up in him and he wondered if he was crying, if that was possible in this body, swirling in the deep, dancing and singing and alive in more ways than he thought possible.

He was pulled from the water back to the room and slumped to the floor, tears on his cheeks, mind spinning.

<Welcome, Sandy-Oscar partial. Sandy-Oscar partial will help human-Enceladon whole?>

He swallowed, tried to find his voice.

'Yes, I'll help you.' He looked at Lennox and Vonnie, then at Sandy. <Of course. Of course I'll help you.>

33
AVA

<Chloe?>

Nothing. She sat in the detention block, tears in her eyes. She couldn't go on like this, but she was powerless to do anything.

After the bullshit in the research room, she'd been hauled away by Turner and dumped back here. They'd increased security on the door, removed the knives from the kitchen.

She had to think of a way to escape, but they'd deliberately separated her and Chloe to make her compliant. If they could hurt Chloe at any time, how could Ava do anything but go along with them?

She sent out feelers into the ether, alert to anything Chloe might give off. Back in the research room, the Enceladons were drawn to her. It was clear what Gibson was trying to do – use Chloe in a distressed state to lure Enceladons into a trap. Ava couldn't let that happen.

The front door opened and she tensed up, ran to the doorway, but it was just one of the two guards. He was short and Hispanic, *MENDOZA* on his lapel.

She slumped back to the living room and he followed her in.

'Hey.' He looked apologetic. 'Just checking you're OK.'

'What?'

He nodded behind him. 'I heard what happened at research. That's rough.'

'Screw you.'

Mendoza nodded. 'I have a family. I get it.'

Ava softened her gaze and her voice, one of her old tricks for dealing with Michael. 'Can you help me?'

'There's nothing I can do.'

'Let me have Chloe here. A mother shouldn't be separated from her daughter. You're a parent.'

Mendoza ran a hand through his hair. 'There are strict orders.'

'Why?'

Mendoza looked uncomfortable. 'They don't want you … influencing the baby.'

'How do you mean?'

'Is it true you can speak to her?' Mendoza tapped his head. 'Like, in your minds?'

Ava wondered how much to say. 'It's not speaking, she doesn't have language yet. But I can sense things from her, I feel it in my head and heart.'

'Doesn't sound too different from a regular mom.'

Ava angled her head. 'I can't compare it. But it's agony being apart.'

'What about the others? Lennox and Heather? And the creatures?'

Ava held his gaze for a long time, then nodded. 'Yes.'

He rubbed his chin. 'What does that mean for the rest of us?'

'I don't know.'

He smiled. 'Can you tell what I'm thinking now?'

She fluttered her eyelashes. 'No. You need to tell me.'

She glanced at the rifle hanging from his shoulder. He was a trained killer, of course, but she had nothing to lose.

He saw where her gaze fell and shook his head. 'Please, don't do anything stupid. I'm still a United States marine.'

Ava waved a hand around the room. 'You don't believe in all this, I can tell. You're a hypocrite.'

Mendoza seemed genuinely hurt by that, shifted his weight. 'I'm sorry.'

She looked at the gun again, wondered how to fire it.

The front door opened and Mendoza went on alert. He lifted the rifle and stood in the doorway. Fellowes came in, dishevelled but somehow energised.

'Mendoza, I need to speak with the prisoner alone.'

Mendoza shuffled his feet but held his ground. Ava wondered about Fellowes, he was different from the guy she first met at Ullapool harbour. He'd rescued her and Chloe from Gibson earlier and she wasn't sure why.

'Sorry, sir, but I'm under strict instructions not to let anyone in here.'

Fellowes puffed his chest out. 'Then why are *you* in here?'

'Just making sure she had everything she needed.'

'Soldier, I'm ordering you to let me speak with Ava alone.'

Mendoza stiffened. 'With all due respect, I don't take orders from you.'

'Of course you do.'

'You're a British civilian,' Mendoza said. 'And from what I heard, you're not going to be around here much longer.'

Fellowes tried to walk past Mendoza in the doorway but Mendoza blocked him.

'Sir, you need to leave.'

He strongarmed Fellowes, bending his arm behind his back and marching him down the hall. Mendoza reached the front door and opened it. Fellowes arched his neck and looked at Ava.

<Hold on.> His voice in her head made Ava reach out to the wall for balance. <I've spoken to Sandy. I know where Lennox is. We're going to get you and your daughter out of here.>

Mendoza pushed and Fellowes was gone, the door closed behind them, Ava alone in the darkness.

34
LENNOX

The fire had burned down to embers and Vonnie cuddled into Lennox's shoulder under the blanket they were sharing. The salty smell of her hair from the sea. The presence of a pretty girl next to him on the sofa made this feel like a dream.

Vonnie squeezed his arm and looked at him. Her eyes glimmered in the fading light. He needed something to be sure of in his life, and he wondered if that was her. Two days ago he was locked up with Heather. Now he was free, had been swimming with Sandy, met with Xander and the rest, done all this with Vonnie. He felt connected to her in a way that would've seemed impossible a few days ago.

Sandy was through in the kitchen, resting in the sink. Lennox didn't know Sandy's age, had no idea how long Enceladons lived for. Given what Sandy had done to Heather's brain tumour, Enceladons must be able to cure themselves of some diseases. Sandy talked about transformations of energy from one state to another, so they understood death. Some of the captured Enceladons died, almost gave up on living. Being disconnected from their community, from their family, meant they just didn't want to live.

He felt sick with guilt about Ava and Heather. Ava and Chloe were back in New Broom, but Heather was still free somewhere. Lennox had tried sending messages to her, but she must be too far away. She could be injured and alone out there, and here he was playing happy families with Vonnie.

'Do you trust Oscar?' Vonnie's voice was sleepy.

'I don't know. Sandy was willing to connect with him, and they're a pretty good judge of character.'

Vonnie squeezed his arm again. 'So you only decided to like me when Sandy decided I was OK?'

Lennox liked the fun in her voice. 'I never said I liked you.'

'Hey.' She punched him in the ribs, and he flinched and laughed. 'Plenty of guys would be ecstatic to sit in front of a romantic fire with me.'

'Really?'

She punched him again and he pushed her away, but it was all flirting.

'Sure. Alone on a remote island, in a cosy, firelit bothy.'

Lennox threw a log on the fire. 'It feels good.'

'It does.' He sat back and she kissed him on the cheek. Blood rushed to his face.

'This is crazy,' Vonnie said. 'I guess you're used to it, you met Sandy months ago. But this all happened to me in the last few hours. There are creatures up there.' She threw a thumb towards the window. 'I might be able to see Enceladus from my telescope. There's been another world in the solar system full of life all this time. There's so much to know. How did they evolve? What about their culture, art, politics? And all this insane stuff about telepathy, quantum-wave collapse. Reality is connections, not things.'

'Did that make sense to you?'

'I think so. It's like Buddhism, right? We're all part of an interconnected system, everything in the universe. They just found a way to manifest that.'

He'd never heard anyone talk like her, so different to how his brain worked. He loved it.

'Can I try something?' he said.

'Sure.'

He sat up. The log crackled in the fireplace, threw out some smoke.

<Can you hear me without Sandy here?>

Her eyes widened. <Yes! And you can hear me?>

<Sure.>

Vonnie shook her head. <This is insane.>

Lennox shrugged. <We'd better get used to it, it's just who we are now.>

<And we can talk this way to the others?>

<If we're in range.>

Vonnie smiled. <But what does this mean?>

<How do you mean?>

<For our future? The future of humankind?>

<I don't know.>

The fire cracked again, and Lennox thought he heard something else. Maybe from outside. He tensed up and listened.

'What?' Vonnie said.

<Wait. I think—>

The door burst open and Sandy scuttled across the room, flashing red and yellow as they flailed three tentacles behind them. They knocked into a chair and fell over and five armed soldiers came behind, spotlights from their rifles strobing the room.

Lennox hauled Vonnie up from the sofa and pushed her behind him. 'Go.'

Sandy righted themself and lashed out a tentacle at the closest soldier, a spark of light arcing from their limb to the guy's head. He shuddered and collapsed, his spotlight swinging, gun clattering on the floor.

Another soldier had something on the end of a pole, one of those cages they used to capture Enceladons, that blocked their powers. Another guy had a long-handled taser and he scorched Sandy's body with it. Sandy was going crazy, lights flashing up and down their body, distressing patterns and ridges across their head. The taser guy got Sandy again, and Lennox lunged for the rifle on the floor, but another soldier smashed him in the face with the butt of his gun and Lennox collapsed in a heap against the wall. The soldier pointed his gun at Lennox's face.

Lennox turned to Vonnie, standing by the window. <Go, please. You can help us later, but you have to get out.>

She hesitated, looked at the gun on the floor, but she was too far away.

<Go.>

<I'm sorry.> Vonnie hauled the window open and leapt out as a soldier lunged for her and missed.

The other soldiers overpowered Sandy, pushing them into the cage, which slammed shut. Sandy was squeezed inside, tips of their tentacles poking out, light display fading to nothing.

He heard Vonnie's voice in his head. <I'll find you both, I promise.>

Lennox stared at the soldier standing over him and hoped that Vonnie would stay well away from him.

35
HEATHER

Heather sat on the beach and watched Rosie play with a red bucket and spade. She filled the bucket and flipped it, plonked it on the ground and tapped the edges to loosen the sand. Slowly lifted the bucket to reveal the sandcastle, her squeal of delight filling Heather's heart. It was summer, Rosie was five, the sun hazy. A colossal monster with tentacles and tendrils burst from the Forth and lunged for her. She screamed as it grabbed her and dragged her to the water's edge. Heather leapt up and chased, but Rosie was under the surface before she could even cry out. Heather ran into the water, splashing past her waist to her chest, but there was no sign of anything. She screamed for help but there was no one else on the beach, the world was empty.

She woke with her chest rising and falling rapidly, a panic attack in her sleep. It always happened when she dreamed of Rosie. She tried to calm herself. As her breathing slowed, deep sorrow engulfed her, the loss of her daughter hitting her all over again. She'd been happy and healthy in the dream, now she was dead and gone, and Heather couldn't stand it.

It took a long beat for her to realise she was in the bedroom of the B&B, morning light fuzzy through the thin curtains. She eased out of bed, walked to the window and pulled a crack in the curtains. A sunny day, land and sea in harmony in the dappled sunshine. There was something profound about coastlines that she couldn't put her finger on – where land met sea was special. Maybe it reminded humans of their aquatic ancestors, deciding to take that first step onto land.

She walked to the open kitchen and living area, Paul under a blanket on the sofa, heavy breathing. The sofa wasn't long enough for him, his feet sticking out one end, neck cricked at the other.

He snuffled then opened his eyes. He'd always been a light sleeper, a useful survival tool.

'Hey,' he said.

'Hey.'

They'd greeted each other like this every morning for two decades. It was nothing but it was everything. Now it was Iona's turn to wake up next to him, to share her dreams and fears.

'Won't Iona be wondering where you are?' She hadn't had the heart to ask him last night, worried that he'd remember about his real life and leave.

'I explained to her on the phone.'

'That you were spending the night with your ex-wife?'

Paul sat up and angled his head to say she was being stupid. 'She knows the trouble you're in, what you've been through.'

'And she trusts you?'

'Of course.'

She put on a stupid smile. She was wearing a long T-shirt she'd found in an old cupboard, her bare legs goose-pimpled. No one would ever know her body as well as he had. 'But does she trust *me*?'

He pushed the blanket aside and stood. He was in shorts and a T-shirt, still pretty fit for a guy in his fifties. Heather wondered how she looked to him, then chastised herself for that. Who gives a shit, right? Except she did.

'Sleep OK?' he said.

'Bad dream.'

Heather went to the kitchenette and put the kettle on. She didn't want to face him because he knew what she meant.

'I still get them sometimes,' Paul said. 'It's hard to wake up from that. Feels like…'

'…losing her all over again.'

She turned and looked at him. Pictured Iona at home, hands on her baby bump, no idea what was coming – sleepless nights, anxiety and stress, breastfeeding, incontinence pads, nappies and colic, burps and pukes, tantrums. She thought of Ava with Chloe, able to curb the worst meltdowns by sharing her feelings. If only all the human race could do that.

'Do you think the journalist will write our story?' Heather said.

'Will anyone publish it? And even if they do, will anyone believe it?'

Heather nodded. 'Maybe we should introduce her to Sandy.'

Paul looked out at the landscape, mountains framing the sea. 'We need to find them first.'

'Find Lennox and we'll find Sandy.'

A knock on the door made Heather jump, but it was the triple knock they'd used yesterday in the FBI room with Freya and Vicky.

Paul put a hand out for Heather to stay back and went to the door. Opened it a crack, breathed out and opened it further.

Freya came into the room, running her hands through her hair then down her face.

'I've just come from Camp Outwith,' she said. 'Lennox and Sandy were on Isle Martin with the campsite owner's daughter. But they're gone.'

Heather frowned. 'What do you mean?'

'The girl staggered into camp late last night. Soldiers busted in and took Lennox and Sandy.'

36
OSCAR

He stared at the scrambled eggs on the plate. Looked around the canteen, not many seats taken. It was busy earlier when the shifts changed at seven, the night shift desperate for food before bed. The American troops had taken to a Scottish fry-up, square sausage, black pudding, haggis and potato scones.

He stared at the loch out of the window. So beautiful, yet this place had a heart of darkness, he realised now. He'd been creeping towards the realisation for ages. He'd felt uneasy for a long time, and the events of the last few days had crystallised things. Then last night's connection with Sandy sealed it. He understood.

He'd imagined meeting an alien millions of times, but it was even more mind-blowing than he expected. He felt at one with Sandy, part of them in a way he'd never felt before. Boarding school, university, scientific research and the civil service – these were all pathetic constructs that kept people in conflict. They were like chimps battling for supremacy of their social group, with their ulterior motives, power struggles, a million subterfuges and slights, hang-ups and grudges.

But not Sandy, not the Enceladons. They didn't understand war or lying. No wonder they seemed like a threat to military and political forces – they pointed towards a new way of being, and that was threatening to the status quo.

He couldn't support that anymore. He'd meant what he said to Ava last night. What he'd *thought* to Ava last night. *That* was mind-boggling. He didn't know how it worked, but he presumed that everyone who'd connected with Sandy could subsequently communicate with each other telepathically. There was obviously limited range, he couldn't speak to any of them now. The scientific part of him wanted to put himself on the slab, cut his skull open and find out how it worked. But that was the old, human way of thinking. That was a way of existing that seemed pathetically out of date now.

He was snapped out of it by two soldiers taking the table next to him. Southern accents, plates of bacon and sausage.

He was about to leave when he overheard something. 'Excuse me, what did you just say?'

The soldier was muscle-bound, brown buzzcut, narrow-set eyes. He looked at Oscar as if he was dirt, the way they all did. 'This is a private conversation, sir.'

'Just tell me.'

He looked at his friend and shrugged. 'It's not classified or anything. We captured one of the illegals last night, playing happy families with that mixed-race kid and some girlfriend on an island north of here.'

'Sandy and Lennox are here?'

Buzzcut guffawed and raised his eyebrows at his friend. 'Sandy? You giving them little pet names now?'

'Where are they?' Oscar said, standing up.

They shared a look again. 'Far as I know, the boy's in the stockade and the thing is in research.'

Oscar ran out of the canteen and across the courtyard to the research block. Swiped his card at the door, but it flashed red. Tried the door anyway, locked. Swiped again, same thing. Did it three, four times, the lock beeping each time. He banged his fist against the door.

'Gibson!'

Fuckers had restricted his access.

He strode over to the stockade and it was the same there. Red flash, beep, door stayed locked. He banged the door over and over, there would be a guard inside.

Eventually the door opened and a guard filled the doorway, gun raised. It was Turner, the worst possible scenario.

'I'm here to see Lennox Hunt.'

Turner smiled at him. 'No, you're not.'

'I'm ordering you to let me speak to the prisoner.'

Turner nodded at the electronic lock. 'Your card has been deactivated.'

'I've been given express permission by General Carson—'

'Let me stop you there,' Turner said, stepping forward and forcing Oscar away from the door. 'I have direct orders from Carson not to allow you anywhere near the kid.'

'There must be some mistake.'

Turner tapped his rifle barrel with his fingers. 'I need you to step back, *sir*.'

Oscar moved to push him aside. 'If I can just—'

Turner jabbed a fist into Oscar's guts, enough to wind him and send him back a couple of steps. He doubled over and sucked in air.

'This is a big mistake.'

Turner stepped back into the building. 'Take it up with Carson.'

The door closed and Oscar righted himself. He had a rock in his stomach as he walked to Carson's office. Tried to think how to play this but honestly couldn't think of any way it would come out well.

He was ten yards from the office when the door opened and Carson came out, flanked by two guards, guns raised. His face was implacable, which was somehow worse than angry.

'What's going on?' Oscar said, waving his keycard. 'I've had my access blocked.'

'You're lucky you're not in the stockade.'

'What's this about? I have the same right to access the Enceladons as Gibson, that was agreed at the highest level.'

'That changed when you became a traitor.'

Blood rushed to Oscar's cheeks. 'What do you mean?'

Carson stared at him for a long time and Oscar squirmed.

'We tracked you,' he said eventually. 'You think we'd let you run around without surveillance after how you've behaved?'

Oscar swallowed. 'Wait...'

'Thank you,' Carson smiled. 'You led us right to the kid and the illegal.'

'But—'

Carson held a hand up. 'Enough.' He nodded at the soldiers. 'They'll escort you to your accommodation. You're under house arrest. But don't get too comfortable, we're going on a little trip later.'

The soldiers stepped forward and Oscar felt defeated. 'What do you mean?'

Carson smiled and Oscar didn't like it one bit.

37
AVA

She'd barely slept, stomach tight as she tossed and turned, worrying about Chloe. Who was looking after her? At least when Ava was in prison she knew Freya was caring for her. Up here, it would be a stranger who didn't give a shit if she cried all night or lay in a dirty nappy.

She sat at the kitchen table in the detention block, hands wrapped around a mug of chamomile tea. Scrunched her eyes shut and tried to sense Chloe's mood, any sign. She cursed this extra connection she had, it was worse than being a normal mum. Mostly she loved having a sixth sense about her baby, but being separated was so painful. She'd been gifted a new way to communicate, only to have it taken away.

The Enceladons on the base withered away in captivity and she understood why. Those poor creatures spent every moment inseparable from their community, couldn't conceive being alone. For them to come here looking for a new home and be treated like this was disgusting.

But humans had been doing this forever, right? Slavery and subjugation, torture and murder. History was a brutal march of domination. The Enceladons were a new way of thinking, a new way to live. But the humans here were stuck in the same old patterns, razor-wire fences and machine guns, military muscle and hatred, hurting for the sake of it.

She tried to contact Chloe again. Nothing. Then she thought of Fellowes. He'd spoken to her in her mind, which must mean he'd connected to Sandy. Either that or they'd found a way to replicate the Enceladons' telepathy. But it felt like he was on their side now, wanted to help.

She heard the beep of the front door lock and tensed.

Two soldiers she didn't recognise, just kids really. What had led a pair of fresh-faced teens to become gun-toting cogs in the military machine?

'Time to go,' the shorter of the two said. He was more scrawny than the other, bulky guy.

She didn't move. 'Go where?'

'Classified,' Scrawny said.

'Then I'm not going.'

Scrawny tilted his head and looked at Bulky for assurance. Got a nod.

'We can do this the easy way or the hard way, ma'am. But we have orders to get you.'

'I want to see my daughter. I'm not cooperating until I see Chloe.'

Bulky stepped forward. 'You're in luck, that's where we're taking you.'

'Really?'

They marched her across the courtyard, away from the research block and towards the dock. They walked round the warehouse then past the RIBs tied up on the jetty. Kept walking to a larger ship, *USS Sallis* on the side. It was sombre grey, prominent bridge and radar tower, cannons mounted front and back, two more down each side. At the stern, the deck was cut away, the space filled with water like a swimming pool, crane hanging over. Another enclosed platform was built in the middle of the ship, looking down at the swimming-pool space, like an observation deck.

The guards ushered her on board. She paused with her hand on the railing. 'Where's Chloe? You said you were taking me to her.'

'She'll be here.'

Bulky shoved her forward so hard she stumbled. She grabbed at the railing and righted herself, and Scrawny pointed his gun at the observation deck.

She stepped inside and saw Lennox looking towards the rear of the ship, another armed guard keeping an eye on him.

<Lennox.>

He ran to her and hugged her, and she welled up. She'd missed their connection.

<I thought you got out,> she sent to him.

< I did, but they tracked us down.>

<You and Heather?>

<Me and Sandy.>

<So where's Heather?>

Bulky pulled her away across the room.

Lennox looked at her. <I don't know.>

<And where's Sandy?>

<Don't know that either.>

She looked around the room. <What's this all about?>

38
LENNOX

Lennox had a sinking feeling about Ava's question. He looked around the observation deck. This must surely be an Enceladon fishing trip. They'd been terrible at catching them so far – in several months they'd picked up around two dozen octopoid creatures. Lennox knew from his swim there were thousands more out in the water.

He wondered where Vonnie was. He presumed she'd got off the island, otherwise she'd be here. He hoped she didn't attempt a rescue.

He looked at Ava, on the verge of tears, but couldn't think of anything to say to make her feel better. He was as defeated as she was – they'd both briefly been free.

She turned to the two guards with her. 'You said my baby would be here.'

The small one shrugged. 'That's what we were told.'

<It'll be OK,> Lennox sent.

<You don't know that.> Ava stared at him so hard he had to look away.

They were all hurting, but she had Chloe to think about into the bargain. He couldn't begin to imagine. He was sixteen years old, what did he know about life? He remembered back at school when Ava was Mrs Cross, a maths teacher. It was a different world, a different universe.

He glanced at the mouth of the loch, then at the back of the ship. The odd swimming pool inside the rear end made him feel ill. If this was a fishing trip, it was a different scale to what they'd done before. And why bring him and Ava?

The door opened and Carson strode in, flanked by two armed

guards. Behind him skulked Oscar. When he saw Lennox, his eyes went wide.

<It wasn't me, I didn't tell them where you were.>

Lennox flinched at Oscar's voice in his head, and a fire burned in his belly. Of course it was him, how else could they have found them on Isle Martin?

<Fuck you.> Lennox launched across the room and grabbed Oscar by his shirt, rammed him against the wall. He punched him in the stomach then the face before two guards hauled him off. He stumbled and fell, smacked his head off the wall.

He sat up and saw Carson smiling at him.

'Happy families, eh?'

<Please,> Oscar said in Lennox's mind. < He had a tracker on me. I didn't know, I swear.>

Lennox felt sick to have this voice in his mind. For the first time since all this started he wished he couldn't hear other people's thoughts. Maybe Sandy and the others had a way of tuning this stuff out, a way of being alone. He'd always assumed being connected like this was a better way, but not if you were tied to arseholes like Oscar. Humanity had a shitload of growing up to do before all this could work. He imagined all the online bigots and trolls, all the hate-filled monsters spewing bile directly into your brain with no filter, no ability to block it out. Unbearable.

Oscar smoothed his shirt down and turned to Carson. 'Why are we here?'

Carson looked supremely confident as he waved a hand at Lennox like a Roman emperor. 'I think Mr Hunt knows what we're doing.'

Lennox cleared his throat. 'It's a fishing trip. For Enceladons.'

Carson coughed out a laugh. 'Illegals.'

Oscar pushed himself away from the wall. 'General, I strongly—'

Carson held up his hand. 'Enough.'

So maybe Lennox was wrong, maybe Oscar was fucked like the rest of them.

'But this is much bigger, right?' Lennox said. 'This is different scale. Something's happened.'

Carson nodded. 'Very good, Mr Hunt, something has happened. And we're going to test it out.'

'Where the hell is my daughter?' Ava said, blocked by guards from approaching Carson.

Carson unhooked a radio handset from his belt. He lifted it to his mouth and pressed the button.

'It's time,' he said. 'Let's catch some fish.'

39
HEATHER

From a distance, Camp Outwith reminded Heather of the Faslane Peace Camp, the permanent anti-nuclear protest site outside the submarine base at Gare Loch. She and Lennox had been driven past it on their way into the base, where they were held before New Broom was built. She liked the idea of folk living outside of society because of their principles. She admired them for doing what they believed in.

Paul parked his truck in the layby by the beach and Freya jumped out, took them to a campervan further along the peninsula. A black woman sat on a foldout chair warming a pan of water over a gas stove. Standing beside her was the journalist Vicky, arms akimbo, unhappy face.

'This is Jodie,' Freya said, waving at the woman. 'She runs this place.'

Jodie jutted her chin out in acknowledgement. 'No one *runs* this place. But I've become the mother, I suppose.'

'I'm Heather and this is Paul.'

Vicky threw an annoyed glance at Heather and Paul. 'Can you tell Jodie I need to speak to the girl.'

Jodie cleared her throat. 'She's been through a lot.'

She lifted the bubbling pan and poured water into a teapot. Stirred it, put the lid on. Heather saw a collection of mugs at her feet, carton of milk.

Jodie stood, surprisingly sprightly. Dungarees, grey quiff, twinkle in her eye.

'You're one of the original ones,' she said, stepping up to Heather.

Heather ran her tongue around her teeth. 'Yes.'

Jodie smiled and it felt like the woman was staring into her soul. Heather wondered briefly if she was telepathic.

<Can you hear me?>

Jodie didn't acknowledge anything.

'How's the girl?' Heather said.

'Traumatised.'

Heather nodded. 'They're bastards.'

Jodie looked down the coast in the direction of New Broom around the headland. 'Have you been kept there the whole time?'

'Since it was built.'

'Can't have been easy.'

'Nothing is.'

'True.' Jodie glanced at Vicky. 'Is this woman on the level?'

Vicky threw her a look but Heather shrugged. 'I think she's on our side. What other options do we have? We're powerless.'

'We're never powerless.' Jodie waved a hand around Camp Outwith. There were about twenty campers and tents, maybe fifty people. 'People have power when they work together.'

It was like something she might've got from Sandy. But Heather doubted it was true, really. She struggled to see how this little congregation of outcasts and dreamers could do much against the military might round the coast. She thought of the Faslane protestors, they'd been there for decades and the nuclear subs hadn't left. What can ordinary people do in the face of greater power?

'Hey.'

A young woman came out of the campervan, and Jodie walked over and enveloped her in a big hug. She was thin and tall, striking eyes and black hair.

'You OK?' Jodie said, rubbing her arms. 'I'm making tea.'

Classic mother role. That had been Heather once, hugging a teenage girl, making sure she was OK. Except she'd failed at that.

Now she was surrounded by people who felt like strangers, even her ex-husband. She glanced at him and he smiled, but she felt empty.

The girl sat on a bench and waved Heather over.

'I'm Vonnie, you must be Heather. Lennox told me about you.'

'Don't believe a word of it.'

Vonnie stared at her. <I can't believe they got him.>

Heather flinched and straightened her shoulders at Vonnie's voice in her mind. <You can do this?>

Vonnie ran a hand through her hair.

The others watched them carefully.

<I connected with Sandy. I still don't really understand.>

<Yeah, they have that effect.>

<What does all this mean?>

Heather shook her head. <I wish I knew.>

Vicky threw a hand in the air. 'What are you doing? Is this what you told me about? Voices in your mind?'

Heather's heart swelled knowing Vonnie was another one of them, someone she didn't have to hide her true self from. In comparison, hearing Vicky's reedy voice was like being buzzed by an insect, just background noise. But that was a terrible way to think of another human being. She was supposed to be open minded, that's what Sandy had done to her.

'Yes,' she said to Vicky, then looked at the others.

Paul and Freya knew, of course. Jodie took it in her stride, handing mugs of milky tea to Vonnie and Heather. Heather sipped from hers, felt the burn on her lips and liked it. She pictured the atoms of the liquid going to her stomach, being absorbed into her body, becoming part of her. Everything we consume, everyone we interact with, becomes a part of us. They always had, she'd just been blind to it.

A phone rang and Paul looked apologetic as he answered it, walking to the water's edge.

Heather watched him go, and she knew.

'So where is this thing now?' Vicky's voice brought her back.

Vonnie hunched her shoulders and gripped her mug tight. ‘They’re at the base. Lennox too. We have to rescue them.’

Freya spoke up. ‘Ava and Chloe are there too. We have to get them out. But look at us.’

She waved a hand around the camp.

‘It’s not just us,’ Vonnie said, staring at her tea. She looked at Heather. <I went swimming. The other Enceladons are nearby. If they understood the situation, they would help.>

‘What are you saying?’ Vicky said. ‘Stop keeping secrets.’

Vonnie looked at her with a pity that Heather recognised, and Vicky shrank.

‘I went swimming with Lennox and Sandy,’ Vonnie said. ‘We met the other Enceladons. There are thousands of them. If we can get them to understand, maybe they would help.’

‘But how?’ Jodie said.

Heather was distracted from the conversation, watching Paul’s body language as he ended the call. He stayed looking out to sea for longer than necessary, his shoulders tense. She got up and walked to him, knew from the look on his face.

‘I have to go,’ he said.

Heather nodded. ‘Iona.’

‘She’s gone into labour. She’s quite far along already.’

He looked apologetic but she sensed something underneath. This was his way out. It wasn’t his problem anymore, his ex-wife and her crazy nonsense with aliens and telepathy. She was relieved. Glad she wasn’t responsible for him being here any longer. He could go and they would both have guilt-free consciences.

‘I’m so sorry.’

‘It’s OK.’

‘I just—’

She grabbed him in a hug before he could say anything else. She didn’t have a telepathic connection with him but she knew him inside out. He would always love her, just as she would always love him. But that chapter of their lives was finished, their daughter was dead and it was time to move on.

She swallowed hard and held on too long.

40
AVA

They'd been twenty minutes at sea and she still hadn't sensed Chloe's presence on board. She wondered if the guards had just told her Chloe was here to get her to come quietly.

<Baby, it's Mummy.>

Nothing.

She looked at Lennox glowering at Oscar, who'd shrunk into himself. Carson gave demands in a low, calm voice down the radio to someone on the bridge.

The observation deck faced the back of the ship, so they'd been watching the banks of Loch Broom get smaller as they headed out to sea. They passed an island, Lennox craning his neck in that direction.

They were further out to sea, the loch mouth widening, then they were surrounded by islands, rocky outcrops in the water that only served to emphasise the expanse of ocean around them. They cleared the islands and the ship headed right, towards a bleak headland of stony beaches, inlets and coves. She spotted the occasional whitewashed house amongst the vast moorland and hills, and wondered what it was like to live there. Scotland was only a small country, yet had so much remoteness.

The engine cut out. Everyone in the room tensed with the absence of noise, as if the silence was pressing down on them.

Ava heard something, faint at first, but she recognised Chloe's cries. Her body tensed at each wail.

'Tell me where she is,' Ava said. She tried to step towards Carson but was blocked again.

'Let's see if Gibson knows what he's talking about,' Carson said to himself. He waved at Ava's two guards. 'Take her down.'

They rough-housed her out of the door and down the steps. Chloe's cries grew louder and she felt each one across her forehead, in her belly.

Round the corner on the open deck beside the pool she saw the creep Gibson, with Chloe in the same cot as before, the same restraints on her head, wrists and ankles. Her face was purple with rage as she cried and cried.

Ava tried to send calm feelings towards her, but Chloe was obviously being blocked again. Ava got no sense of her mental state.

The cot was on a large metal trolley with wheels, angled outward again, pointing Chloe over the rear of the ship, the water container and the sea beyond. Ava got closer to the edge and saw there was a large metal cage suspended in the pool on the end of thick metal chains from a crane on the side of the ship. The cage was submerged in the water and inside were a group of Enceladons.

She tried to run to Chloe but was stopped by Bulky, who gripped her arm hard. She lunged to grab at his rifle but he swung it away and punched her in the stomach. She crumpled to her knees, tears in her eyes.

'Careful,' Gibson said, frowning. 'We need her.'

He was standing at a laptop on another metal table, its wheels locked in place. The same set-up as he'd had in the research lab, Chloe still in the skull cap with electrodes poking out. It looked like some crazy shit the Nazis might've done. Ava couldn't let this go on but she couldn't stop it. She looked at Scrawny, thought about what it would take to overpower him. But there was also Bulky and Gibson, and the guards back in the observation deck, the rest of the crew. There was no way.

Ava heard something in her mind, a painful cacophony, conflicting messages and ideas, signals and feelings. Realised Gibson had stopped blocking the Enceladons in the water below and amplified them. She thought back to last time in the research lab and realised what this was all about.

She screwed her eyes shut and threw her hands over her ears. Then she felt Chloe's mounting distress, the baby was obviously experiencing the same things as Ava, except she was only six months old, for God's sake. This was torture for an adult, it was obscene that they would subject a baby to it.

'Please,' Ava cried, staggering to her feet and holding her hands out to Gibson. 'You're torturing her.'

He typed on the laptop, the banality of evil, that he could do something like this with a keystroke.

'Trust me,' he said, barely looking at her. 'I know what I'm doing.'

'How can you?' Ava could barely speak with the chaos of voices and emotions, screams and ideas and sorrows and fears in her mind. She literally couldn't hear herself think. She tried again to send Chloe a feeling of calm, but knew it was no use. The baby was screaming out loud as well as sending her emotions into the ether, and Ava didn't know which was worse.

She stepped towards Gibson but was sideswiped by a slap from Bulky. She barely cared anymore, bring the physical pain to go with the mental anguish. She glanced down and saw the Enceladons frantic in their cage, obviously sensing Chloe's distress the same as Ava. Gibson was amplifying them to the humans and vice versa, it was obscene.

Gibson nodded at Bulky, who dragged Ava over into Chloe's eyeline. Chloe's eyes widened and her cries became louder and more angry, unbearable.

Then Chloe blasted a silent scream that made Ava collapse. At the same instant she stopped making any noise with her mouth, her face already starting to go back to a calmer colour, the echoes of her telepathic howl ringing in Ava's mind and somehow getting louder. She glanced at the Enceladons and, just like before, they were clambering and grabbing at the bars of the cage trying to get to Chloe, trying to calm her and make sure she was OK.

'OK,' Gibson said to himself. 'Let's see if this works.'

41
OSCAR

Oscar watched everything going on below with growing horror. They were torturing a baby, for fuck's sake. He would never have agreed to this and Carson knew it, but Gibson seemed to be enjoying it. Chloe was strapped in, getting more upset, Ava down there too, obviously she was needed to set Chloe off. And the Enceladons were craving contact with her. Oscar heard a mess of noise in his mind, distorted anguish from Chloe and the Enceladons, but at least he was a distance away.

'This is disgusting,' he said to Carson, who was staring at the action below.

Carson turned. 'Do you like steak?'

'What?'

'It's a simple question. I love a juicy ribeye, medium rare, lots of green peppercorn sauce.'

'That's not the same, you know—'

'Why not?'

Oscar looked at the Enceladons tangling their tentacles in the bars of the cage.

'These are intelligent creatures from another world, for God's sake. You can't compare them to livestock.'

'I've never understood how folks differentiate between animals. Why is it OK to eat a cow but not a dolphin or your pet dog?'

'That's not what this is about.'

'You're a hypocrite, Fellowes. You claim to have these things' best interests at heart, yet you happily inflict pain and suffering on all the animals you eat, just for your own pleasure.'

'I'm not responsible for factory farms and the way they treat animals.'

'And I'm not responsible for the wellbeing of these things,' Carson said. 'You seem to think they're some kind of special case, but to me they're nothing more than rats – an infestation to deal with. Bigger than rats, but it's the same thing.'

'They're smarter than us.'

Carson flexed his fingers. 'If that's true, then it's even more important we don't let them overrun us. Don't let them take over our goddamn home.'

Oscar glanced around. Lennox was subdued in the corner, maybe trying to communicate with the Enceladons in the cage. He was staring at the water in the enclosed area, then the water of the loch.

Carson and the guards were looking that way too. Oscar saw his chance and bolted for the door. He heard shouting behind him as he ran down the steps and round the corner, waiting for gunfire or the searing pain of a bullet in his back.

Out on deck he was pelted by the noise in his mind, a cacophony of screams and cries fighting for attention. He staggered and shook his head, then took in the scene, Gibson fiddling with his laptop and looking out to sea, the guards distracted by something out there, Ava reaching for Chloe and trying to undo her restraints. A sucking noise came from the sky and Oscar saw a helicopter hovering over the back of the ship, downdraft blasting them. Two soldiers were up there in the open side door, guns trained over the back of the ship.

He ran to the enclosure and the frantic Enceladons, his mind scrambled by their distorted cries. Gibson had changed their messages somehow, increased their volume and intensity, making Oscar double over at the handrail.

He blinked away tears and jumped into the water of the enclosure, heard more shouts behind him and didn't care. He swam to the top of the cage then dived down to the metal grid and started yanking at the locked door, but it didn't budge. He heard gunfire and saw bullets trace through the water around him, sending bubble threads into the deep. He scrambled up for air then back down, examined the cage, the Enceladons clamouring, their voices overdriven in his mind, but he couldn't see any way of getting them out.

Then the noise shut off and the creatures all turned and faced the stern of the ship. Oscar swam to the surface and gasped in air. The guards were looking out to sea along with Gibson. Even Ava was staring over his shoulder.

He hauled himself out of the enclosure and saw it.

One of the giant Enceladon creatures he'd only seen once before, when the thing they called Xander rose out of the sea at Ullapool harbour. He'd forgotten how massive they were. A gigantic jellyfish with an extraordinary light display across its cigar-shaped body, thousands of tendrils dragging behind as it shimmered and glowed and climbed over the stern of the ship into the enclosure.

The cannons at either side of the enclosure fired what looked like rockets over the creature. They popped above it and burst open, shooting out thin metallic nets, spreading their corners in the sky as they floated down and landed on the creature's body. When they touched, electrical flashes like lightning strikes shot across their flesh. There were six of these huge nets, overlapping and flashing, tightening around the creature so that its skin was pressed through the gaps in the mesh. Their light display faded to a dull grey and they just sat there, motionless and trapped in the back of the ship.

Carson had done it, he'd caught a big one.

42
LENNOX

It was Xander. When the chaos from the Enceladons below was amplified, he knew Xander would come. He'd sensed Sandy amongst the melee of creatures, their howling distress, tried to block it out but he couldn't.

He watched Xander's light display fade and tried to send something. <Xander-Sandy-Lennox OK?>

Nothing back. The noise had died, they'd re-activated the cage, and those nets must be EM blockers too. The silence was brutal.

He looked at Carson staring at Xander. The general had never seen one of the big Enceladons in real life.

The Enceladons didn't understand the stupidity and violence of the human race. But they must've experienced something similar once before, with whatever it was that invaded their home world and made them leave. That time, they'd run rather than fight. Maybe they didn't understand the concept of fighting. If they'd never had to do it in their evolution, how could they? How could you explain the fucked-up nature of humanity to creatures who'd lived in harmony with their environment for millions of years?

Sandy and the others had access to the internet here when they weren't inhibited by these EM cages and nets. But did they understand it? How can you explain the depths of humanity to something like Sandy or Xander? The conspiracies, hatred and anger, the violence, deviousness and dishonesty.

The sight of Xander trussed up made Lennox sick. Like the pathetic sprawl of fish in the back of a boat when the nets are released. Sifting through the dying animals, working out which ones people wanted to eat, which ones would make you enough money to come back out and do it all over again.

He breathed deeply and looked around the deck. When Oscar had left, the guards dithered and looked at Carson, who'd barked at them to catch him. That meant it was just Lennox and Carson left in here. Carson was still watching the scene below, couldn't believe he'd pulled it off.

Lennox edged away from the window, saw Carson's pistol on his right hip. It was only a few feet away and Lennox was fast. He couldn't see if the holster was fastened, how easily it might come free.

He closed his eyes, opened them again and decided. Lunged for the gun.

Carson sensed his movement and turned away at the last second, but Lennox still got his fingers on the gun, realised there was a button to release it from the holster. Carson swung his elbow into Lennox's jaw, knocking him to his knees, but his hand was still on the pistol. He stretched a finger and pressed the button, whipped the gun out and rolled away, sat against the window.

Carson was four feet away, hands out. A flicker of panic in his eyes replaced by a smile.

'Don't be stupid, kid.' He waved a hand around the room. 'There's no way out for you.'

'This isn't about me.' Lennox nodded at the window. 'Let them go. Xander and the others.'

Carson narrowed his eyes. 'You know the big one?'

'Let them go, now.' Lennox tried to stop his hand shaking. The gun looked oversized in his grip. He glanced down to look for the safety, had no idea.

'You know I can't do that.' Carson arched his back and stood taller.

'What if I shoot you?'

'You won't do that.'

'You don't know me.'

'I know you're not a killer.' Carson examined him and Lennox squirmed under his gaze. 'It changes you. Trust me, I know. You don't want that, not someone like you.'

Lennox pressed his lips together and pushed at a sliding switch on the gun handle with his thumb. He had no idea if that was the safety. Tried to judge from Carson's face, but he was unreadable.

Lennox aimed the gun at Carson's crotch. 'Maybe I won't kill you. Maybe I'll just blow your dick off.'

Carson swallowed.

'Now,' Lennox said. 'Let them all go.'

Carson sprang at him and knocked Lennox's hand but the gun went off, the noise huge in Lennox's ears as Carson slammed his body against the glass. A punch to the gut made Lennox double over, then he felt a boot on his knee and buckled, another smack on his arm and he dropped the gun. A kick to his groin made him roll onto his side, pain radiating through his body like fire.

Carson cleared his throat, straightened his tie and put the gun back in its holster.

43
HEATHER

She stood in the gloom at the far end of the beach, the tents and vans of Camp Outwith in the distance, and remembered Yellowcraigs Beach on another night, on the other side of the country. She'd stood there looking at the North Sea rather than the Atlantic, but felt just as alone.

She'd never been one to join in. She had friends at school, but none of them could see into her soul, and she'd kept a distance from them, kept something to herself. Then she was at Edinburgh University studying environmental science and had the same feeling – a caring group of friends, but they easily drifted apart afterwards. And working at the Scottish Environment Protection Agency too, by then she'd established a pattern. She loved the work and got along with her colleagues, but she was never in their hearts.

The only ones she'd really let in were Paul and Rosie. Now one of them was dead, the other had a new life. And she had no one except Lennox, Ava and Sandy, locked up in New Broom.

She felt dizzy, stars blurring in her vision, moon shifting and the horizon tilting. She put a hand to the back of her neck, where a familiar pounding pain had sprung out of nowhere. Her stomach tensed and she crouched, lowered her head, then vomited on the stones, splatter hitting her trainers, wind flicking at her. She held her hair away from her face and puked again, muscles clenching until her stomach was empty. Her legs quivered. She spat several times then waited a full minute before standing upright and looking around. Her head was still pounding, that would take longer to fade. So the tumour was back for good.

She thought about what Sandy had done for her in the room at the Ceilidh Place. Cured her cancer. But that was bullshit, it turned out, there was no curing this. Anyway, it wasn't about 'curing'. The cancer cells were as much a part of her as the healthy ones, as much her as the microbes in her gut or her scalp, the shit in her colon or the snot in her nose. She was ashamed that she'd bought into that bullshit, the idea of a battle against herself. She should've known better. We can't fight ourselves. If we do, we always lose.

She ran her tongue around her gums and spat some more, then walked along the beach to the fires. She found Jodie, Vonnie and Freya in animated discussion.

'Are you OK?' Jodie said. 'You look pale.'

Heather was touched that she really seemed to care. Maybe not everyone was like Heather, some people were born to be part of something.

'I'm fine.'

'Have a seat.' Jodie pulled over a chair and Heather sat. Everyone's faces were shifting in the firelight and she thought of them as ghosts, haunting this land while they still could.

Jodie handed her a mug of tea and she held it tight, the heat of it warming her against the wind.

'What did I miss?'

Jodie looked around the fire. 'We were just discussing what to do next.'

Heather nodded but didn't speak, afraid her voice would give away her hopelessness. Vonnie and Freya were much younger than her, and Jodie was a force of nature. Heather couldn't stand their positivity in the face of all this. She just wanted to crawl into a hole, close her eyes and never leave.

'We have to get them out,' Freya said, leaning forward.

'Agreed,' Vonnie said, playing with her hair.

Her voice was so assured. She was just a kid, really, about the same age as Rosie when she died. Same age as Lennox. But that made

Heather correct herself. Rosie was confident and self-assured, smart and resourceful before cancer took her. And Heather had seen so much of that in Lennox too. He had so much insight into what the world could be like. Maybe these teenagers should take over the world and leave the rest of them to die in peace.

'But how?' Jodie said. 'These are trained military men with weapons. The place is secure.'

'Sandy got us out,' Heather said, surprised at her own voice. Apparently, she had an opinion here. 'They didn't think it was such a problem.'

'But now Sandy is inside,' Vonnie said. 'You were there, they must have a way of keeping the creatures contained.'

Heather thought about the research lab, the cages, the listless and dying Enceladons. The way no one gave a shit.

'Maybe if we get in touch with the other ones,' Jodie said, nodding at the sea. 'Out there.'

Her eyes widened as she stared, making Heather turn.

Darting across the sky were green and orange tracers, the orange shifting to red and pink, the green fading and re-emerging as blues of a million different shades, strands and tendrils like delicate clouds. The aurora swept from the open ocean down the loch, flickering and flashing, intertwining and interlocking, drifting apart, a dancing pattern that made Heather laugh. She stood to take it in better, then saw everyone else had done the same, all of them gazing at the northern lights as if they meant something, as if they were a message from the universe that they were on the right path.

Heather glanced at the faces around the fire and knew in her heart they would find a way to make everything right. She tried to hold on to that feeling, but it slipped from her just like the aurora fading from view.

44
AVA

She watched the sun's early rays hit the hilltops across the loch and felt bone tired. Chloe was in her arms, feeding hungrily. If the baby didn't need her, she might give up. It was the same for millions of new mothers across the planet, that bond pulling her from one moment to the next, balanced with exhaustion unlike anything she'd ever known, weariness in her soul, in every cell.

But they were together, the two of them in the detention block. She guessed Lennox and Oscar were over in the stockade. Presumably Carson had let her be with Chloe because they didn't need her for now, having captured Xander. Ava wondered about long-term damage to Chloe from what happened on the ship. Ava herself was traumatised, had slept badly, nightmarish visions of humans and aliens in pain.

She sent out feelers to Chloe now, got back calm contentedness, which made her feel more happy than she could've imagined.

Having Chloe had amplified her life a millionfold. She hadn't realised how big her heart could be before Chloe, now she feared it would explode with all her feelings. The good moments were so much more than anything she'd experienced, but the bad moments were too.

She shifted Chloe's weight in her arms, felt a painful tug on her nipple but enjoyed it, it reminded her of their connection. A day would come when that wasn't the case and she felt tears welling up at the thought. Every parent wonders what life will be like for their baby but it would be different for Chloe, with the power they both shared. But Ava loved her extra connection with Chloe, couldn't imagine life any other way.

She watched sunlight spread down the hills then closed her eyes, dog tired.

She was startled by a thump.

She opened her eyes and saw two tentacles spread across the window, suckers clinging to the glass, shimmering gold and black, blue to green. Sandy pulled their body into view, head stretching and narrowing, ring patterns descending as the other three tentacles stuck to the glass.

<Sandy-Ava-Chloe partial welcome.>

She felt tightness in her chest and realised it was joy.

<Sandy, how are you free?> She stood up and Chloe grumbled but stayed attached.

<Short time, small gap, simple movement.>

Ava smiled, she'd forgotten how oblique Sandy's communication was.

She lifted Chloe from her breast and pulled her top down. Chloe grumped and burped, but she was content. Ava looked behind her at the doorway.

<You have to get out of here, Sandy.>

<Sandy-Ava-Chloe partial leave.>

<What about the others? Lennox and Oscar, Xander and the other Enceladons?>

Sandy's light display flickered through purple and orange, back to aquamarine. <Too difficult. Many humans with violence.>

<You mean guns?>

A moment's pause. <Reverse Enceladons and humans to original energy state.>

They meant killed. They could do wonderful things, but they couldn't reverse death. Sandy had tried with Ewan at Ullapool harbour, but he was too far gone.

Ava looked round. <There's a guard outside the door.> She stepped to the window. <You'll be seen.>

Sandy's tentacles thumped against the glass. <Open from inside.>

Ava released the catches, but the window only slid open a few inches because of its security locks. Sandy's tentacles went to the opening and began squeezing through, suckers springing back into shape once they were inside the room. But there was no way they could get their whole body through like that. Sandy's head was ten times wider than their arms.

<Sandy, you can't get through there.>

<Simple shape transformation.>

Sandy's head flattened and their light display stopped for a moment, then came back a glimmering cream and brown. Their first two tentacles were through into the room, waving in the air, touching Ava's face. Chloe giggled as she grabbed one and put it in her mouth.

Then two more tentacles and the start of their body, squeezing through the gap like slime, and Ava was briefly reminded of old horror movies. Sandy closed their eyes as they slipped through the gap, then the back of their head eased through like a pancake and immediately sprung into a spheroid shape, followed by the last tentacle.

Their light display was bright again, yellows and reds, and Chloe clapped her hands, the tip of a tentacle still in her mouth. Sandy wrapped their tentacles around Ava and Chloe in a hug, removing the tentacle from Chloe's mouth so gently the baby didn't fuss.

<Are you sure about the others?> Ava sent. <Can't we help them escape?>

Sandy dimmed a moment, blinked those big eyes. <Too many humans with violence.>

Ava heard a noise, realised it was the front door opening. She pushed Sandy away, looked around. <You have to hide. Human with violence is coming.>

Sandy shuffled back against the window, looked around, but there was nowhere. They shrunk down, wrapping their tentacles under their body until they were football sized, but they were still totally noticeable.

'Hey there, I was just checking to see if you needed—'

Mendoza stood in the doorway and stared at Sandy. His gun hung loose on his shoulder and he didn't raise it. He looked at Ava and Chloe then back at Sandy, who'd grown back to normal size.

'How did that get in here?'

Ava glanced at the slightly open window.

'For real?' Mendoza sucked his teeth. 'These things, man.'

'They're not things,' Ava said. 'They're people.'

'They're not like any person I've met.'

'They're not human, but they understand everything. What's happening here is cruel. You're different from the other guards, you care.'

'I don't know about that.' Mendoza shifted his weight and glanced at Sandy.

'You know what's happening here.' Ava stepped forward. 'None of us deserves this.'

'I just do what I'm told.'

'You know how that sounds: "Only obeying orders." You're better than that.'

'I'm not sure that I am.'

Ava shook her head. 'Everyone has to stand up for what they think is right.'

Mendoza looked at Sandy for a long time. Sandy's tentacles waved in the air, their body pulsating with colours, growing and shrinking.

'You talk to this thing?' Mendoza said.

Ava nodded.

'And it feels pain?'

Ava angled her head, didn't want to overplay it. 'Absolutely. They're very empathetic, much more than us.'

Mendoza chewed his lip and looked out the window, then at Sandy, then to Ava with Chloe squirming in her arms.

'I got a little girl,' he said. 'Eighteen months. It's tough.'

'You must miss her.'

Mendoza stayed silent for a long time, then looked her in the eye.

'I was on the *Sallis*, manning one of the cannons. I saw what they did to that creature. I saw what they did to your daughter.' He looked around the room, as if for an answer. Eventually he turned back to Ava. 'I know a way you can get out.'

Just as he spoke, an alarm began to sound outside.

45
LENNOX

Lennox looked out of the barred window of the stockade, saw a couple of soldiers throwing their uniform jackets on as they ran out of sight. It was the same alarm sound as when Sandy broke them out the first time, and that gave him hope.

<What can you see?>

Lennox turned and frowned at Oscar, who was in the adjoining cell, thick metal bars between them. He closed his eyes for a moment and felt into the mental space between them, blocked him, though he wasn't sure how.

'Use your voice,' he said opening his eyes.

'Why? We've got this amazing—'

'I don't want you in my head, OK?'

Oscar narrowed his eyes and Lennox sensed he was trying to communicate.

'How do you do that?' Oscar said. 'How do you block someone?'

Lennox ran his tongue around his teeth. They were fuzzy and his mouth was dry, he couldn't remember when he last had a drink of water.

'Practice,' he said.

The alarm kept blaring outside, and Lennox closed his eyes and focused. Felt for a presence.

<Sandy, did you escape? Xander, are you there?>

'I can hear that,' Oscar said.

'Good for you.'

Nothing from Sandy or Xander. He hated not being connected. This power had already changed the way he thought, his brain chemistry, his outlook. He could never go back, humanity could never go back. But the fact he, Oscar, Ava and Chloe were all locked up suggested there was a lot of resistance to evolution.

'Did you get a reply?' Oscar stood and rubbed the back of his neck.

'No.'

'Would you tell me if you did?'

'Probably not.'

Lennox looked outside again.

Oscar wrapped his hands around the bars. 'Look, we're on the same side.'

'Really?'

Oscar looked ashamed. 'Stuff happened in the past that was very regrettable.'

'You're not accepting any blame?'

'Of course I'm to blame,' Oscar said. 'I did it all, OK? Is that what you want? I was wrong. I chased you across the country and I'm sorry. If I'd known then what I know now, I would've left you in peace.'

'And Ewan would still be alive.'

'Yes, Ewan would still be alive. God knows what would've happened. I mean, an entire ecosystem landed here from another world in broad daylight. Political and military forces were always going to get involved.'

Lennox stared at him until Oscar turned away.

'I made a lot of mistakes,' Oscar said. 'And I'm truly, deeply sorry.'

Lennox listened outside for something to indicate what the alarm was for.

'You saw me on the ship,' Oscar said. 'I was trying to set them free. I had no idea Carson and Gibson had built a trap for Xander. I want to find out about them, not capture them. It'll take decades, centuries probably, to learn about their culture, biology, society. We must look like savages to them.'

Lennox waved a sarcastic hand around the stockade. 'You think?'

'That's what scares us about extraterrestrials. Or any intelligent creatures, whether they're from Enceladus or here on Earth, like chimps or dolphins, or even AI. We hate that something else will see humans for the monsters we really are. Seeing humanity from the outside, what we do to each other and our planet, that's terrifying.'

Lennox hadn't considered that. Since he met Sandy, it'd been personal. It gave him a purpose and a family, both human and Enceladon. But what Oscar said made sense. Humans were nasty, craven, violent and selfish, and the Enceladons brought that into sharp relief.

'I envy you,' Oscar said.

Lennox laughed. 'We're both locked up, in case you hadn't noticed.'

'Sandy chose you.'

'They didn't choose me, it was chance.'

Oscar shook his head. 'I don't believe that. Others died of the strokes you all had. But you, Ava and Heather recovered.'

'Just our brain chemistry according to Sandy.'

'You were the first human in history to communicate with something from another world. That means something.'

'It means nothing if we let Carson continue what he's doing.'

'But how can we stop him?'

Lennox rubbed his head. 'I don't know.'

Oscar smiled.

'What?' Lennox said.

'So you do acknowledge we're on the same side?'

Shit. They had to work together if they were going to get out.

<Yeah,> Lennox sent him. <I guess we're on the same side.>

Oscar's smile widened. <Now all we need to do is work out how to beat these fuckers.>

The door to the stockade opened and two guards came in, the alarm briefly louder. One of them was that bastard Turner. He rattled their bars, smiled and pointed at Oscar, gun raised.

'Carson wants to see you.' His tone was unpleasant.

Lennox watched Oscar being led away.

46
AVA

Mendoza rubbed his chin as the siren blared. 'The alarm means the base is in lockdown.' He pointed at Sandy. 'They must've realised this thing has escaped.'

Sandy scuttled to the window and looked out.

'Get down, man,' Mendoza said. 'Jesus.'

Ava stared at Sandy. <More humans with violence outside. Make yourself small.>

Sandy shrunk their body to the size of a watermelon and scuffed comically away from the window, tentacles feeling the way.

Mendoza watched them move, then went to the hallway cupboard, returned with a backpack. 'Can it get in there?'

Ava thought of Lennox carrying Sandy halfway across Scotland in a similar bag at the start of all this. 'No bother.'

<Sandy, get in.>

Chloe squirmed in Ava's arms as she watched Sandy climb into the backpack and pull the zip closed themself. The alarm filled Ava's belly with anxiety.

Mendoza lifted the backpack over his shoulder and waved at the doorway.

'Just follow my lead.'

Ava looked in his eyes, trying to see if she could trust him. Maybe this was bullshit, and he was just going to hand Sandy over. But sometimes you just needed to have faith in humanity.

She walked out of the detention block, shifting Chloe onto her shoulder, where the baby burped then settled. Ava turned and saw Mendoza with his gun raised, pointing at her.

'It's OK,' he said under his breath. 'Just go with it.'

Ava blinked twice, thinking. 'Which way?'

Mendoza nodded. 'Towards the offices.'

Ava started walking. The siren was ear-splitting out here, soldiers jogging across the main square, guns at the ready. An officer spotted them and came over.

'Just stay quiet,' Mendoza whispered.

'What's this, Sergeant? We're in lockdown, detainees to be kept inside, you know protocol.' The officer was tall and thin, blond hair in a parting. He spoke with confidence but had a shaving rash on his neck that made him look like a kid.

'Yes, sir.' Mendoza sounded like a different person, a cog in the machine. 'But General Carson expressly requested to see the prisoner immediately, sir.'

The officer stared at Mendoza then Ava, who was rubbing Chloe's back. The baby wriggled and Ava thought she might be filling her nappy. The officer looked at the activity around him, the air full of noise. He nodded at Mendoza's shoulder.

'What's in the bag?'

Ava tried not to flinch but Mendoza answered straight away. 'Things for the baby, sir.'

Ava could start to smell Chloe's nappy then saw on the officer's face that he smelled it too. He cringed and took a step backward. Macho military men hated to be confronted by the day-to-day of baby shit. But this was good.

'OK, carry on,' the officer said.

Mendoza spoke to Ava. 'Move.'

They were fifty yards away when Mendoza spoke.

'Good timing,' he said, and Ava could hear the smile in his voice.

They walked round the corner towards Carson's office, and Ava began to think she'd made a mistake, that Mendoza was going to screw her over.

But Mendoza told her to keep walking. They reached the end of the block and she saw officers' toilets.

'Wait.' Mendoza checked no one was watching, then went inside. Came out a moment later. 'In.'

They squeezed into the last cubicle and Mendoza took the bag off and placed it on the toilet seat, unzipped it. Sandy sprung out, blues and greens, tentacles running over the cistern and walls. Ava thought about germs.

Mendoza tapped the side wall with his rifle. 'On the other side of this is the perimeter fence. It's out of sight from the rest of the base.'

'But how do we get out?'

Mendoza nodded at Sandy. 'I've seen what this thing can do. Burned a hole right through the fence the first time you escaped.' He tapped the wall again, it rattled. 'This is just metal sheeting. Not too thick.'

They both looked at Sandy. Chloe was struggling in Ava's arms, uncomfortable in her dirty nappy. She'd have to sit in it for now. Ava touched one of Sandy's tentacles and held it.

<Can you get us through this wall and the fence behind?>

Sandy pulled themselves over to the wall and their tentacles ran across the surface. <Simple material-state transfer.>

Ava looked at Mendoza, felt bad he was left out.

<Do it.>

Sandy turned to the wall and their light display intensified, reds and oranges, browns and blacks, then suddenly switching to blazing pink-white on their arms. They laid their tentacles in the shape of a large circle and the glow intensified, then the suckers began to sink into the metal, which was bubbling and sparking at the edges. This went on for a minute or so, the tentacles slowly disappearing into the dissolving wall, the smell of burning metal overtaking the dirty nappy, Ava making sure Chloe was looking the other way from the furious light.

Then the wall gave way and an oval shape fell to the ground

behind. There were only a few inches of rocky ground to the fence, and Sandy did the same again on the mesh links there, but quicker this time, the glow so bright and obvious that Ava hoped Mendoza was right, this wasn't visible from the rest of the base. Sandy seemed unharmed by the heat emanating from their tentacles.

The fence came away from its surrounds and Sandy clung to the loose piece and lowered it to the side. They slid back into the stall and stood erect on two tentacles.

<Sandy-Ava-Chloe partial leave.>

Chloe giggled and stuck out a finger. Sandy wrapped it with the tip of a tentacle, and Chloe again shoved it towards her mouth.

Ava looked at Mendoza.

He was staring at the hole in the wall and fence, shaking his head and whistling under his breath. He turned to Ava. 'Be careful. Stay away from the roads.'

'I have a plan,' Ava said, looking at Sandy. 'What about you?'

He shrugged.

'You were seen helping us,' Ava said. 'They'll punish you.'

'I'll be OK.'

Ava pointed at the hole. 'Come with us.'

Mendoza sucked his teeth. 'My place is here.'

Ava heard more commotion outside, wondered if they'd been spotted from outside the bathroom. If they had, this was all pointless.

'Go,' Mendoza said, pushing her towards the opening.

Ava threw her arm around him for a moment, pressing Chloe into his shoulder in the process.

'Thank you,' she said in his ear.

She grabbed Sandy's tentacle and ducked through the hole in the wall, then the fence. They were down near the water, a few feet of rocks then a small drop to a gravelly shore. An expanse of water beyond that, hills and sky and oceans forever.

<Sandy, can we swim together?>

<Sandy-Ava-Chloe partial?>

<Yes, like you did with Lennox before.>

Sandy pulled at her hand and they clambered to the water's edge. Ava glanced back and Mendoza was watching from the hole in the wall.

Sandy stood upright and wrapped their tentacles around Ava and Chloe. <Hold on.>

Sandy's skin expanded to wrap around her, then solidified so that she felt absorbed into it, becoming part of them. The flesh covered her face but she could breathe, tasted Sandy's skin and ideas and mind all inside her, and she was inside them. She turned to see Chloe happy and giggling and stretching her fingers in the pink and grey and blue flesh, wiggling her toes.

Sandy leapt into the water and Ava didn't feel a splash, then they were racing through the loch, the three of them a single entity, spiralling and diving and swerving, and it was the easiest thing in the world.

<Where to go?> Sandy's voice in her head.

She knew exactly where to go.

47
OSCAR

The alarm cut out as Oscar was being led across the square. Soldiers were sweeping both sides of the perimeter fence.

<Sandy? Xander?>

Nothing.

Did the other Enceladons have names? There was so much about them he didn't understand. Lennox had named Sandy and Xander, but what did they call themselves? Did they even differentiate themselves from each other? He couldn't comprehend a world where there was no individuality, so counter-intuitive to the human mind. But maybe that was the point, utterly alien intelligence.

Oscar slowed to watch the soldiers around the perimeter fence, but Turner prodded him in the back with his gun. They reached the office and Turner rapped on the door then stepped back.

Inside, Carson was looking out of the window. There was silence for a long time. Oscar remembered a seminar he went to once in the civil service, about letting the other person speak first in negotiations, a power play. It was bullshit but it worked, because he couldn't stand this.

'What's going on out there?' he said.

Carson turned and Oscar didn't like the smile on his face.

'What makes you think you have the right to know?'

Oscar stuck his chest out but it felt pathetic. 'I'm an employee of His Majesty's Government, you don't have the right to—'

'Can it.' Carson stepped to his desk and waved for Oscar to sit. He got his whisky and two glasses out of a drawer and poured big drams. It had to be about nine in the morning, but Oscar was tempted. He was bone-tired and thirsty, needed the Dutch courage. So he sat and took the glass, drank a good gulp and felt the burn.

Carson drank too and admired the whisky in his glass. It was all a show, but Oscar was just the same.

'One of them escaped somehow,' Carson said. 'Smart little guys, ain't they? But it hasn't breached the perimeter, it's still on the base. We just need to find it. What is it about them, Fellowes?'

Oscar didn't answer, didn't want to contribute to this shitshow.

Carson leaned forward. 'Why do you care so much? You were on their tail at the start, you were as keen as anyone to capture them. What happened to change your mind?'

Oscar was ashamed about all that now. He'd been the first official from the UK government to contact Sandy and he felt sick about how he'd behaved. But he'd always just wanted to understand.

'I got to know them,' Oscar said.

Carson snorted and shook his head. 'Jesus, it's all touchy-feely with you, isn't it? You know, I never used to understand the phrase "culture war". It felt dumb to me, folks arguing about stupid, insignificant stuff when there were bigger fish to fry. But now I see it's about whether you think things should all be equal, or whether you appreciate that there's a natural order, survival of the strongest.'

'Fittest.'

'What?'

'It's survival of the fittest, not strongest. It's a common misconception, it doesn't mean fittest as in strongest, it means the best fit, as in the most appropriate.'

'What's the difference?'

Oscar didn't know how to get into it, and he knew Carson didn't want to hear it anyway. 'It doesn't mean that the strongest always wins.'

Carson pointed his glass at Oscar. 'But that's exactly my point. Might *is* right, that's all there is to it. Humans were designed to take what we can and exploit it. It's kill or be killed, eat or be eaten.'

'No,' Oscar said. 'There are countless examples of altruistic behaviour in the animal kingdom, creatures helping other species, cooperation between animals. That idea of kill or be killed is completely wrong.'

Carson finished his whisky. 'Bullcrap. It's us or them, Fellowes. That's what you've never understood. They are an existential threat to humanity, and we have to deal with it.'

'You're so wrong,' Oscar said, his chest tightening with anger. 'They're smarter than us. We have to learn from them. They evolved on another world, they have a completely different—'

'That's just it,' Carson said. 'I don't agree that they're smarter than us, smarter than *me*, but they have abilities that could destroy us. They can speak to each other in their minds, kill people just by touching them with their tentacles. They worked out how to come all this way in space without a ship. We all know what happened to the natives when the Spanish arrived in the Americas. When a more-advanced race meets a less-advanced one, it's not good news for the weaker one. I can't let that happen here.' Carson smiled. 'But now I've got one of the big ones down at the dock, and we know how to catch the rest. We don't even need the baby anymore, Gibson has worked out a way to simulate her signals. We just go out there blasting that noise, and they'll swim right into our laps.'

Oscar pushed his chair back and stood. 'You can't do that.'

'Sit down.'

Oscar stood for a long time, wavering. Thought about throwing his whisky glass into Carson's face, but Turner was outside. Eventually he took his seat again.

'I can do whatever the hell I want here,' Carson said. 'I'm in charge.'

'There will be consequences.'

'No, there won't.'

'I want no part of this,' Oscar said. 'And I'm lodging an official complaint with MI7. You can't stop me.'

He finished his whisky, felt the heat in his stomach, wanted to fight.

'Yes, I can,' Carson said. 'I'm blocking all contact with MI7, with the outside world. Your phone and laptop will be confiscated immediately. And I'm going to court martial you for what you did on the ship. It was treason, punishable by death.'

Oscar laughed. 'That's insane, you can't court martial me, I'm not American and I'm not in your army.'

Carson placed his glass on the desk and poured a refill. 'Haven't you been listening, Fellowes? I can do whatever I want.'

48
HEATHER

She stepped away from the group and walked along the beach. She was tired of the discussions. Jodie, Vonnie and Freya were cajoling the rest of the Outwithers to help in breaking the humans and Enceladons out of New Broom. It was a lost cause, Heather had seen the firepower at the base. But she had to go along with it or she'd be a coward. They were talking about driving a convoy of campervans and cars to the front gate and hoping for the best. Heather understood they needed to do something. To their credit, the Outwithers were up for it. They were here for a reason, maybe this was it.

Her head throbbed and she felt sick. With the brain tumour, she didn't know how long she had left, and she was so fucking tired of it all, just surviving, living without her daughter, all of it.

She saw a disturbance of the water's surface out at sea, watched as the ripples and eddies came closer to shore. Before she even had time to send out a message, Sandy was clambering out of the water, their head and body hugely inflated. As they reached the shore they shrank to normal size, and Ava and Chloe emerged from inside, like stepping out of fog. Ava stood dripping on the shore, Chloe squirming in her arms, Sandy touching their heads with lingering tentacles.

Ava spotted Heather and ran to her, Chloe bouncing in her arms. They hugged for a long time, Heather smelling the sea, feeling the joy and relief shivering through Ava.

Eventually Heather pulled away, shook her head. 'How?'

'It was just like Lennox did with them. I was *inside* Sandy.'

They both laughed while Chloe gurgled. Sandy was investigating the space between rocks on the beach, shuffling tentacles around.

Heather looked over Ava's shoulder at the water, surface rippling in the breeze. <What about Lennox?>

Ava frowned. <He was in the stockade with Fellowes, according to Sandy. We couldn't do anything. They were thrown in there after the business on the ship.>

<Ship?>

<It was awful. They used Chloe, tortured her. Distressed her then messed with her internal voice somehow, and the Enceladons came to her. Then the Americans used her to catch Xander. It was horrible.>

Heather chewed it over. They had to get Lennox out, of course, and she supposed Oscar too. But Xander was even more important. It felt like being a traitor to humanity, but the Enceladons *were* more important. They had to rescue Xander, reunite them with the other Enceladons, and get them far away from here, somewhere safe.

She looked at the group along the beach. 'They're talking about rescuing them all.'

'How?'

'God knows.'

'Ava!'

Freya broke away from the discussions and ran to them. Ava opened her arms and the two sisters enclosed Chloe in their embrace.

Heather watched Freya and Ava and thought about Paul with his new wife. She'd probably given birth by now.

Freya touched Ava's cheek, then they both turned to Chloe, who Ava passed to Freya for a cuddle. They were a normal family, two sisters caring for the next generation, the same scene millions of times over across the planet.

<Sandy-Heather partial not happy?>

Heather turned and Sandy was next to her, upright on two limbs, the others tasting the air like always.

<No.>

Sandy slid closer, clacking stones under their tentacles. They reached for Heather's hand, a second tentacle round her neck, the tip hovering at her ear.

<Do we have your permission?>

The suckers of Sandy's tentacle stuck to the hair at the back of her head.

<Yes.>

The tentacle entered her right ear and she flinched and shivered. Sandy was examining her blood cells, neurons, plasma, marrow, all of her.

<Heather-Sandy partial neural network not full efficiency.>

Heather swallowed, she'd been subconsciously waiting for this since she sat in the doctor's office days ago. <My brain tumour is back, yes.>

<Heather-Sandy partial requires simple restructure of materials.>

<Wait.> Heather breathed deeply.

Sandy paused and loosened their grip. <Sandy-Heather partial not desire full efficiency?>

She didn't want to think about her answer. <Sandy, Enceladons die, right?>

Sandy flashed spots and stripes over their head, black and white moving into zebra stripes, then colourful again. <Yes, return to original energy state.>

<Could you prevent it?>

Sandy seemed to be thinking how to answer, or maybe accessing the internet. <No. Cell reorganisation is possible, we age differently to humans. We can repair for a long time, but eventually must return to original energy state.>

Heather knew that some animals on Earth didn't age like humans – jellyfish, flatworms, lobsters. But they died all the same.

She held on to the tentacle round her neck, imagined it squeezing tighter until she couldn't breathe. She felt the blood running under Sandy's skin, wondered what colour it was. There was so much she didn't know.

<It's the same for humans,> she sent. <Sometimes, it's our time to … return to original energy state.>

<This is Heather-Sandy partial's time to return?>

<The tumour is part of me. You made it go away before, but it came back. Am I just meant to have you fix me every time? There's something in my cells, something built into me. We all have a shelf life.>

<Unclear, shelf life.>

Heather smiled. <Never mind.>

Sandy's tentacle retracted from Heather's ear and loosened from her neck. Her chest rose and fell. To think these things even to herself, let alone to tell someone else, was new to her. And in thinking them, she realised they were true. This was her time, she didn't want to go on.

'Hey.' Jodie was standing a few feet away. 'You two OK?'

Heather nodded. 'We're fine.'

Jodie looked at the gathering behind her. 'Because we're doing it. We're going to New Broom. No time like the present, right?'

Heather heard the waves on the shore, opened her eyes wide to let in more beautiful Highland light, felt the stones under her feet.

'Sure,' she said. 'Let's do it.'

49
LENNOX

'Come on.'

This was a soldier Lennox didn't recognise, a black guy with a tight flat top and a scar on his cheek. He opened the barred door and walked Lennox out of the stockade and into the courtyard, Lennox blinking from the sun, the piercing blue sky, wind in his face. Compared to the gloom of the stockade, the sharpness of the hills and the smell of the sea were too real, like a vivid dream.

<Sandy, are you near? Can you hear me?>

Nothing, and he felt that Sandy was far away. He couldn't explain how. He was flooded with joy and sadness – it was great that Sandy had escaped New Broom, but Lennox felt all alone. He looked at the detention block.

<Ava? Are you there?>

Nothing, but no sense of how far away she was. That was the thing with these comms between humans, they were like toddlers learning to speak.

Lennox turned to the soldier. 'Where are we going?'

The guard was impassive. Lennox wondered what he thought about this place. Beautiful surroundings to indulge in torture and oppression. Maybe he didn't care, or maybe he believed what he was told. The last few years had seen the far right create a war out of everything. Loony lefties were trying to hug an alien octopus, while people in their right minds were dealing with a military threat.

The soldier took him round the offices and accommodation block. They passed the *USS Sallis* and walked to a large, floating dock, two cranes at the mouth, a hangar roof overhead, floodlights beaming inside.

They stepped through the entrance and Lennox saw Xander, floating in the middle of the structure with those nets still stretched over their body. There was a line of armed guards on either side of the water, some on raised platforms.

Lennox was nudged past them all, staring at Xander the whole way. Their rubbery flesh looked almost fake, like a giant latex monster from an old scary movie.

<Xander, are you OK?>

But he knew they were being blocked, that metallic mesh was using the same tech that blocked Sandy and the others in the cage.

Lennox saw Gibson and Carson on another raised platform at the back of the dock, along with a table of apparatus, laptops, electronic boxes, flashing lights. They'd spent all their time and resources coming up with a way to fuck with the Enceladons.

The soldier walked Lennox to the platform and up the steps.

Gibson was showing Carson something on the screen, and they turned.

'Good of you to join us,' Carson said.

'I didn't have a choice.'

Carson nodded at Xander. 'Impressive, isn't it?'

Lennox gave Carson a death stare.

'I used to fish for blue marlin off Hawaii,' Carson said. 'Caught some big brutes, but never anything like this.'

There was a laugh in his voice that made Lennox sick. He pictured Carson holding a huge dead fish in the back of a boat, shit-eating grin on his face, another triumph over nature.

Behind Carson, Gibson was readying a skull cap.

Lennox glanced at Xander. <Can you hear me?>

Nothing.

'Don't bother,' Carson said. 'It's isolated until Gibson flicks his switch.'

Gibson walked over, holding the skull cap.

Lennox backed away, but the soldier stepped up behind him, prodded him with his gun.

Gibson placed the cap on him and went back to his desk. Tapped on the keyboard, a box to his right with a digital display and flashing red lights.

<Test four point zero three.> The metallic voice in Lennox's mind made him jump.

'What the fuck?'

Gibson smiled and Carson nodded. 'I presume you're getting something.'

Lennox swallowed and didn't speak.

Gibson stared at the screen and confirmed with Carson. How the fuck had they done this?

Gibson got the nod from Carson and flicked a switch on the box. A shiver ran through the mesh around Xander. Their light display started up, oranges and reds flashing like billowing curtain folds across their skin, fading and glowing, back and forth.

<Xander, don't say anything to me, these other humans, they can detect what we're doing and they mean you harm. You and the rest of the Enceladons.>

Xander's body pushed against the mesh, it looked painful, like the metal strands would slice through their flesh.

<Xander-Lennox partial welcome.> Their voice was happy and welcoming and Lennox's heart sank to his stomach.

<No, don't speak. They'll use this against you. Against me too.>

<Xander-Lennox partial in trouble.> A moment of silence, then: <Where is Xander-Lennox-Sandy partial?>

<I don't know, please stop talking.>

<Communication is connection, life is connection.>

<I know, but you don't understand, these other humans, they'll kill you all.>

Lennox saw Gibson turn a dial on the box then felt a rush of emotion fill his chest so that he thought he would explode. His eyes closed and he was gone, shooting into the atmosphere faster than any rocket, past the moon, accelerating at a terrifying rate. He looked down and realised he was in Xander's body, heard the discussion and chatter of their limbs, the tendrils dangling from their body, the different tastes and smells and signals that he couldn't even describe, things there were no human words for. He realised how pathetic the human senses were, a mere five, exploring only a tiny sliver of the universe. He shot through the solar system towards Enceladus, surrounded now by thousands of similar creatures, the conversations between them reassuring him that he wasn't alone. Then he was there, in Saturn's rings. Caught sight of the blue-and-white stripes of Enceladus's surface, then he was diving through the vents on the southern pole, into the deep, blue water, the ice roof above a temporary heaven, seafloor volcanoes like gods beneath him, providing warmth and energy in a giant, moon-wide ocean so far from the sun.

He danced through the water alongside thousands of octopoid creatures like Sandy, swimming through his tendrils, moving in and out of his giant body with ease. Nothing was separate, they were indivisible as creatures, an entire ecosystem that understood itself, that gained huge comfort from its own co-dependence. But there weren't even words for this, because there was no other way to be.

Then there was a moment of worry, something dark on the horizon, the ice overhead breaking up and millions of small, dark objects dropping into the water, creatures of some kind, but not part of this community, destroying everything in their path, relentless, unthinking, incommunicative, and the Enceladons had to go, escape their home of a billion years, leave through the southern vents into space, a giant exodus through the dusty rings of Saturn towards Earth.

And before he knew it, they were descending back through Earth's atmosphere over Ullapool, landing in Loch Broom, swimming away from the humans to a safe space, a hidden area behind a huge undersea ledge, not far up the coast. Lennox recognised it, he'd swum there with Sandy, it was their secret place and Xander was offering it up on a plate in his mind.

He opened his eyes and realised he was on the floor, his hands on the cold metal, hip sore where he'd fallen, dizzy and confused, his mind human again, the disappointment of that, feeling like an empty shell.

He looked at Xander, the mesh activated across their body again, light display gone, just a giant grey ball of flesh floating in the water.

Gibson spoke to Carson. 'I know where they are, sir.'

50
AVA

Ava sat in Freya's campervan, the side door open. Chloe was lying in a makeshift crib, a plastic laundry basket lined with blankets. She grabbed at her toes and shoved two in her mouth. Ava looked around and remembered Heather's old banger, the one they'd taken from Dirleton across the country, chased by police, Ava's husband and others, staying one step ahead. Until it broke down at Urquhart Castle, then been impounded by Highland police. The van was probably still there. Ava thought about how little of their old lives were intact. With Michael dead, she wondered if she was in line to inherit their Longniddry house. Probably not, given that she was found guilty of his manslaughter. And anyway, there was no way she would ever set foot in that house again. Every mark on the carpet, every scuff on the woodwork would remind her of him.

All their lives were changed. Ava, Heather and Lennox were at the vanguard, but there would be others. No one on Earth could be the same after the discovery of life on other worlds, especially not life like Sandy and Xander.

She watched Heather and the others getting ready. She understood their desire to do something, but she couldn't believe this was it. A bunch of ordinary, unarmed people driving a convoy of beaten-up vehicles into the front gate of a heavily defended military facility. It was suicide.

Heather spotted her and came over. She was wielding a metal-headed golf club with a sharp wedge. She swung it aimlessly and smiled.

'This is madness,' Ava said, waving a hand at the activity. Two young men were tying a piece of metal sheeting that had washed up on the beach to the front grill of someone's van. Like it would make a difference.

'I know,' Heather said.

'Please don't do this. I can't believe this is your plan.'

'What else can we do?'

Ava looked at Jodie and Vonnie, making Molotov cocktails with wine bottles and diesel-soaked rags. 'Anything but this.'

Heather shrugged. 'Like what?'

'Go to the police.'

'You know as well as I do the police won't do anything. In fact, they'll probably arrest us.'

'Then get the word out there,' Ava said. 'Tell the press.'

Heather shook her head. 'We tried that, nothing came of it. That journalist told Freya she couldn't get a single editor to take her seriously. Either they thought she was crazy or they didn't want to attract the wrong kind of attention from the authorities. No one in the press is interested in rocking the boat, not when they're run by billionaires friendly with the UK government, who are friendly with the US government, who want their men to take charge. That's the way the world works.'

'It shouldn't be.'

Heather placed a hand on the roof of the camper as Freya appeared alongside.

'Besides, it was taking too long,' Heather said. 'It's all very well campaigning and getting journalists interested, but that takes forever. We don't have time now. Lennox is in there, so's Xander. Gibson has made a breakthrough – if they can catch Xander, they can catch the rest of them.'

Ava glanced at Freya then Chloe. 'You think they'll kill them all?'

'They don't give a fuck about the Enceladons, never have. And now, with what you saw on the ship, the Enceladons need our help.'

'Can't you get them to help themselves?' Freya said. She ran a hand through her hair. 'I don't have the connection you guys have, so I don't really understand, but they seem pretty incredible, all sorts of powers. Can't you just tell them to run away, or get Xander out?'

Heather shifted her weight. 'I tried. I spoke to Sandy, explained the situation. But they just don't understand.'

Freya cleared her throat. 'Why not? What's wrong with them?'

Heather gave Ava a look and Ava knew what it meant. They were so alien, they just didn't comprehend how humanity worked. They were too innocent, open and caring.

'They just don't get it,' Ava said.

Heather pointed at the sea. 'Sandy went off after I spoke to them. But they didn't give any indication of understanding or getting help. They just said they had to be with the others. I think they're finding it traumatic being separated from Xander. It's like an illness to them.'

Ava looked at the preparations and felt forlorn.

'I better go help,' Heather said, swinging the golf club like it was a piece of driftwood.

'Heather, you can't do this,' Ava said.

'I have to.'

'You don't *have* to.'

Heather gave her a long look. <I want to.>

<I can't go with you.> Ava reached into the crib and tickled Chloe, who giggled.

<I know,> Heather sent. < I understand.>

Ava's cheeks flushed, tears came to her eyes. <What if you don't come back?>

Silence in the air between them and in their minds.

Eventually Heather spoke. 'You, Chloe and Freya need to get out of here. If it doesn't go according to plan, they'll come here and take you.'

Ava stood, her eyes wet. 'Don't go.'

Heather wrapped her in a hug, the golf club dangling awkwardly.

<Stay safe,> Heather sent, and Ava burst into tears.

51
HEATHER

They bounced along the rough tarmac and the growl of the engine filled Heather's mind. Jodie was driving her camper, Heather in the passenger seat, Vonnie and half a dozen young Outwithers in the back. The tension was palpable, and Heather smelled nervous sweat. She thought about how Sandy tasted the air, the water, everything, with their tentacles. Humans were so blind.

They reached the outer area fence and stopped. There was a convoy of ten vehicles – six campers, two cars and two pick-up trucks, containing around forty people. One of the trucks had metal sheeting tied to the grill, along with two old sewage pipes tied to the chassis at either side, makeshift battering rams sticking out the front. Two young men and a woman sat up front, four more in the flatbed at the back with large rolls of carpet. The driver revved the engine then gunned for the gate, smashing into it with a shocking noise. The battering rams tangled in the fence as it swayed and collapsed, then dragged parts of the fence out as they backed away.

Heather looked round. They were still a couple of miles from New Broom, this fence was just here to deter people from having a snoop around. The defences of the base were much sturdier.

The pick-up rammed into the gate twice more, wheels bouncing over the collapsed fence as it drove forward and back, the guys in the back holding on.

The fence finally flattened and they all drove forward, chugging along the narrow road. Loch Broom stretched out to their left, the rocky slopes of Meall Mòr on the other side. Heather felt trapped between hills and sea, but there was no other way of doing this.

They reached the rise before the base and paused. Heather glanced at Jodie, who was hunched over the wheel, hands gripping tight. They shared a look. Jodie didn't look scared, but she looked as if she knew what was coming.

Before they left, Heather had drawn out a detailed map of the base, from the detention block to the stockade, the research centre to the soldiers' quarters. The idea was for the leaders to get to General Carson and take him hostage. They couldn't hope to defeat all the soldiers, but they could negotiate the release of Lennox, Xander and the Enceladons. They'd take boats, and once they were safely away, release Carson. Then they'd try to get the Enceladons to leave the loch, go thousands of miles away and live somewhere humans could never find them. Earth was a big place, three-quarters water, surely they could find somewhere.

Heather looked at the kids in the back of her camper. They had a perverse, youthful excitement, naïve, invincible energy. They didn't realise how serious this was and no amount of explaining would help. To them it felt like a game, fuelled by righteous anger.

Heather was much more cynical. She wasn't crazy, but felt resigned to the fact she had to do this. How could she live with herself if she didn't? Also, she didn't honestly care if she died. She'd died once already when Rosie died, then had another death sentence placed on her with the brain tumour. She'd tried to kill herself and was only alive because Sandy saved her. Twice. Now the tumour was back. She wasn't going to live long now anyway, so what difference did it make? She might as well go out in a blaze of glory if she could.

She looked at the other vehicles. It didn't seem like a blaze of glory at the moment. It seemed like a bunch of misfits who felt they had to do something. Jodie was older, and Heather wondered if she was taking advantage of the younger ones. It was easy to be the outsider, see yourself as fighting the system. Or maybe Heather was being unfair. Jodie was here for the same reason as the rest, they'd felt something, they were given a sign by the Enceladons.

Jodie nodded to the man in the pick-up and he took off, engine racing as he jolted forward over the rise in the road, Jodie slamming the camper into gear and following, the other vehicles right behind, engine noise filling the air as they accelerated down the slope, the fenced-off New Broom laid out in front of them. They bumped over the track and Heather saw a couple of guards at the gate stand up. The front pick-up was only a few yards from the gate already, then smashed into the fence hard, the vehicle juddering to a halt, then reversing and ramming again.

Jodie angled their camper towards the weakened fence to the side of the pick-up and they smashed into it at speed, the jolt throwing Heather forward against her seatbelt. The ones in the back were thrown around as the camper slid to a stop sideways, halfway over a collapsed piece of fence. Vonnie and the others jumped out and threw sections of carpet over the razor wire along the top of the fence, then clambered over, waving baseball bats, golf clubs, lengths of pipe. Some of them were lighting and throwing their Molotov cocktails. Alongside them, the guys from the pick-up had done the same. Heather looked the other way, saw two more campers sitting on top of destroyed fencing. Outwithers swarmed across the carpet laid over the razor wire and ran into the base.

Gunshots rang out and Heather flinched. She and Jodie undid their seatbelts and jumped out of the camper, clambered over the fence into the base, Heather waving her five iron around her head. There were whoops and hollers all around, the sound of breaking glass and spray of flaming fuel across the ground. Gunfire made her duck and crouch-run towards the stockade. The others were heading for Carson's office then down to the dock where they presumed Xander was being held, some of them heading for the research block where Gibson had the other Enceladons. But Heather was going for Lennox.

<Lennox, are you here?>

More gunfire made Heather flinch as she ran along the outside of the catering building, staying out of the main square.

Then she saw the first person fall, the driver of the pick-up, blood spurting from a wound in his chest as he spun and crumpled to the ground. Then a woman behind him doubled over clutching her stomach, staggering in the dust before collapsing. Then two more in quick succession – a middle-aged man hit in the leg, screaming and holding his knee, his foot pointing in the wrong direction. Then a woman Heather's age fell forward as a spurt of blood came from a bullet in her back.

This was a fucking massacre and they were so stupid to even be here, these people were sacrificing their lives for nothing. Armed soldiers against civilians, people who had normal jobs until their lives were upended by a message from aliens.

Heather saw Jodie diving for cover behind Carson's office. She looked around for Vonnie, spotted her and three others running to the dock area, bullets spitting up dust around them.

Then she felt it before she heard it, a searing pain in her shoulder, blood spraying from a hole in her jacket, the burning of a thousand suns in her arm and chest. Her knees buckled and she fell to the dirt, hand at her shoulder, covered in blood and dust and the world spinning around her as she lay on the ground and waited to die.

52
OSCAR

The stockade was crammed with people, not designed with a mass attack in mind. Oscar looked around the four small cells. There were fourteen people, some asleep, amazing given what happened last night.

Oscar, Mendoza and Lennox had been in here since before the attack. Sometime after the alarms and gunfire, guards brought the bound Outwithers in at gunpoint, shoved them into the cells and left without a word. Lennox hugged the girl, Vonnie, and Oscar recognised some others from the camp. Jodie was amongst them, and she threw Oscar a despairing look, shook her head, then slumped in the corner. The adrenaline buzz for some of the younger ones took a while to wear off, and their talk of a prison breakout faded as they realised their situation.

Mendoza had sat silent through the whole thing, Oscar quizzing the Outwithers about what happened. A crazy plan in the first place, but they'd felt compelled to do it.

Many Outwithers had been shot in the attack, including Heather. The injured had presumably been taken to the small infirmary on site, but it wasn't equipped for much. Maybe Carson was just letting them die. Oscar and Lennox had both tried to contact Heather with their minds, but nothing.

Oscar watched the sky brighten outside the window at the far end of the stockade.

The door to the prison opened and Turner came in with three other guards.

'Fellowes and Mendoza, up.' He opened the door.

Oscar caught a look between Mendoza and Turner. This time yesterday they'd been on the same side.

Lennox stood and came to the bars of his cell.

Turner put wrist restraints on Oscar and Mendoza.

'What is this?' Oscar said.

Turner eyed him with disgust. 'Your court martial.'

'But I presumed that was a joke. How the hell can he—'

'Shut it,' Turner said, and shoved him towards the door.

Oscar lowered his head and fell in behind Mendoza, then heard Lennox in his mind. <Good luck.>

They were taken to the meeting room. Oscar had sat in this room for months, put up with Carson's bullshit, and where had it got him? In front of an illegal court martial.

Carson sat at the top of the table, Jeong on one side, Gibson on the other. Oscar had gathered from Mendoza that a US army court martial needed three officers. But this whole thing was obviously a kangaroo court, Carson had gone fucking mad.

Jeong looked like he wanted to crawl under the table and hide. He obviously didn't want any part of this bullshit. Gibson threw a thin smile at Oscar and ignored Mendoza. Carson was in full dress uniform, chest puffed out with medals gleaming.

'Sit,' he said, waving to the chairs at the opposite end of the table. Turner and the other guards took up position behind them. The restraints on Oscar's wrists cut at his skin.

'I refuse to acknowledge the legitimacy of this,' Oscar said, voice catching in his throat.

Carson stared at him. 'Noted.'

Oscar looked around. There was no one taking an official record here. 'And I demand to speak to your superiors immediately.'

Carson laughed. 'My superiors?'

'This is illegal.'

Carson shook his head. 'You still don't get what's going on here, do you? This is a security emergency. I have no superiors, and I make the law.'

'You've lost your mind.' Oscar looked at Jeong and Gibson. 'Why are you going along with this maniac?'

Jeong squirmed in his seat, Gibson just smiled.

Mendoza piped up, voice calm. 'What are you going to do with the others in the stockade?'

'That's none of your concern, son.'

'Are you going to murder them?' Oscar said.

Jeong looked sick.

Carson shook his head. 'No one is *murdering* anyone here. This is a military base, we do things by the rules.'

Oscar waved around the room. 'I'm not military, so this is illegal.'

'You were seconded to us, and as such are subject to US military law.'

'That's bullshit and you know it.'

Oscar glanced at Mendoza. He'd explained what he did for Ava and Sandy, said he had no regrets.

'Look,' Oscar said. 'Do what you want with me, but Mendoza doesn't deserve this. He's a good soldier.'

Carson stared at Mendoza, who returned his gaze, chin up.

'I don't take any joy in this,' Carson said.

Oscar laughed. 'Come on, you love this. Unlimited power to fuck with us and the Enceladons.'

Carson stood and went to the window. 'What am I supposed to do, Fellowes? Let these things overrun the planet? If I don't stop them, God knows how they'll spread. And where does that leave the human race? What about our way of life, our families, our homes? You've seen what these things can do, they could wipe us out if they wanted. And I'm the only one who can stop them.'

'They don't mean us any harm, that's obvious.' Oscar stared at Gibson. 'Tell him.'

Gibson stayed silent. Jeong looked at his lap. Carson had lost the plot and no one but Oscar was calling him out.

This was really going to happen.

Carson pulled at his shirt cuffs. 'They are obviously a profound threat to humanity. We've been over this.'

'They are nothing of the sort.' Oscar pushed his chair back and stood. He felt a rifle butt in his back, buckled, the chair pushed under him as he slumped.

'Anyone aiding and abetting them is guilty of high treason.' Carson's voice was as calm as the water outside.

Oscar placed his bound hands on the table. 'You are on the wrong side of history, Carson.'

'I don't think so. History is written by the victors, and I'm about to be victorious.'

'What do you mean?'

'There will be no more illegals this time tomorrow.'

'What are you going to do?'

Carson shook his head. 'No concern of yours. You won't be here anyway.'

He looked at Mendoza for a long time.

'I'm sorry, son,' he said in a low voice, then walked back to the end of the table. 'You are both traitors to the United States and to humanity. You've been found guilty of treason by this court martial and sentenced to death by firing squad at fourteen hundred hours today.'

Oscar felt like he was trapped in a nightmare, this couldn't be happening. 'You're a fucking psychopath, Carson.'

Carson nodded at Turner. 'Take them away.'

53
AVA

She sat at the water's edge on the verge of tears. She'd had a fractious sleep in Freya's camper, waking up often to check on Chloe, anxious of news from round the coast. But there was nothing, just the wind rocking the van, the sound of the sea, same as it had been for millions of years, long before humans were ever here.

When Chloe woke, Ava brought her from the crib into her narrow bed, hugged her close, sent messages of comfort as she fed her and felt the love flowing back. She was constantly anxious and full to overflowing with emotions she could barely express.

She'd got up at sunrise, changed Chloe's nappy, wrapped them both up warm and walked down to the shore. Sat on a blanket waiting for trouble to come, only a matter of time. The others had gone ten hours ago, it was surely all over one way or the other. The fact she hadn't heard told her which way. Which meant soldiers were coming for them.

As she sat there now, she heard the last straggling Outwithers who didn't go to New Broom preparing to leave. She didn't blame them. Why risk their freedom and safety? Many of them had camped here for months and what had they got? No connection to the Enceladons, who didn't seem to understand the pull they had on the Outwithers. They didn't understand how humans worked at all. They didn't understand the danger they were in, the way people could harm them.

But no wonder the Enceladons didn't understand. If you gave an Earth-bound octopus all of the internet, would it understand? If you gave that information to a dolphin or chimp, dog or worm, would they?

For that matter, *Ava* didn't understand how humanity worked, didn't understand why there was inequality, violence, poverty, hatred, wars, famine, disease, destruction. Hate, hate, hate, all the way down to the core of what it is to be human. She didn't want to be a part of that, things had to change.

'Hey.' Freya sat down next to her and took Chloe, who burbled and stuck a finger in Freya's nose, making her laugh.

Freya nodded behind them. 'We should go.'

Ava shook her head in a non-committal way.

'Heather was pretty clear,' Freya said, tickling Chloe's tummy. 'If we don't hear anything by sunrise, we need to leave.'

'They could've come for us already,' Ava said. 'The attack was last night. Soldiers don't wait for daylight.'

'Maybe they don't have enough room in their prison?' Chloe struggled in Freya's arms so she put her on the blanket. The baby grabbed a stone.

'She'll eat that,' Ava said.

Sure enough, Chloe's hand went to her mouth. That's how babies explore the world, tasting it. Just like Sandy.

Freya gently pulled Chloe's fist from her mouth. The baby's face soured and Freya laughed to make a joke of it for her.

'I don't want to go,' Ava said. 'Heather and Lennox. Xander, all the others. I can't leave them.'

Freya kept her voice light. 'You have a daughter now, sis. You have to put her first.'

'You think I don't do that already?'

'I didn't say that.'

Ava started crying. 'I love her so much, but I can't just go.'

'Hey.' Freya put an arm around her shoulder. 'It's OK, we'll figure something out.'

The sound of an engine starting made Ava jump, and she realised how tense she was. A balloon fit to burst. Maybe some of the others could handle this better, but she felt one step away from crumbling to dust.

The driver of the campervan behind them waved at her and Freya, worried look on his face.

Ava stood and arched her back. She wiped tears from her eyes with the backs of her hands, flapped at her face to cool her cheeks.

She looked at the waves, like a meditation mantra of endless repetition, constant movement yet stillness.

<Sandy, are you there?>

More engine noise behind them, another vehicle leaving the camp.

She looked at Freya, then back to sea. Isle Martin to the right, the stretch of coast further north. Across the loch mouth, mountains now ablaze with light from the east. She imagined being up there, sunshine filling her heart.

<Sandy. Please.>

Nothing.

She sighed. <Sandy.>

More silence.

Then: <Ava-Chloe-Sandy partial welcome.>

Ava burst out laughing at Sandy's voice, it felt like a cool pillow on a hot night.

Sandy emerged from the water, head then tentacles, gliding over the stones. They looked around the beach, empty now except for Freya and Chloe on the blanket. Chloe saw Sandy and stretched out her hands. Sandy scuttled over and extended a tentacle, tickled her feet. Freya sat wide-eyed. Ava felt sorry for her, without the connection this must seem so crazy.

Sandy's colour dimmed to dark greens and blues. <Sandy-Heather partial?>

Ava shook her head. <She and the others tried to get Lennox and Xander out of New Broom.>

Sandy shimmered in gold and yellow. <Sandy-Xander partial too stretched. Not at full efficiency. Sandy-Lennox partial also.>

<They're being held prisoner. We have to help them.>

Sandy's head changed shape, a ridge like a frown running down the middle between their eyes. <Other humans blocking stretched partial. Must allow return.>

Ava touched one of Sandy's tentacles. <They won't, that's the problem.>

<Meaning unclear.>

Ava looked around. They were four tiny figures in a giant landscape, like fleas on a dog, but this situation couldn't be bigger.

<Sandy, I need to meet everyone,> she sent. <Enceladons-Ava whole.>

Sandy was still playing with Chloe while talking to Ava, tasting the air with their other limbs. <We will take you.>

Ava gripped the tentacle tighter and stepped towards the water, but Sandy didn't move.

< Ava-Chloe-Sandy partial.>

Ava looked at Chloe. <You want me to bring her?>

Sandy flashed orange and purple. <Sandy-Ava-Chloe partial become Ava-Chloe-Enceladons whole. Enceladons keen to connect with human juvenile.>

Ava stared at Freya and Chloe, then at Sandy. She reached down and picked Chloe up, turned to Freya. 'We'll be back soon.'

She turned to Sandy. <Let's go.>

And they walked into the sea.

54
LENNOX

Lennox was screaming underwater, unable to move, chained to the bottom of the deepest ocean. The water was crystal clear and somehow he could see all the way to the surface, to the shore alongside, where everyone he knew was standing laughing at him. Sandy and Xander were there too, bodies flashing with joy, splashes of colour mocking him for being unable to breathe. He pulled at his chains but they didn't budge. He screamed and his mouth filled with water. He gulped it down, happy finally to be part of the oceans of the world, to be a tiny drop in this vast expanse that dominated Earth and had brought the Enceladons here.

<Are you awake?>

His chains loosed and he drifted to the surface of consciousness. Heard the murmur of voices, smelled sweat and fear, light against his eyelids, Vonnie's voice in his mind like a beacon.

He opened his eyes and sat up, looked around the cell. Vonnie was across the room, smiling at him.

<I am now.>

He wondered if Sandy dreamed, if Enceladons could feel each other's dreams. He remembered when they'd first met on Yellowcraigs Beach. He had no idea what was coming, yet at the same time he'd felt something profound, something he couldn't explain. As they travelled across the country and grew to know each other, he was completely changed. He loved Sandy, he realised now, in a way he'd never experienced before. He'd never known his birth parents, never had that connection.

He looked at Vonnie. Maybe this was the human connection he

craved. They got each other, and maybe that's where love grew from.

She stood up. <Are you OK?>

He ran a hand over his hair. <Weird dream.>

She smiled. <Yeah, I've been having a lot of them. Think it's to do with Sandy?>

He'd never thought of that but it was possible, Sandy had rewired their brains. A part of them was Enceladon now, so maybe their brains were adjusting.

<Maybe.>

He stood and went to her. She rubbed his arm and he remembered kissing her in the bothy on Isle Martin.

There was something so intimate about communicating this way. They were surrounded by people and no one else could hear them.

Lennox spotted Jodie at the window, looking out.

The Outwithers formed the camp because they'd felt something, same as Lennox at Yellowcraigs. He, Heather and Ava had strokes but recovered. He'd asked Sandy about that, and never really got a satisfactory answer. Something about a comms signal that was too strong. Some folk in Ullapool had passed out when the Enceladons landed, but they didn't have strokes. Sandy said something about Lennox's brain chemistry being different. Presumably there were only some humans who could understand the Enceladons, who could hear each other's thoughts like Lennox and Vonnie. Did that mean that only some people were capable of evolving like this? What happened to everyone else?

Also, the fact that Sandy and Xander had accidentally killed people suggested the Enceladons had powers they hadn't yet revealed. If that was the case, why didn't they just bust out of here? Maybe because they didn't understand that power. They were in a new world, everything completely different. But they'd left Enceladus because of some strange invading horde or swarm, that's what Sandy had shown him. They surely understood the concept of aggression from that example. Why couldn't they just fight back against the humans enslaving them, threatening annihilation?

Thinking of Heather and Ava made his heart hurt. He found out last night when they all came in that Heather was shot but not killed. Hopefully they were treating her properly. He knew that Ava hadn't come and he was glad of that. Hopefully she was miles away by now, the other side of the country. There was no saving the rest of them, that was obvious now.

He turned to Vonnie. When they first met she was so strong, sure of herself. Much more than *he'd* ever been. He pulled her into a hug, long and hard, smelled her hair, dust and sweat.

<Why did you do all this?> he sent, waving around the room. <Why come back?>

She pulled away, looked confused. <For you.>

He squirmed and shook his head, couldn't accept that.

Vonnie pointed out of the window.

'And for them,' she said. Maybe she sensed she'd given away too much, been too honest. 'I felt it too, when me and Sandy connected. This is the next chapter of life on Earth, right? I want to be a part of that, whatever it is. Everyone here does. That's *why* we're here. You think we all wanted to attack a military base? What choice did we have?'

Lennox swallowed and felt ashamed. He'd been selfish. He was the first human to connect with an Enceladon and he'd wanted to keep that to himself as long as possible. But this wasn't his secret to keep, this was for everyone. Sandy wouldn't understand selfishness, he was sure of that.

'I know, I'm sorry. I just don't want to see you hurt.'

He implied all of them with a wave of his hand, but really he meant Vonnie. Selfish again. But fuck it, he was still human, at least for now.

Jodie walked over and touched Vonnie on the shoulder. 'How are you kids doing?'

'We're OK.' Vonnie looked around the stockade. 'What do you think they'll do to us?'

Jodie sucked her teeth. 'Nothing good.'

'What about Sandy and the others?' Lennox said. 'What will they do to the Enceladons?'

Jodie stared at him until he had to look away.

55
AVA

Ava was dizzy with the thrill of swimming inside Sandy. With Chloe in her arms, both of them enveloped by Sandy's body, they shifted through the currents like a torpedo. She saw a pod of dolphins alongside as they skirted the Summer Isles. She could taste the water, smell a pair of seals darting through the water behind them, hear the clicks and chatter of the dolphins, somehow understand their energy. Did the Enceladons connect with dolphins too? They were a more obvious point of first contact for a marine species.

Chloe giggled and Ava could hear it, even though they were both encased in this weird liquid skin of Sandy's. Ava had panicked when she first went into the water, struggled to breathe, then submitted. They were inside Sandy, and Sandy was inside them. There was no closer connection possible.

She saw lights as they ducked under a jutting headland and swerved behind a huge lip of rock. The lights got close quickly, then they were amongst the Enceladons, hundreds of giant jellyfish creatures, thousands of smaller octopoid animals, a mass of tendrils and tentacles, flashing lights and throbbing bodies, and she and Chloe were part of it.

She sensed happiness and anxiety in Sandy as they approached one of the jellyfish. Sandy extended tentacles, which were met with long, pink tendrils, intertwining with each other. She felt the throb of love between them. Chloe wiggled her fingers to copy them, and Ava reached over and clasped her hands.

Ava didn't even know where to start. <Sandy, we need your help.>

<Ava-Chloe-Sandy-Yolanda partial welcome.> Something in Sandy's voice was cautious, she hadn't detected that before.

<Yolanda?> She presumed this was the giant jellyfish, similar to Xander.

<Arbitrary identifier for human understanding.> Yolanda's voice was deeper and more resonant, rattled Ava's brain a little.

Chloe's eyes went wide at Yolanda's voice in their minds, then the baby laughed. Ava held a hand out, still inside Sandy's stretched body, and waved at the display around them. They were drifting in and out of Yolanda's body while also inside Sandy. It made the idea of individuality irrelevant.

<Yolanda, Sandy, all of you.> She tried to think of how to bridge this gap. They sort of shared a language, but neither humans nor Enceladons had any frame of reference for each other's experiences.

<We need to save Xander and the other Enceladons. We need to save Heather, Lennox and the others. There are people who feel connected to you, who tried to rescue Xander, but they've been captured.>

Silence for a few moments. A sprinkle of yellow and orange spots ran from Yolanda's tendril to Sandy's tentacle, then back again. Their background colours complemented each other. However they were communicating, it was beautiful.

<Sandy-Heather-Lennox partial stretched too thin.>

<That's right, Sandy.> Ava pulled Chloe closer into a hug, as if to demonstrate. <Sandy-Heather-Lennox partial is too thin. Sandy-Xander partial is too thin. Do you remember what it was like when we first met on Yellowcraigs Beach? You were on the other side of the country from your kin, from Xander and the others. You could barely function. The same is happening to the others at New Broom. The humans there can't be trusted, they want to keep your partials stretched thin, even break them.>

<Not understand break.>

They were so connected, they couldn't imagine being apart forever.

<You'll never see Xander again. Or Lennox or Heather. Or any of them.>

Silence, more flashes and stripes of bright purple light. They were drifting near the sea bed, and Ava saw a large shadow above them somewhere. For a moment she thought it was a ship come to attack, but then she recognised the outline of a whale. Another intelligent sea creature attracted to the Enceladons. Of course. If she could talk to Sandy, and Sandy could talk to whales and dolphins, did that mean...?

<Why are humans stretching Enceladon-human partials?> This was Yolanda, confusion in their voice.

How could she explain this? <Other humans are bad.>

Yolanda rippled with light. <Meaning unclear, bad.>

Of course, it implied a moral judgement. If you had no moral framework, because everyone in your history had always cooperated and got along, how could 'bad' make sense?

<Other humans want to break Enceladons-humans.>

<Break?> This was Sandy. Ava kept a tight grip on Chloe, this conversation made her want to hold her close.

<Stretch too thin. Then stretch more. And more and more, until broken.>

She hugged Chloe, who was flexing her fingers in the substance of Sandy's body. None of this made sense, inside an alien creature under the sea, trying to persuade them that humans could be evil. A few months ago, she'd been a victim of someone evil herself.

<Return Xander to original energy state?>

<Yes, they'll kill Xander. Return to original energy state. And Lennox and Heather and all the others – humans and Enceladons. And all of you.> She tried to wave around, stretched Sandy's skin from the inside. <Enceladon-human whole. Broken, returned to original energy state.>

Some subdued shimmers of grey and off-white across Sandy's

head, then along their tentacles. A flurry of colours up Yolanda's tendrils, their body pulsing in red and orange eventually, ridges forming along some of their body, stretching from the top of their dome down the tendrils. It looked almost like a temporary spine forming. More flashing spots and circles and stripes, colours that there weren't names for. Then it spread to the other giant Enceladons around them, then the smaller ones too, all of them flashing a simple red and orange, in a single pulse that seemed to sweep around the whole population, like a song spreading through a crowd. Tendrils swaying, tentacles swinging and interconnecting, wrapping around each other's bodies in a writhing mass of life.

One of Yolanda's tendrils snaked through Sandy's skin and raised up to Ava's face. Chloe snorted and grabbed it.

<Already this happened on Enceladus, with Enceladon-Other. Enceladons don't understand, but we must prevent. How?>

Ava grinned and stared at Chloe, who smiled back.

<OK, I have a plan.>

56
HEATHER

Jackhammer pain at the base of her skull. Her stomach muscles clenched and the tension spread up her body to her throat. She just managed to turn her head to the side before the vomit came, flowing out of her like poison. If only it was that easy. She was poisoned and going to die, no amount of vomiting would change that.

A new, brutal pain in her right arm. She carefully rested her head back on a pillow and opened her eyes. She was in the infirmary at New Broom, bright strip-lights overhead, a handful of beds in a long corridor, each containing an Outwither, some unconscious.

She looked at her shoulder. Her shirt had been cut away and a large bandage wrapped around her upper arm. She placed her fingers on it, felt for the pain. Right at the shoulder joint. A few inches across and it would've been through her heart. A few inches up and it would've been through her brain.

Her wrist was handcuffed to the bed frame. She rattled to check it.

She ran a tongue around her dry mouth, looked for a glass of water. Spotted Dr Sharp coming towards her with a bottle of Lagavulin and two glasses.

'Long time no see,' she said, although it had only been about a week since she sat in his surgery and received her tumour news.

He nodded at her shoulder then at the whisky. 'Thought you might need this, medicinal purposes.'

Heather looked around the room. 'How many were killed?'

Sharp looked like he'd just sucked a lemon. He placed the glasses on the bed and poured, held one out to her. His eyes flickered away from hers as he spoke.

'I don't know.'

'You're a terrible liar.'

His hand was trembling, the whisky in the glass making ripples. Heather felt a jolt of shoulder pain, her body on fire with it. She tensed every muscle to ride it, but kept her eyes on him.

Sharp swallowed, hand still shaking. 'Four.'

All the New Orleans sass had left his voice.

'Vonnie and Jodie?'

'Who?'

'My friends at Camp Outwith. Teenage girl and an older black woman.'

Sharp looked at his lap, as if for an answer. 'There's no one fitting those descriptions in the morgue.'

Heather blinked, felt pain across her neck. 'You are murderers.'

Sharp shook his head. 'I had nothing to do with it. I'm just a doctor, I helped you.'

'No, you're part of this.'

He took a big glug of his whisky, still holding hers out. His hand was shaking so much she thought it might spill.

She took the glass from him, cradled it in her lap.

'Why did you do it?' Sharp said eventually, waving his glass to take in the others in their beds. 'You must've known it was a lost cause.'

Heather stared at her whisky. 'We had to.'

'Why?'

She couldn't explain, didn't really understand it herself. Sandy and the others had changed things for the Outwithers, for her, Ava and Lennox most of all. And for the rest of humanity too, they just didn't know it yet.

'Sometimes, you just have to do what you think is right.'

Sharp shook his head and sipped his dram. 'But you could've disappeared. You were out of here, after months locked up. You could've gone anywhere, somewhere they couldn't find you.'

Heather finally took a sip of whisky. Goddamn, it was good. The burn in her throat felt like ecstasy. She licked her lips, felt it warming her soul.

'Run away.'

Sharp studied her. 'To fight another day.'

'And when would that be?'

He took another hit of Scotch. 'I don't know – whenever.'

'Exactly.' Heather swilled the whisky in her glass, her shoulder throbbing with pain. 'I don't have a future, you know that better than anyone. So putting shit off until tomorrow was not an option.'

'Even if it got you killed?'

Heather felt bile rising inside her, took another sip of whisky.

'You act all friendly, walking in here with your whisky and your accent, but you're just the same as the rest. You might as well have fired the gun that killed those people.'

'No, I'm trapped, same as you.'

'Bullshit. We're not the same at all. You're an alcoholic medic who lost his fucking spine somewhere down the line.'

'Hey—'

'Fuck you. You know that what's happening here is wrong, yet you go along with it. Keep your head down, ignore the human-rights abuses, the violence towards an alien species. We should be celebrating a new chapter in history, instead you're grubbing around with a big fishing net, trying to kill these amazing creatures.'

Sharp finished his whisky then eyed the bottle. 'I can't do anything, I'm sorry.'

'You *won't* do anything, there's a difference.'

'What am I supposed to do?'

Heather waved her glass and spilled whisky on her bedsheets. Pointed at her handcuffed wrist. 'Get me out of here. Get us all out of here. Then everyone in the stockade. Then all the Enceladons in the research centre. Just do the right thing.'

Sharp stared at his empty glass. 'They'll court martial and execute me.'

'No, they won't, this isn't the Dark Ages.'

'Yes, they will. They're executing Fellowes and Mendoza in half an hour. For exactly what you're talking about.'

Heather stared at him and tried to comprehend what he'd just said.

57
AVA

Ava was wrapped inside Sandy's skin at the head of the convoy, Yolanda next to them, hundreds of Enceladons on either side and behind them. She missed Chloe already, but this was no place for a baby. She'd persuaded Sandy to go back to Camp Outwith, where Freya was the only one still on the beach. She hadn't had the heart to tell Freya the plan, just told her to look after Chloe for a while. But Freya knew, Ava realised from the look on her face. They'd hugged, Freya holding on too long, Chloe fussing between them, until Ava had to pull away, wiping tears as she strode back into the water.

So now here they were, the entire Enceladon community swimming around the Summer Isles, slicing through the water like it wasn't there. Ava looked ahead, where a large pod of dolphins was leaping from the water as if they understood what was happening. Beyond them, the giant shadow of the whale she'd seen earlier. She wondered if the Enceladons had spoken to them, if they knew.

The Enceladons outstripped the dolphins and Ava realised how fast they must be going. And getting faster.

Sandy spun and leapt from the water as if mimicking the dolphins, and for a brief moment Ava inside them caught sight of land, hills to her left, scattered crofts and houses. Even sparsely spread amongst the landscape, it still felt as if humans were separate from nature, that they didn't understand how to be a part of anything. In comparison, Sandy didn't know any other way except to be part of something.

Back in the water, Ava turned but she couldn't see the end of the convoy, just Enceladon light displays as far as she could see.

They all swerved to the left then back again, as if reacting to some current or force she was oblivious to. She looked at her hands. Her vision was tinted a strange pink from inside a canopy of Sandy's skin. She knew Sandy tasted the world with their tentacles, and she wondered about everything she was missing. Magnetic fields radiating from the centre of the Earth, telepathic signals she wasn't privy to, tidal forces, the gravitational tug of the moon on the Earth's oceans.

<Are you sure about this, Sandy?>

When she'd suggested attacking the base, she had in mind something like when they'd all come down to land around Loch Broom. She knew from her own experience that a miscalibrated friendly electromagnetic signal could cause strokes, and that certain people would recover. But some would not. She thought maybe they could carefully direct these signals, but Sandy told her that wasn't an option. Instead they'd come up with their own idea. It wasn't foolproof, but it was something.

<Sandy-Xander partial must be restored. Enceladon-human whole must be restored. Ava-Lennox-Heather partial must be restored.>

Sandy spiralled out of the water again with Ava inside them, and she wondered if they were checking where they were in relation to the base. She spotted Isle Martin ahead, which meant they were close.

It had been surprisingly straightforward once Ava managed to get the Enceladons to appreciate the situation. They'd fled some hostile force on Enceladus, and taken a long and perilous journey to Earth, only to have another hostile species try to annihilate them. There was nowhere left to run. If they couldn't be accepted on Earth, minding their own business in the ocean, then where could they go?

As they zipped through the water, Ava noticed there was a structure to the Enceladons' movements. They all started rising and falling in unison, creating a subsurface wave. The giant jellyfish like Yolanda were ballooning out their bodies to create a wall of pressure on the upswing, then narrowing themselves as they dived down, repeating the routine.

Even through Sandy's skin, Ava felt the force of the wave they were creating. On one upswing, Sandy breached the surface and Ava looked out. They had created a giant tidal wave, forcing the water in front of them as they hammered through the wash, the water level sucked way down behind them. It reminded her of footage from Japan or Bali, the tsunamis that destroyed landscapes and killed people. She suddenly panicked that this was a terrible idea as Sandy dived back in and joined the others.

<Wait, Sandy, you're going to wash the whole base away?>

<Enceladon water home. Human land home. Obvious.>

<But what about all the humans? You'll drown them.>

Sandy waved tentacles in both directions along the front line of the Enceladon attack. The force of the wave was propelling them all forward faster, like a snowball rolling down a hill. They were gaining momentum at a terrifying rate.

<Enceladon partials will connect with good humans.>

<Good humans?>

Cresting waves and roiling tumbles of water, they must be very close to land now.

<Humans who want Enceladon-human connection.>

What had she done? Introduced the concept of good and bad to these innocent creatures. But there had to be a way to discriminate between different humans and their intentions. Human kids learned it over years, decades, and some remained naïve and trusting forever. Ava felt sick at the thought she might've made these creatures somehow cynical and worldly.

<How will you know good from bad?>

<We will know.>

Sandy leapt out of the water and flew through the air and Ava inside saw New Broom up ahead, armed soldiers along the perimeter fence, readying guns, some down at the dock on the ship doing the same, a few further back in the courtyard standing watching, one or two already running in the opposite direction.

They landed back in the water and darted through the crest of the giant wave, which thrust them onward, then they were rolling and splashing and crashing over the shore then up to the perimeter fence and Ava heard gunfire. Bullets thudded into the water as Sandy rode the wave, Yolanda and the other jellyfish Enceladons reaching what had been the shore but was now the seabed. Then they were easily over the crushed fence, thumping down into the courtyard, some buildings' walls crumpling like paper, roofs shifting with the tsunami, wave after wave pushing Sandy, Ava and the others forward, water everywhere thrusting them up the slope, the toilet block crumpling, canteen doors bursting from their hinges. Ava saw that three jellyfish Enceladons were already at Xander, ripping them free of their cage down at the dock. She tried to orientate herself in the tumbling water, inside Sandy's body, and spotted the stockade at the far end of the base, already pummelled by water like everywhere else.

<Sandy, let's find Lennox and Heather.>

Sandy immediately swung them in that direction, as Ava tried to ignore the carnage all around.

58
OSCAR

He breathed deeply and opened his eyes. He and Mendoza were standing at the perimeter, hands bound to the fence behind their backs. They faced four nervous-looking soldiers with guns. Next to them was Turner. Carson had given him the duty of running the firing squad, recognising his inner psychopath.

Turner had explained to them that capital punishment was technically still legal in the US armed forces. It hadn't been used in decades but could be brought back in extreme circumstances. It sounded like he was parroting Carson, justifying it to himself. Psychos needed to do that – no one is ever the bad guy in their own story, even the monsters.

So they were about to be shot for 'siding with the enemy' even though the Enceladons weren't the enemy, this wasn't a war, and Oscar wasn't even a soldier.

He looked at Mendoza, strong jaw set firm, blank face.

Oscar's bowels felt loose and he worried he might shit himself. What the hell did it matter? No one would ever know about this, he had no immediate family. He'd signed a new secrecy agreement when the base was set up. Things had gone so badly since then he could barely grasp it.

He thought about Sandy, Xander and the rest. What if Carson managed to wipe them out? A single human death was a tragedy, and he was selfish enough to hate that it was his, but the extermination of an entire alien species was the worst decision in history.

'OK,' Turner said, voice steady. 'You are to be executed by firing squad, having been found guilty of treason.'

Oscar looked at Mendoza, then at the gunmen. Mendoza must know some of them. And, of course, he knew Turner well.

'Ready,' Turner said.

'Wait,' Oscar said. Sweat dampened his armpits, his shoulders ached. 'Don't we get a last request?'

'This isn't a movie, asshole.'

Oscar turned to Mendoza. 'Don't you want to say anything?'

Mendoza didn't look at him, just stared at Turner. 'Proud of yourself?' He turned to the others. 'You're all going to hell for this, I hope you're ready.'

He spat on the ground and Oscar thought he might faint.

'Aim,' Turner said.

'Fuck's sake, wait a minute.' No plan, just keep talking. They wouldn't shoot a man in the middle of a sentence, would they?

Something was happening behind the firing squad, soldiers coming out from buildings, the guys in the watchtower pointing out to sea. Some shouting, Oscar couldn't make out what. Turner and the four shooters looked behind Oscar and Mendoza, eyes wide, mouths open.

Then they started shooting, not *at* Oscar and Mendoza but over their heads. Oscar heard a loud roar, smelled the salt of the sea.

He craned his neck and saw a colossal wave careening towards the base, at the shore already, the bodies of hundreds of Enceladons visible below the surface of the wave, smaller ones like Sandy leaping into the air.

Bullets were flying and fizzing into the wave crest.

Oscar didn't even have time to think before water hit him on the back like a jackhammer, lifting him and Mendoza off their feet and tearing the fencing from the posts, throwing them towards the firing squad, who were immediately engulfed, then Oscar was upside down, water down his throat and up his nose, lost in the churn as he spun and tried to take in air, then he was thrown back down and forward, across the courtyard, pieces of fence and lighting swinging around him, sharp metal almost slicing him in two.

He tried to keep his eyes open but water engulfed him as he kept pounding forward. He looked for Mendoza but couldn't see him, glimpsed an Enceladon's tentacle as it slid by. This was an attack, they'd finally realised the danger they were in and done something about it.

The water thumped him into a wall, then the force of it lifted the roof off the building and crumpled the wall like paper, and Oscar felt his lungs squeezed, his wrists still bound behind him on a ripped segment of fence. He yanked at his hands as he was swept into the canteen, flipped upside down, hips banging into a table then the water dragging him away. A pocket of air and he gulped it in before he was washed away again, up and out of the canteen ruins. He thought his shoulders would burst with the pain as he was pressed into another wall. He saw more Enceladons in the water around him, moving like torpedoes, precise and accurate, while he was tossed about. He saw Mendoza swim to a floating roof, scramble on and clutch at the corrugated iron like a surfer, then another wave smashed into him, thrusting his head against a wall and everything went black.

59
HEATHER

She was woken by noise in the ward, saw two soldiers turn and rush out of the building, lifting their guns to their shoulders.

She looked down the row of beds, everyone handcuffed to their guardrails. Heard shouting then shooting outside, sat up and felt the ache of her shoulder. She stretched her neck to see out of the window, shuffled onto her knees to get more height. She caught a glimpse of water, impossibly high and near. A gigantic wave sweeping through the fence lower down and bludgeoning its way across the courtyard and up the slope towards the infirmary. In amongst it she saw giant Enceladons billowing and flattening, the smaller creatures at the vanguard of the attack. They were destroying New Broom, doing what the Outwithers had failed to.

'Jesus.'

She looked around the room. The others had seen it too and were struggling with their handcuffs, the infirmary filled with the clatter of metal. Heather braced herself as water flooded in through the windows and door, busting the glass and taking the frames too, then the surrounds, bricks and masonry crumbling into the corridor as Heather ducked and used the headrest of the bed for cover. Then the whole wall was gone and parts of the roof as well and a wall of water smashed into Heather's bed and threw it forward, almost overturning it, crashing through a hole in the far wall already, propelling her bed out into a cresting wave that tumbled and fought with itself over the last bit of New Broom until she hit the far fence, which held under the onslaught. The waves battered in behind and her bed spun and dived, nose first along the length of the fence, riding the tumult like she was white-water rafting, her wrist cut to pieces from the handcuff, shoulder burning with the pain.

She yanked again at her hand, wondering if it was better to stick with the bed or not. At the moment, it was keeping her above the rising tide, but if it tipped upside down and she was still cuffed to it she would drown.

She gripped the mattress, the bed rocking and shaking along the perimeter fence, hurtling down towards the dock. Crates and barrels of supplies were ricocheting off each other in a chaotic dance, and one thumped into the bed, spinning it and dipping it underwater. The foot of the bed started to sink and Heather panicked, her survival instinct kicking in, and scrambled to the head end.

Another surge of water flooded in and she gripped the bed frame, yanking again at her handcuff as it cut further into her skin, blood seeping into the wash around her.

She looked back at what had been the courtyard, now a massive muddy lake, dirt kicked up into silt, huge slabs of masonry jutting out, roofs drifting around, some military vehicles sliding away. The watch towers had toppled, giant scaffolding strewn across the lake.

Her bed was still spinning and sinking, splashes over the sheets becoming a constant current, the bed rushing downward to the dock. She saw that the military ship wasn't there, was in fact a hundred yards up the hill on its side, a gaping hole where it had run aground on a cliff.

The bed sank some more, her lower body submerged as she clung to the headboard, her arm outstretched where it was still cuffed to the guardrail. The pain was unbearable, flashing through her like a blinding light. They bumped over something then a wash of water broke over her head so that she spluttered and gasped, then air again, then another big wave.

She surfaced and spotted Xander still in their cage, several Enceladons surrounding the enclosure, a swarm of tendrils like a box of worms, writhing and pulling and twisting.

Then she was underwater again and this time the bed didn't resurface. Her lungs burned as she smashed the cuffs against the bed frame. She kicked at the frame with her feet but it wouldn't budge, and the metal and sodden mattress were dragging the bed down, waves still tumbling and collapsing over her.

The bed clunked along, bouncing as it was forced to the dock, skidding against flotsam. The body of a soldier rushed past Heather's head, his arm at an impossible angle, gun strap tangled round his neck.

Her lungs were bursting and her arm burning and she couldn't hold on a moment longer. She opened her mouth and tried to breathe but there was only water, choking her and filling her lungs, making her a part of the wave, and she pictured Rosie as a little girl at the swimming pool, removing her armbands and jumping into the deep end, thrashing her way back to the surface and grinning, two missing baby teeth giving her the most beautiful smile, doggy paddling to the edge of the pool. Heather felt dizzy and blinked, eyes stinging, then she saw a trail of long pink and orange and violet and purple fingers reaching out to her, and she remembered a few months ago, in the water off Yellowcraigs, when she tried to drown herself and Sandy saved her, and she thought they were seaweed or a water spirit, and she was enveloped now in the soft caress of a giant creature that effortlessly snapped the cuff from her wrist and wrapped its whole body around her and squeezed her so that her lungs emptied of water and somehow replaced that with something she could breathe and she gasped and panted and blinked and cried and laughed safe inside this wonderful, strange, impossible creature.

<Welcome Heather-Yolanda partial. All will be well.>

60
LENNOX

<Holy fuck.> This was Vonnie in his head.

He turned and saw her standing on the bench in the cell, looking out the barred window. She beckoned to him. 'Quick.'

He ran over, hearing a low rumble like thunder, jumped onto the bench and looked out. It was like something from a disaster movie, a massive wave flooding down the loch and barrelling into the shore in an immense crash of foam and spray, millions of gallons of seawater racing up the land and smashing into the fence, swamping New Broom, crushing buildings as if they were tiny pieces of trash.

The stockade was up the far slope of the compound, but the water careered towards them, through and over the buildings below. Lennox saw Enceladons amongst the wavefront, flashes of colour sparkling through the spray, as if a rainbow tsunami was coming to kill them.

Vonnie gripped his hand.

'What is it?' Jodie said behind them.

He jumped down with Vonnie and ran to the opposite end of the cell, tried the door.

'A tidal wave,' he said. 'Everyone get away from that wall.'

The others in the cell looked incredulous, moved slowly.

He banged on the bars. 'Hey.' But no guards came.

The glass in the windows over the bench blew out with a smash, the bars still in place, water rushing between, pouring into the room as everyone scrambled against the far wall.

The other windows smashed and water cascaded in, thrashing to the ground and swilling around them, already up to their shins, murky with dirt.

The concrete window surrounds cracked and crumbled under the weight of water, then chunks of masonry tumbled into the cell, making people jump out of the way.

Lennox pulled at the door bars. 'Hey!'

The water was at their waists already, surging through large holes in the wall, then the window bars collapsed and launched across the room, almost hitting Vonnie, who ducked just in time.

Then the whole wall caved in and a waterfall of debris and seawater and junk swelled into the space and shoved them all against the far wall, Lennox clunking his head against the concrete, then he was suddenly underwater. He tried to open his eyes but the salt stung them, and the water was full of mud and debris like soup.

He was flung to the left then upward, gasped for air, looked for Vonnie and Jodie, then was dragged down against the cell bars, his head thunking against them. He found some purchase with his feet on the ground and pushed up, broke the surface, spotted Vonnie across the room, tried to swim to her.

<Vonnie.>

She'd seen him, was splashing across the room, other heads bobbing to the surface then getting swamped again by new waves. Lennox swallowed a lungful of water and coughed, reached out to Vonnie.

<Lennox, shit.>

Then he was pulled backward by the undertow as more water swept in, swirling round the cell, and he was dragged out of a hole in the wall, smacking his back off a brick edge, flipping him upside down, turning him round, churning him in the mayhem.

He tried to gasp for air, thrust himself what he thought was upward.

<Vonnie?>

He was shoved hard in the back, turned to see a car floating on its side. It slammed into him so that he was under again, struggling to breathe. He tried to move but his ankle was stuck between the car's wheel and the arch above it. He could barely see in the murk, excruciating pain up his leg. He yanked and pulled but couldn't get free, lungs bursting, the car suddenly sucked downward in another riptide.

The car hit a block of masonry and spun and he was dragged underneath, his body scraping against what used to be the ground. Then it tumbled again and he was flipped upward, grabbed a breath of air, looked around.

'Vonnie!'

Dragged back under, the car moving fast down the slope on a cascade heading towards shore, or where the shore used to be. He tugged at his foot stuck in the wheel well, knifing pain telling him something was wrong.

The car smashed into the remains of a toilet block, jammed against the wall, water thrashing over him as he held his breath, thinking maybe this was it.

<Lennox?> Ava in his mind, holy shit.

<Ava, where are you?>

<Don't move, we're coming.>

<We?>

<Sandy-Ava-Lennox partial no longer stretched.>

A voice he knew so well. <Sandy, fucking hell.> He gagged, stopping himself from opening his mouth. <Where are you?>

Silence for a moment, agony in his ankle, dizziness from holding his breath.

<Sandy? Ava?>

He saw a light through the gloom then Sandy was around him, with Ava too, then he was inside Sandy's skin, like all those times before, and he took a massive gulp of whatever he could breathe. Sandy's tentacles played with the car wheel, and he felt a tingle up his leg then his foot was free.

Ava smiled at him.

Lennox shook his head. <What the fuck is this?>

<I persuaded them to fight back.>

Sandy broke the surface with the two of them inside. Lennox looked around, through the pink opacity.

<We have to help the others.>

Ava grinned. <It's all in hand. The Enceladons are saving them.>

<Are you sure?>

The water was ebbing around them, the wave receding, leaving a vision of destruction.

Sandy beamed a familiar blue-green colour, stripes and spots across their body.

<Enceladons-good-humans partial connected. Enceladons-good-humans whole.>

61
AVA

She splurged out of Sandy's skin and flumped onto the sodden mud, Lennox alongside her clutching his ankle. She slowly stood and looked around.

New Broom was gone.

They were standing in what used to be the courtyard, in thick sludge, deep puddles all around, pools of water amongst the ruins. The wave had receded and left a vision of hell. Most of the buildings were demolished, walls gone, large chunks displaced up the hillside amongst the gorse and rocks. There were several metal roofs up there too, piled up in a crevice. Cars and trucks were overturned and leaning in swamps of mud and water. Scaffolding, wood and metal from the watchtowers were scattered all around, and Ava wondered about electricity. There were cables running through the puddles, but this place ran on generators, so maybe they'd packed in when the wave hit.

The courtyard area was full of debris – tables and chairs from the canteen, bunkbeds torn to pieces, kit bags, crates of food, three large fridges down by the shore. Bedding, clothes, screeds of broken glass glinting in the ooze. Fish slapping and floundering, having been dragged from the sea.

And bodies, human bodies.

Ava swallowed, looked at a few nearby for any familiar faces. But they were all in uniform. One guy was impaled on a piece of wood, another's neck was snapped, a third one missing a leg, blood pouring from the wound into the silt.

She looked away.

'Where's Vonnie?' Lennox said, sitting up and wincing with pain.

Ava couldn't take it in. This had been a military base a few minutes ago, with a research station, doctor's office, canteen and toilets and a shower block, detention block and a stockade. Now there was just a claggy wasteland, scattered with the detritus of human life and death.

'Vonnie,' she shouted.

Then Lennox in her mind. <Vonnie, are you OK?>

But there was more than Vonnie to worry about. What about all the other Outwithers, what about Heather? Sandy had said they would be protected, but how would they know who to protect? And where were they?

A couple of octopoid Enceladons emerged from the old stockade, supporting some injured Outwithers. They walked gingerly down the slope. Ava could hear the rush of water back into Loch Broom behind her. She smelled salt and seaweed, dead fish and petrol, which worried her. What if something blew up or went on fire? She'd seen footage of fires after the Japanese tsunami.

This seemed more localised than a tsunami, more targeted by the Enceladons. She wondered about Freya and Chloe back at Camp Outwith.

She heard a noise coming from the dock, saw several giant jellyfish sliding into the water. The dock itself had crumpled like paper.

<Xander, is that you? Where's Heather?>

One of the jellyfish waved tendrils in Ava's direction, flashing purple and gold, then slid into the water and floated, like they were sunbathing.

<I'm here.> She spotted Heather walking up from the dock, climbing over debris and rubble, waving her hand in the air. <I'm OK.>

Ava ran towards her, clambering through the carnage. Heather's right arm was limp at her side. Her shoulder was bandaged and she had deep lacerations at her wrist. They hugged and Ava held on for a long time.

Eventually they parted and Heather pushed a strand of Ava's hair behind her ear. 'Where's Chloe?'

'With Freya at Camp Outwith.'

Heather looked around. <Did you do this?>

It was so natural to switch between voice and thought, and Ava wondered if she would feel this strongly connected forever. With Heather, Lennox, Chloe. Her heart glowed. <Sandy and the others did it.>

Heather gave her a look. 'But you persuaded them.'

She looked out to sea, where dozens of the big Enceladons were sitting, waiting, Xander amongst them. They turned the surface of the water into a fireworks display, immense colours, patterns and shapes rippling from one to the other in the shallow water.

'I met Yolanda,' Heather said. She looked over Ava's shoulder. 'Is Lennox OK?'

'I think so.'

They walked over arm in arm, and Ava smiled as Sandy came to greet them. They had mud all over their tentacles, but the happy light display underneath shone through.

Ava tried not to notice the dead soldiers, but Heather stared and Ava felt ashamed. She'd persuaded the Enceladons to do this, now these people were dead.

<It's not your fault.> Heather had read her mind.

Ava shook her head as Heather helped Lennox to his feet, hugging him hard. They were all injured, distressed, shocked. But at least they were together, the three humans who started this, and Sandy.

'I need to find Vonnie,' Lennox said, scanning the Outwither survivors stumbling down the hill.

'Is this who you're looking for?'

Ava whipped round and saw Carson standing in the wreckage, holding Vonnie's arm tight, his gun pointed at her head.

The look on Carson's face made Ava feel sick.

62
OSCAR

Oscar rolled onto his side and puked seawater over the mud. Put a hand out to steady himself and realised he wasn't bound to the fence anymore. The salty taste burned his nose. His shoulders ached and the back of his head pounded. He felt a lump on the side of his skull.

He opened his eyes and saw Mendoza on his knees, panting. Realised Mendoza had performed CPR on him.

Mendoza shrugged. 'I saw you go under, still lashed to the fence. I had to help.'

'You risked your life for me.'

'Just what anyone would do.'

Oscar sat up, looked around. 'What the hell?'

It was like a nuclear bomb had hit New Broom. Buildings destroyed, debris everywhere, murky pools and endless junk amongst the sludge.

Dead bodies.

Mendoza sat down next to him as Oscar tried to orientate himself. They were sitting in what used to be the canteen, he thought. Some of the kitchen counters were still in place along a crumpled wall. He wondered about gas leaks.

'We should be dead,' he said.

Mendoza crossed himself. 'A sign from God.'

Oscar squinted at him. It seemed insane that the sun was still in the blue sky overhead. It felt like an extreme storm had passed through, the lightness of not being under its oppressive power anymore.

'You think?'

'Sent down some angels.'

'They were Enceladons.'

Mendoza smiled. 'Angels come in all shapes and sizes.'

Oscar shook his head. 'You saved my life. Thank you.'

Mendoza helped him up. Oscar rubbed at his wrists, raw where they'd been tied. He wondered about the firing squad, if some of them were dead. He thought about Carson.

He took in the chaos for a long time. Couldn't see anyone else alive from here. He spotted umpteen giant Enceladons in the loch, glowing and shapeshifting like they were having a party. He saw that Xander was no longer down at the dock, which was buckled and destroyed.

'Are we the only humans left?'

Mendoza shook his head. 'Don't think so. I heard voices round the other side.'

Oscar started to walk that way and Mendoza grabbed his arm. 'Wait. We were about to be shot for treason, remember?'

'So?' Oscar waved at the scene. 'This changes all that.'

'You think?'

Mendoza led the way to the edge of a crumbling wall. They both slowly looked round the corner.

Amongst the debris of the courtyard, Oscar saw what looked like a stand-off. Heather, Ava, Lennox and Sandy at one side, huddled together. A few yards away was Carson, gun pointed at Vonnie's head. He was talking but Oscar couldn't hear what he said.

'What's he doing?' Oscar whispered.

Mendoza spat in the mud. 'Ending things.'

'Look around. It already ended.'

'Not for him. Guys like Carson can't ever admit they lost.'

'We have to help them.' Oscar felt a surge in his chest, finally able to do the right thing. His whole time at New Broom had been compromised, his whole life, really. Now he could stand up.

He looked around for a gun, anything he could use. Couldn't see anything useful amongst the wreckage.

Then he realised something.

<Lennox, Sandy, I'm over by the canteen with Mendoza. I can see you with Carson.>

Mendoza looked at him, realised what he was doing. 'That shit is crazy.'

Lennox glanced over, trying not to make it obvious. Oscar wondered if Ava and Heather had heard him too. He had no idea how this worked, had barely used it.

'We need a distraction,' Mendoza said.

Oscar looked around then out to sea, all the giant Enceladons there.

<Lennox, can you speak to Xander? Get some of the big guys to cause a distraction to Carson's right?>

Mendoza had followed Oscar's gaze. 'Really?'

'What's more distracting than that?'

'Hello, scum.' The voice made Oscar jump.

Turner stepped out from the side of the broken wall, machine gun pointing at them. 'Look what the tide washed in.'

Oscar's heart sank, but Mendoza just stood still as a rock.

Turner grinned. 'You two were supposed to be dead.'

Mendoza shook his head and spat again into the mud. 'You always were a fucking asshole, Turner.'

Turner waved with his gun. 'Move.'

63
HEATHER

She wondered if she should just rush the bastard. She'd had a lifetime of arrogant men doing what they wanted, fucking up humanity and the planet for their own gain and egos. Life was just one big pissing contest for these clowns. Carson was the latest in a ten-thousand-year-old line of patriarchal bullshit that women had had to put up with, roll their eyes or bow their heads, shut the fuck up and get on with it.

No more.

But she wouldn't get to Carson before she was killed. Honestly, she didn't even mind that idea, she could lie down here in the mud and sleep for a million years. But Carson would kill Vonnie too, then Lennox and Ava, just to show he was in control.

Carson was still talking but she'd tuned out. Eventually he paused for breath.

Heather shook her head. 'Look around, it's over.'

Carson seemed surprised that a middle-aged woman would even dare talk to him. 'It's not over until I say it is.'

Heather waved a hand at the destruction. 'New Broom is gone.'

'We can rebuild it.'

'What are you going to do, shoot us all?'

Carson smiled. 'Thanks, great idea.'

She wondered how many bullets he had.

'Look who I found.' She turned at Turner's voice and felt a rock in her stomach. He was marching Oscar and Mendoza over, gun at their backs.

In the other direction, a handful of Outwithers were watching, keeping a safe distance, along with the Enceladons who'd rescued them from the stockade. They were scared, of course, but surely if they all acted together they could overcome these two pricks with guns. These two throwbacks to cavemen with clubs. But that was the key, wasn't it? Working together. That's what the Enceladons had worked out millions of years ago, cooperation. This individual way to live was going to kill humanity.

Turner shoved Oscar hard in the back, Mendoza walking calmly. He'd always been a nice guy to Heather and Lennox, despite being a guard. Right now, he looked as if he might rip Turner's head clear from his neck given half a chance.

Heather still thought about the numbers. There were five humans and Sandy on this side, against two guys with guns and a hostage. But if they rushed them and Vonnie died, Heather would never forgive herself.

Lennox and Sandy had been weirdly quiet throughout all this, and she wondered if they were talking privately. They'd all seen what the Enceladons could do with the wave. Ava had somehow persuaded them into this attack, could Lennox persuade them to help out again?

'Execution time,' Carson said, nodding at Turner.

Heather put a hand out. 'What the hell?'

Carson looked at Oscar and Mendoza. 'These two were found guilty of treason.'

'You're the guilty one here.'

Carson grinned. 'This is my base.'

Turner raised his gun and pointed it at Mendoza.

Heather heard a rushing sound like a waterfall, turned to see a dozen giant Enceladons rising into the air over the edge of the loch, seaweed falling from their bodies. They darted over to hover above the humans' heads, throwing them all into shadow and drenching them with dripping seawater. The Enceladons' tendrils dragged beneath their bodies across the mud and silt like a giant luminous forest, blocking the view.

Mendoza and Oscar rushed Turner, running in a zigzag through the tendrils. Heather heard gunfire, saw a muzzle flash and felt a bullet whizz near her ear. Lennox and Sandy had bolted from the other side towards Carson, but she couldn't see what was happening through the tendrils. More rapid gunshots made her crouch alongside Ava. More gunfire, tendrils flashing and swaying and flapping left and right, seawater still raining down from the Enceladons' bodies overhead, the whole thing in shade.

The gunfire stopped and she heard Carson yell.

'Call them off, or the girl is first.'

The Enceladons floated to a safe distance away, but stayed airborne, subdued colour flashes across their bodies. Heather wondered if they understood.

In their wake, Heather saw Lennox and Sandy just a few yards from Carson, who was backed against a wall, holding Vonnie by the throat. A few yards to the right, Mendoza stood over Turner's body, neck clearly broken. In front of them both was Oscar, lying face up in the mud, blood pouring from bullet holes in his chest and stomach.

Mendoza went for Turner's gun but Carson fired a warning shot.

'Don't.'

64
LENNOX

The power always lay with the guy who had the gun.

Lennox looked at Vonnie. She seemed a lot calmer than he felt.

When Oscar suggested a distraction, he'd passed it on to Xander and the others in the water. Looking at Oscar now, all that did was get him dead.

'You killed him,' Heather shouted at Carson, pointing at Oscar's body.

Carson straightened his shoulders. 'Technically, Turner killed him.'

'Let us help him,' Heather said.

'He's gone.'

Heather shook her head. 'Maybe Sandy can bring him back.'

Lennox knew that wasn't true. Sandy had tried with Ewan at Ullapool harbour. They could do incredible things, but they couldn't bring someone back to life. Lennox wondered if Heather was trying to trick him.

She stepped forward but Carson fired another warning shot.

'I will kill all of you,' he screamed, waving the gun. His grip on Vonnie's throat was white-knuckled and she was struggling to breathe.

Lennox held his hands out. 'Hey, go easy on her.'

Vonnie gave him a look. <I'm OK.>

<I know you are. Just stay cool.>

<Always.>

'Are you talking to her?' Carson said. 'Freaks. This is what's become of the human race. You're all infected.'

'We *are* infected,' Lennox said. 'But it's not a disease, it's the cure.'

Carson gave a manic laugh. 'Cure for what?'

'For everything humans have done wrong. It's a chance to start again.'

'You sound like a goddamn communist.'

'You have no idea. You've been next to these things for months and you haven't learned a thing.'

'I've learned that they can be caught. That they're stupid enough to climb straight into a cage. They're easy to defeat.'

Lennox shook his head. 'You can't defeat the future.'

'Fuck your future,' Carson said, squeezing his hand tighter around Vonnie's throat. He started to move along the wall. Up beyond the entrance to the base, vehicles were scattered around. Some of them looked in a decent state, maybe drivable. So this was his plan, use Vonnie to get away, live to fight another day. Same old human mindset.

Lennox couldn't let that happen.

<Sandy, we need another distraction. Just something to put Carson off for a second. But don't get shot. Vonnie, get ready.>

<I was born ready.> But he could hear the stress in her voice.

<Sandy-Lennox-Vonnie partial ready. Simple chemical realignment.>

Lennox wondered about that, then Sandy's body ballooned up, flashing blue and white zigzag stripes, switching to muddy brown and grey, knobs and bumps emerging on their skin as they dashed across the courtyard faster than Lennox could follow, and he realised Sandy had turned the colour of the debris-strewn wasteland around them, camouflaged against the jumbled brickwork and mud.

Carson aimed the gun and pointed, shot three times but Sandy didn't stop and launched themself at Carson's face, landing on his chest, tentacles wrapped around his throat. Vonnie thrashed herself free, peeling his fingers from her neck and kicking his knee so that he buckled. Sandy smothered him with their body and pried the gun from his fingers, flung it into the detritus somewhere.

Mendoza pick up Turner's gun and Heather and Ava ran towards Oscar on the ground, as Vonnie kicked Carson again, twice for good measure, then pulled the cuffs of her hoodie and strode over to Lennox.

Sandy pushed Carson to the ground and sat on him for a long time, his legs thrashing in a puddle, his body writhing. Eventually he stopped fighting and Sandy scuttled over to Lennox, camouflage gone, flashing blue and green, just like the first time they met.

<Sandy-Lennox-Vonnie partial not stretched anymore. Enceladon-human whole.>

'Is he dead?' Lennox said, pointing at Carson.

Sandy flashed in thin streaks. <Not returned to original energy state. Partial rest phase.>

Heather looked up from Oscar. 'What about him? Sandy?'

Sandy scampered to Oscar's body, placed their tentacles on the bullet wounds. Lennox saw blood mingling with mud and seawater on the ground. Sandy gently climbed on his chest and flashed through a rainbow of colours, then dimmed for some time, before sliding off and sitting alongside Oscar in the mud, two tentacles still resting on his chest.

<Oscar-Sandy partial returned to original energy state.>

Lennox swallowed hard. Sandy's words didn't come with any emotional expression in them, as if that was just a part of life. But that's exactly what dying was.

They were all silent for a long time, Heather kneeling by Oscar, Ava standing over them, Mendoza with his gun at the ready, keeping guard, flashing looks at Carson's unconscious body. Lennox and Vonnie stood a few feet away, holding each other. Sandy sat in the mud.

Behind them, Xander and the others had lowered themselves back into the loch.

The Outwithers up the hill were slowly walking towards them. Lennox stared at the ruins around them, his mind empty.

65
AVA

She squeezed Chloe to her chest and felt whole again. Closed her eyes to concentrate on her baby's feelings, sent waves of love and devotion and comfort to her, felt simple joy coming back. She couldn't wait for Chloe to learn words, arrange sentences, express how she felt through the clumsy, inefficient use of language, the way humans had done forever. But this connection they had now was Ava's whole world.

She opened her eyes. Ardmair Beach was in a much better state than New Broom. Freya and Chloe had stayed in the camper, parked on the road up from the shore. Freya had seen the tidal wave out in the loch. The overspill here was just an extraordinarily high tide, throwing seaweed and driftwood up the stones, splashing over the road, but nothing dangerous. The houses on the coast had taken a battering, like they might in a winter storm, but nothing they couldn't handle.

Now, they were sitting round the campfire Freya had built. Also around the fire were Lennox and Heather, Vonnie and Jodie, Mendoza, and Sandy off exploring the flotsam washed up by the waves.

There were three other fires nearby, each surrounded by Outwithers drying off, still in shock about what happened.

They'd managed to get a couple of military trucks to work back at the base. Maybe they should've called the police or ambulance, but it seemed better just to get out of there. The only concession to a possible aftermath was that Mendoza tied Carson's unconscious body to a large fencepost, to give them time for whatever was going to happen here.

This felt like the end.

All the Enceladons had drifted round the coast, and were now sitting in the water between Ardmair and Isle Martin, filling the ocean. They had subdued light displays, smaller creatures mingling between the giant ones. The whole thing was the greatest natural display Ava could imagine. David Attenborough would kill to narrate this. But the rest of the world had no idea what had just happened.

Only Sandy was out of the water, staying close to Lennox, who was similarly not letting Vonnie get far away. They sat holding hands at the fire, not speaking. Heather and Jodie were in a low discussion with Mendoza, and she wondered what he would do now. The rest of them could disappear into the Scottish Highlands, but he had a family back in the US, a treason charge still hanging over him.

Maybe they should've killed Carson, but she couldn't have lived with herself if they were just like the soldiers. Of course, others at New Broom had been killed by the wave, but that felt unavoidable. The Enceladons had to do it. Besides, Jodie and some of the other Outwithers had gone around checking the bodies, and many of them weren't dead, just unconscious like Carson.

Ava felt guilty, but she would get over it. She felt guilty about Michael too, but the years of bullshit she'd lived through meant that she also felt justified.

What the military had done to Lennox and Heather, to Sandy and the rest, to her and Chloe, was brutal. They all deserved this moment of peace, even if it was laced with shock.

Chloe started gurning and Freya offered to take her. Ava shook her head, instead stood and bounced Chloe in her arms until she giggled. Just like every other mother and baby on the planet. She and Chloe had these powers, but they were just normal too. There would be tantrums and tears, bust-ups and fights, reconciliation and hugs, millions of tiny moments that made up a life of connection.

Lennox stood, cleared his throat.

'Hey.' He addressed everyone around the fires. Rubbed his hand over his hair, glanced at Vonnie, who nodded in reassurance. He looked older than when Ava first met him. 'I've been speaking to Sandy, and the Enceladons are leaving. All of them.'

Jodie frowned. 'What do you mean? Leaving Earth?'

Lennox shook his head and glanced at Ava. 'Once Ava got them to understand what was happening at New Broom, that seems to have opened their eyes. They understand now that if they stay near humans, they'll always be in danger.'

'Not all humans,' Jodie said, waving a hand around the beach. 'That's why we're here. Some of us want to stay connected.'

'Yeah, they understand that too.'

Ava felt Chloe wriggle, shifted her weight and kept bouncing her a little. 'Where are they going?'

Lennox looked at Sandy, flickering in the sunshine. 'The Arctic. I'm not sure where exactly. Either they don't know themselves, or they don't want to tell me, just in case. But it makes sense. They come from colder water than most of the oceans here. They're used to having an ice cap overhead. Plus it'll provide protection while the ice remains.'

Jodie shifted her weight in her fold-out chair, then stood. 'But what about us?' She looked at the other fires, the other Outwithers. 'We've been here for months because we felt something. If they leave, what are we supposed to do?'

Lennox nodded, again looked at Vonnie for support. She returned his nod and he swallowed. 'Sandy says that anyone here who wants to can go with them.'

Confused talk around the other fires, Jodie shaking her head. 'How can we go with them if they're going to live in the Arctic Ocean?'

Lennox looked at Vonnie then Ava. 'They say there's a way. I've swum with Sandy, so have Vonnie and Ava. I've been *inside* Xander. It feels like ... I can't explain it. But it feels like you're completely part of them. Like the most natural thing in the world. Sandy says any of us could start off like that, be able to breathe and swim like them, inside one of them. Then gradually ... become one of them somehow.'

Jodie stared at him. 'How...?'

Ava cleared her throat. 'If Sandy says they can do it, I believe them. They don't know how to lie.'

Lennox smiled thanks to her. 'Basically, everyone needs to decide what they want to do. Stay here and stay human. Or go with them and become Enceladon.'

He sat down amongst more murmurings and Ava looked at Chloe, sucking her fingers.

Freya stared at Ava. 'You're not thinking...'

Ava knew her answer. Her experiences with Sandy and Yolanda, with all the Enceladons, would always be the most remarkable moments of her life. But she'd just become free. She wanted to live as a human. A woman, mother, daughter, sister. And she had Chloe. So much future, so much potential, so much life still to live.

'No,' she said, smiling at Freya then Chloe. 'I'm staying right here.'

66
HEATHER

All around her, intense conversations fluttered in the air like birds. The Outwithers had already connected to each other through this shared experience, never mind what came next. She wondered how many of them would take up the offer. It was a big leap, especially since most of them had never even met an Enceladon until today. This was a moment for gut feelings, but maybe they needed more information. Was there a way back if they didn't settle in? Was there a time limit – after a certain moment, could they never return? Like everything about the Enceladons, there were so many unanswered questions. Questions that would probably never be answered unless you became one of them.

She went to speak to Mendoza. 'Hey.'

Mendoza smiled. 'What's up?'

'Just wondering how you're doing.'

'Good.'

Heather looked at the people on the beach, the Enceladons offshore as if it was the most normal thing in the world. She wondered what was happening back at New Broom.

'It's a lot to take in,' she said.

Mendoza laughed. 'Sure is.'

Heather shifted her weight. 'You know, I don't think I ever knew your first name.'

He held out his hand. 'I'm Mateo, pleased to make your acquaintance.'

She laughed and took his hand. 'Thanks for everything.'

He shrugged.

Heather rubbed at her aching shoulder.

'You should get that checked out,' Mendoza said. 'Could be infected.'

'What with me being in the middle of a tsunami, you mean?'

'Yeah.'

They both looked out to sea at the spread of Enceladons.

'I wonder how things are back at New Broom,' Heather said eventually.

'Not good.'

'Do you think Carson woke up yet?'

'I hope not.'

'It can't have been easy for you,' Heather said. 'Some of those guys were your friends.'

Mendoza ran his tongue around his teeth. 'It is what it is. Most are still alive. As for Turner, it was him or me.'

More silence.

'So what's next?' Heather said, waving out to sea. 'I presume you're not taking them up on their offer?'

Mendoza shook his head. 'I got to get back.'

'How?'

'Good question.' He pointed out to sea. 'Reckon they could give me a ride, drop me off in Los Angeles?'

'It's not exactly on the way.'

'I'll find a way. My family is used to working under the radar. I can get back.' He looked her up and down. 'What about you?'

'What do you mean?'

'Their offer.'

'Hey.' Heather turned to see Ava, hands in her pockets, Freya behind her playing with Chloe.

'Hey.'

Ava glanced at Lennox. 'This offer is crazy, huh?'

Heather nodded at Mendoza. 'We were just talking about it.'

'And?'

Heather swallowed. This was why she'd come to talk to Mendoza, if she was honest. This conversation was too hard.

'I'm going,' she said.

Ava nodded at her for a long time, tears in her eyes, which set Heather off.

<I thought you might,> Ava sent.

She threw herself at Heather, wrapped her arms around her. Heather remembered Sandy doing the same thing all those months ago, saving Heather from herself. Heather held on to Ava, smelling the sea in her hair, feeling the warmth of her body, sensing her love.

Eventually Heather pulled away. 'I presume you're not.'

Ava looked at Freya and Chloe. 'I can't.'

'I understand.' Heather looked around the beach. 'I don't have any reason to stay.'

Ava shook her head, tears running down her cheeks. 'You have us.'

'You have each other,' Heather said. 'And that's amazing. But I don't have that. I'm tired, Ava, that's the truth. I'm tired of this life and I have been for a long time. I don't have anything holding me here like you do. And I want an adventure. I want to find out what it's like. To feel what we've felt with Sandy, feel that multiplied a billion times. To see how they live, how they connect.'

Ava was sobbing now, hands over her face. Heather hugged her tight, pushed her hair out of her face, held her tear-soaked hands.

<It's OK, it's what I want. It's a good thing. It's the best thing that could happen to me.>

Ava tried to get her tears under control, breathed shakily, fanned her cheeks. <I know, it's just ... I'll miss you.>

<I know. But we'll always be connected. And maybe I'll come back, who knows?>

Mendoza was giving them space and Heather appreciated that. He was still just human, couldn't communicate like they could. What would happen if this spread to the rest of humanity? Maybe in generations to come it would be normal, and humans would find a new way of living. More like Enceladons. But that was for someone else to worry about.

'What about Lennox?' Ava said, looking over. 'Do you think he'll stay or go?'

Lennox, Vonnie and Sandy were standing close, communicating with each other.

Heather honestly didn't know how to answer.

67
LENNOX

He darted between Xander and Yolanda, sinewy tentacle movements propelling him and Sandy through the water as if it wasn't there. What must it be like to do this on your own? To dive hundreds of metres through the gloom, dance like a maniac through fathoms of water without a care in the world.

The sea outside of Sandy's skin seemed opaque to Lennox as he looked out. He could taste the salt and seaweed with their tentacles, and a million other things too – the tang of crabs and lobsters scuttling along the seafloor, the peculiar taste of a plastic bag floating overhead. Sandy was part of their environment in a way no human had ever been, and Lennox was envious.

They gathered speed, winding through the bodies of the giant Enceladons, avoiding bumping into other creatures, just a passing stroke of tentacles or flash of light in acknowledgement. Lennox wondered what the relationship was between the different sized creatures. It wasn't parent and child, nor siblings, but something closer, like clones or plant offshoots. They were the same creature, which is why he'd called one Sandy and their bigger partner Xander. Yolanda's name was randomly picked to signify a different entity for humans. Did that mean that none of them even had names – that they were all one, interlinked creature?

He could be a part of this. That's what they were offering.

They swung round and darted through more bodies, incandescent with flashes and pops of colour and shapes, pure joy. It was the most incredible thing, these beautiful creatures were happy.

<Sandy-Lennox partial is love.>

He welled up at Sandy's voice in his mind. He didn't know if Sandy meant that phrase like it sounded. They would never fully understand each other like this, with him as a human and them an Enceladon. There was always this barrier. They could talk, sense emotions and feelings from each other, but they saw the universe so differently.

<Yes, Sandy-Lennox partial is love. Enceladon-human partial is love.>

<Partial, not whole.>

Sandy meant not all humans, and they were right. Lennox wondered what would happen after New Broom. A renewed attempt to catch and kill them? An escalation of violence? Or maybe a realisation that they should be left alone. Maybe even some self-realisation that humanity was on a crash-course to oblivion. That cooperation was the way forward, that connecting to each other and the planet around us was the only way.

<Yes, sadly, partial humans, not whole.>

They swam amongst the giants, overwhelming in every way but so familiar now, so comfortable, like home.

<Sandy-Lennox partial join Enceladon whole in new home?>

It sounded like an innocent question, but it was so profound Lennox felt tears in his eyes. He wanted to stay with Sandy, wanted this life. But he thought about Vonnie and the world outside of the ocean, of the life he hadn't lived yet as a sixteen-year-old kid. All the different ways his life could go, countless decisions, messy and complicated. All the connections he would make in the human world.

He swallowed hard, feeling some of Sandy's essence or body in his throat. They were already part of each other and they always would be.

<I can't. I need to stay with the other humans.>

He sensed sadness rippling through Sandy's skin.

<Sandy-Lennox partial stretched thin. But never break. Always connected.>

Lennox was crying now. <Yeah, always connected.>

They swam back to the shore and Sandy scuttled up the stones, Lennox emerging from their body like a magic trick.

The beach was busy, some of the Outwithers saying their goodbyes, ready to take up the Enceladons' offer. Tears and hugs, sadness but pensive joy as well, excitement about what was to come.

Lennox limped to Heather and Ava.

'Well?' Ava said, her voice shaky.

Lennox looked around the beach, shared a look with Vonnie in the distance. He had told her already, of course, she was his new human connection. But he had wanted one last swim, one last connection with an impossible world.

'I'm staying here,' he said.

Ava sighed, relieved.

Lennox turned to Heather, who was smiling.

<You're going with them, aren't you?> he sent.

She nodded. She didn't have to speak, he understood. The three of them all understood each other so well. What they'd been through had connected them forever.

He grabbed her into a huge hug, tears on his cheeks, and felt Ava wrap her arms around them both. The three of them stood by the water's edge, and he thought about them standing over Sandy's body on another beach at the start of this.

He felt tentacles on his back, realised Sandy was wrapping them all in a hug, suckers sticking to their skin, lights flashing, tentacles caressing them.

They stayed like that for a long time, then eventually broke apart, Heather laughing at her own tears.

Lennox looked at Vonnie, who smiled at him, then he looked at the other Outwithers on the beach. Ten of them were ready to go, including Jodie and Heather. He was envious but also relieved. Their life would be incomprehensible, but then so would his. Nobody knew the future and that was the point.

Ava wiped her eyes and Lennox sniffed.

Heather threw them a smile then turned and walked hand in tentacle with Sandy into the water. Neither of them looked back.

<Good luck,> Lennox sent.

The other Outwithers walked into the sea too and were met by Enceladons, who guided them deeper, then they were wrapped up inside their partners and disappeared under the surface.

The larger Enceladons began moving away from the shore. They waved tendrils in the air, splashing and flashing, light displays that Lennox had got so used to, simple happiness.

Freya brought Chloe down to Ava, who took the baby. Chloe looked out to sea, giggling and waving at the receding creatures. Mendoza came and stood with them too, watching the exodus to the Arctic Ocean, Enceladon-human partial.

Vonnie arrived next to Lennox and slipped her hand into his.

The remaining Outwithers stood on the beach and watched as the Enceladons got further away, then they were beyond Isle Martin and out of sight.

Everyone reluctantly started walking up the beach, away from the sea. Mendoza and Freya headed for her campervan. Ava touched Lennox's shoulder and took Chloe away too.

It was just Lennox and Vonnie left, looking at the sea in silence.

<What now?> Vonnie said in his mind.

He turned to her, looked in her eyes, felt the connection.

<Good question.>

ACKNOWLEDGEMENTS

Huge thanks to Karen Sullivan for giving Sandy and their story a home, along with everyone else at Orenda Books for their hard work and dedication. Massive thanks also to everyone at BBC Two's *Between the Covers*, for falling in love with Sandy and bringing their journey to a wider readership. Thanks as always to Phil Patterson and all at Marjacq for their unwavering support, even when I write crazy books. Thanks to everyone who has supported my crazy books over the years, it would all be impossible without you. And all my love, as always, to Tricia, Aidan and Amber.